'So totally absorbing you'll forget absolutely everything until you turn the last page. Absolutely brilliant, can't wait for the next one! Forget food, forget drink, sleep and play . . . just read until the end.'
Jack, age 13

'**Shark Island** is the best book I have ever read. It has a brilliant storyline. I think boys and girls will love it.'
Victoria, age 10

'I really liked it. I read it every night non-stop and my mum had to force me to put it down when it was bedtime.'
Max, age 10

'It covers everything you need in a brilliant story: humour, tension, sadness, happiness and all the other emotions you can fit into a book.'
Daisy, age 12

'I really liked all the characters, especially the bad guys.'
Kieran, age 8

'It's amazing!'
Beth, age 11

'I got really hooked and can't wait to read the next book.'
Charlotte, age 12

Shark Island

DAVID MILLER

OXFORD

UNIVERSITY PRESS

OXFORD
UNIVERSITY PRESS

Great Clarendon Street, Oxford OX2 6DP

Oxford University Press is a department of the University of Oxford.
It furthers the University's objective of excellence in research, scholarship,
and education by publishing worldwide in

Oxford   New York

Auckland   Cape Town   Dar es Salaam   Hong Kong   Karachi
Kuala Lumpur   Madrid   Melbourne   Mexico City   Nairobi
New Delhi   Shanghai   Taipei   Toronto

With offices in

Argentina   Austria   Brazil   Chile   Czech Republic   France   Greece
Guatemala   Hungary   Italy   Japan   Poland   Portugal   Singapore
South Korea   Switzerland   Thailand   Turkey   Ukraine   Vietnam

Oxford is a registered trade mark of Oxford University Press
in the UK and in certain other countries

British Library Cataloguing in Publication Data

Data available

ISBN: 978-0-19-272901-9

3 5 7 9 10 8 6 4 2

Printed in Great Britain by CPI Cox and Wyman, Reading, Berkshire

Paper used in the production of this book is a natural,
recyclable product made from wood grown in sustainable forests.
The manufacturing process conforms to the environmental
regulations of the country of origin.

This is for Su'en and Hanna
with love

Contents

1

The End of the World

Their whispering woke Hanna. It sounded like the hissing of snakes in the blackness. Mum and Dad were over near the window, the outlines of their heads just visible in the silvery reflected light from the waters of the lagoon. Mum had a sarong wrapped round her. Dad, as usual at night, had nothing on. 'Has the boat stopped?' she heard Mum ask.

'I think so. I can't be sure. Just listen!'

There was a tense, tight silence. Hanna felt a sudden, unexpected prickle of fear. She eased up the corner of her mosquito net, strained her ears to hear.

At first there seemed to be nothing out of the ordinary—just the usual island noises: the rasping of cicadas from the jungle behind the hut; the soft lap-lap of wavelets on the beach.

But then she heard the engine.

It was coming from away to the right, from the deep water out beyond Dead Man's Leap: the low *bonka bonka bonka* of a powerful diesel. It had to be from a *kumpit*, one of the big wooden fishing boats they sometimes saw cruising past, searching for horse mackerel and barracuda in the narrow channels between the reefs.

'Are they fishing?' Mum whispered.

Dad leaned further out of the window, squinting between the rows of palm trunks. 'I don't think so. There'd be lights if they were fishing.'

'Maybe they're after turtles.'

'Turtles don't nest on this side of the island, you know that.'

'Then what . . . ?'

A new noise: the high-pitched whine of an outboard motor starting up. Dad stayed at the window for a second or two longer, straining to see, then pulled himself quickly inside. 'They're coming here,' he said urgently. 'They're coming right into the lagoon!'

The sound of the outboard got rapidly louder. Hanna could hear the slap-slap of the waves on the hull of a small boat. Dad was groping around in the corner of the hut, finding his shorts, pulling them on. Sweat glistened on his narrow, bearded face. Mum was at the window now, peering out. 'There are about five of them,' she counted. 'No, six.'

'Are they armed?'

'I can't tell. They've got scarves round their heads, sort of bandannas.'

2

She was silent for a moment. Then she said something that made Hanna's heart lurch with fear. 'Do you think they're pirates, Nick?'

Pirates!

Not Captain Hook. Not Captain Pugwash. Not Bluebeard or Blackbeard or whatever his name was. Mum was talking about *real* pirates, Hanna knew, modern-day pirates. The kind who robbed ships—even big tankers—killed the crews, threw their mutilated bodies overboard. The kind Dad had told her there'd be no problems from, not in a million years. Not on safe, friendly Kaitan Island.

Dad squinted outside again. 'I'm going to go and talk to them, Lin.'

'No!' Mum's terrified reply came out as a shout.

'Well I don't propose to wait until they invite themselves in. If they're just a bunch of fishermen, well and good. If not I can keep them occupied long enough for you three to get away into the jungle. Wake the kids.'

'But, Nick!'

'I'm awake,' Hanna said. 'I've been awake right from the start. I've heard everything.'

'That's all we need!' Dad exclaimed.

Hanna felt a sudden, stupid, surge of anger. 'I thought you said there was no danger from pirates!'

3

'I don't know who they are, OK? That's why I'm going to find out. Now wake Ned and for God's sake don't let him make any noise.'

Hanna glanced down at the dark shape of her brother, hunched on the thin mattress next to the rough planks of the hut wall. He'd slept through everything so far, which was totally typical—it took an earthquake to wake him, especially on school days. Ten years old, three years younger than she was, though it could have been a century. She clapped a hand over his mouth and thumped him in the ribs. He stirred, struggled, and made a noise like a strangled chicken. 'Quiet!' she hissed, only just managing to control her spiralling terror. 'We're in danger!'

Ned wrenched himself free. 'What danger?' he demanded loudly.

Dad dropped down beside him. 'Ned, this is serious. There's no time to answer questions right now. I want you to get up, put some shoes on—not your flip-flops but your trainers—and I want you to do exactly what Mum says, OK? No arguing, no answering back. It's really really important.'

Ned glanced at Mum, then up at Dad's face. Even he seemed to realize the seriousness of what was happening. 'OK, Dad,' he said quietly.

Dad grinned at him, put a hand through the mosquito net, and ruffled his spiky black hair.

Then he stood up, turned, and gathered Mum and Hanna into his arms. For an instant he held them tight to his chest, so tight Hanna could hear his heart beating, smell his special, comfortable Dad smell; then he was gone, slipping quickly out of the side door, and down the ladder into the darkness. 'Be careful,' Mum called out to him. When she turned back, Hanna saw that her face was stretched tight, like a dead woman's.

The boat was coming in fast—very fast—screaming in towards the beach. It sounded like an angry wasp zooming into the attack. If this was home, Hanna was thinking, as she struggled with her salt-stiffened trainers, if this was England, we could dial nine nine nine right now, get the police. There'd be helicopters with searchlights, trained marksmen. Here there was just Dad—Dad with his silly flappy shorts and his bare chest—against half a dozen men with bandannas and, no doubt, guns. She wanted to go to him, be with him. They couldn't just leave him! 'Mum,' she began . . .

But Mum shushed her to silence. She was holding out bottles of drinking water. 'Take these,' she ordered. 'And when I say go, go. Take the path by the well, then go as fast as you can into those bushes on the ridge. And for God's sake be quiet.'

'But we'll need torches,' Ned protested.

'No torches. The moon's quite bright. Switch on a light and they'll spot you straight away.'

Hanna glanced at her mother. She was still in her sarong, still barefooted. She looked so Chinese, so *foreign* suddenly, with her high cheekbones and big almond-shaped eyes. 'But you're not ready, Mum!'

'I'm OK.'

'No you're not. Dad said . . . '

A crunch as the bow of the craft rode up onto the coarse coral sand of the beach. The engine cut. A moment of stillness, then Dad's voice—hard and challenging: '*Nak apa?*' He was frightened of nobody, Dad. Or if he was he never showed it.

'What's he saying, Mum?' Ned demanded.

'He's asking them what they want.'

There was a gabble of shouts in reply, splashes as the men from the boat leapt overboard into the shallow water. Again Dad's booming voice. '*Nak apa?*'

Mum had gone rigid, as if she'd been frozen or something. 'I've got to go to Dad,' she said urgently. 'He's not handling this right. He doesn't know how to speak to these people.'

'But he knows Malay,' Ned protested.

'Not *polite* Malay. Not the right kind of Malay. They'll listen to me, I'm certain of it.'

'But what about us? Dad said you should come with us.'

6

'You're quite old enough to look after yourselves!'

Mum suddenly sprang to life, pushing them roughly out of the hut, down the steps, onto the coconut-strewn grass. She pointed in the direction of the well. 'Now go!' she ordered. 'We'll come and find you when everything's safe.'

Ned gave a sob of terror. 'But I don't *want* to go, Mum. I want to stay here with you!'

Mum sucked in a sharp breath. 'Please, Ned,' she began, 'please don't make me . . . '

'Come on, for God's sake!' Hanna grabbed at her brother's hand, wrenched him away. 'We'll be all right, Mum,' she called back over her shoulder, 'don't worry about us. Go and help Dad!'

They began to run.

Ned was slow at first, reluctant, glancing back at Mum. But then he had to concentrate on the path as it twisted up between the tangled roots of the coconut trees. 'Don't stop,' Hanna kept urging him, shoving him in the back if he started to slow. 'Just keep going.'

It was darker under the trees, a lot darker, and it got harder to run as the path steepened. They passed the well with its sagging rattan screens, the ground around it still wet from the water-fight they'd had while they were bathing earlier. Ahead was the dense wall of undergrowth

7

where the jungle began. Something—a palm rat probably—scuttled across the path in front of them, rattling the dry leaves. There were scorpions in the leaves, Hanna knew, and lots of other nasty things that only came out at night. That was why their hut was built on stilts. That was why . . .

Loud noises from the beach. She grabbed at Ned's T-shirt, jerked him to a halt, twisted back.

It was impossible to see anything—there were too many trees in the way—but the sound carried, crystal clear. There was some kind of argument going on—raised voices, the scuffle of feet in the sand. She heard Dad's tiger growl, Mum's softer tones. Mum was pleading with the men, it sounded like, offering them something, but they seemed to be ignoring her. There was a sudden loud shout from Dad. What sounded like a series of violent blows landing. The splash of a body falling heavily into the water.

Then the scream came.

It was like no other scream Hanna had ever heard. A scream of rage, not fear—harsh, cracked, starting off deep and low, then doubling and redoubling into a brain-splitting, blood-curdling howl. The terrible noise torpedoed across the surface of the bay, bounced off the steep rocks of Dead Man's Leap, seeming to get louder, not softer, as it went.

And then . . . silence.

It was even worse than the scream, somehow, the silence. More shocking, more terrifying. It was as if the world had ended, as if every living thing had been wiped from the face of the planet. There were no voices, no shouts, any more—not even the splash of waves on the beach. Even the cicadas high up in the jungle trees seemed to have been frozen into stillness. For the first time in her life, Hanna quite literally felt her hair stand on end.

Ned's voice, Ned's little-boy voice: 'It was Mum, Hanna. That screaming was Mum.'

'Of course it wasn't! It was one of the pirates. Dad must have . . . '

'It *was* Mum! I know her voice! It *was*!'

Hanna turned back to her brother. He looked like one of those kids you see on the news—those street kids in Palestine or somewhere—staring at the camera with already-dead eyes in the moments before the bullets slam into them. 'I'm going to go and find her,' he said quietly.

'No you're not.'

'I am!'

He tried to push past her, but she was too quick for him. She grabbed him by the neck, wrestled him to the ground, threw herself on top of him.

They'd had fights before—lots of fights—and Ned had almost always won. But this time it was different. Dodging his thrashing legs, she pinned him against the twisted roots of one of the forest trees, forcing his head back until he started to choke from lack of air. 'Mum said stay here, so we're going to stay here!' she hissed desperately. 'If we go down there they'll capture us too, and then there'll be nobody to get help, nobody who'll know what's happened. Mum and Dad are depending on us, do you understand that? *Do you?*'

Ned struggled for a little while longer, then suddenly went limp. 'It *was* Mum,' he said hopelessly.

'It wasn't. I heard it just as clear as you, and it wasn't. Now promise me you won't do anything else stupid. Promise me!'

Ned was crying now, sniffing back tears. 'All right,' he said eventually. 'I promise.'

Hanna released him, stood up slowly. Even though she'd told Ned she was certain about the scream, she wasn't really. She wasn't certain about anything any more—what to do, where to go. Was she being a coward, staying here, keeping Ned here? What if there was something they could do right now? What if they *could* rescue Mum and Dad?

She sniffed once, twice. There was a strange smell. It was like . . . like a barbecue. Were the pirates *cooking* something? Not caring about snakes or scorpions or anything else, she pushed herself quickly through the undergrowth until she got to a place where she could see.

Smoke. A tall column of black smoke was twisting up into the pale, moonlit sky. As she watched there was a flicker of flame at its base. Then another.

They'd set fire to the hut!

For some reason—for some stupid reason—it was her iPod she thought about. She'd had it for her thirteenth birthday from Mum and Dad, and had tucked it under her pillow before she went to sleep. It was the best present she'd ever had—easily the best. And now it was going to get burnt up. Destroyed. It was so unfair, so *totally* unfair!

It seemed impossible for flames to spread so quickly. Within seconds the flimsy hut was a roaring inferno, sparks shooting skywards in a mad swirl. There was a noise like guns going off as the bamboo poles holding the roof cracked and split under the intense heat. Some of the coconut trees nearby had caught fire too, their massive fronds curling and twisting like clenched hands . . .

Now there *was* light—more than enough. It looked like daytime down on the beach, and for the first time Hanna could see their attackers. They were thin, wild-looking men in ragged shorts and singlets. They had *parangs* slung from

11

their waists—long, vicious slashing knives like the one Dad used for cutting bamboo and coconuts—and some of them were carrying bundles. They were moving quickly away from the burning hut, back across the sand to where their boat was drawn up.

But where were Mum and Dad? Surely they weren't in the hut? Surely the men hadn't forced them to go back inside before they'd set fire to it . . .

A sudden movement from the boat caught Hanna's eye. It wasn't empty, as she'd first thought. She strained desperately to see. In the bottom of it, just visible, curled up like caterpillars, were two dark shapes—human shapes. One of them was wriggling, the other was still. It was impossible to be sure, but the moving shape seemed to be wearing a sarong. It had to be them. It *had* to be!

'Hanna?' Ned's voice beside her, hesitant, uncertain.

'They're in that boat,' she said, not taking her eyes off it. 'Mum and Dad are in that boat.'

As they watched, the men reached it, shoved it swiftly out into the water; swung themselves aboard. The engine screamed into life.

The craft surged rapidly into the lagoon, curving out beyond the reef towards Dead Man's Leap and the waiting *kumpit*. To the children it felt as if it was taking their whole life with it—everything warm and comfortable and loving.

To Hanna's surprise Ned's hand crept into hers—the first time he'd willingly held hands with her for years. 'What are we going to do now?' he asked.

She was quiet for a long time, watching until the boat was out of sight, until there was just the flicker of moonlight on the water, and the flicker of flames from the burning hut. Then she took a deep breath. 'Something,' she said in a new, hard voice she didn't know she had. 'We're going to do *something*.'

2
Premonitions

They'd talked about the island for as long as the children could remember. It was usually in the evenings, in winter, when the nights were long and dark and cold, and they were sitting round the woodburner after supper, after homework, watching the dance of the firelight on the rough white walls of the cottage. That's when Dad—tired out from his day's work thatching—would stretch himself and say, 'God, I wish I was on Kaitan right now.'

Then Mum would glance up from her marking, and nod. 'On the verandah in front of the hut, sitting on that bench thing.'

'Watching the sun sink down behind Dead Man's Leap.'

'Magic.'

That would be the cue for stories—stories that both children still loved to hear, even though they'd heard them a hundred times—about the 'Last of the Hippies' as Mum called Dad. How he'd taken a gap year back when gap years hadn't been invented, and the gap year had turned into a gap two years, then five years, then ten . . . How he'd drifted through Thailand and Cambodia, Laos and Vietnam, working in logging camps and on riverboats; how he'd helped set up a sanctuary for orphaned orang-utans in Sumatra, and taught English to a Malay prince in Perak. How he'd crossed Borneo on foot and in Dayak canoes, and been arrested as a suspected spy by the Indonesian authorities when he'd finally got to the other side . . .

And how, on an ordinary beach—an ordinary *boring* beach—north of Malacca, he'd met this Malaysian-Chinese girl student who was so beautiful, and so intelligent, that he'd made up his mind then and there to marry her; and eventually, despite everything her parents could do to prevent it, had.

'I'd heard about these islands, these incredible, fabulous islands, from a German guy who ran a wreck salvage business up in Palawan,' Dad would say. 'They weren't in any of the guidebooks because they were too difficult to get to, and were too close to the Philippine border for comfort.'

'Which is precisely why your dad decided they would be the *ideal* spot for our honeymoon,' Mum would add, with a touch of sarcasm.

That was when Dad would fetch his crumpled,

sweat-stained map of North Borneo out of the top drawer of the dresser, spread it out on the floor, and point to a pair of tiny dots off the coast, way out in the blue expanse of the Sulu Sea. 'There are two of them, see? Kaitan, which was our island, and Ular, a bit smaller. Kaitan means shark— Shark Island. Named after its shape, which looks like a shark's fin sticking up out of the water.'

Mum and Dad had spent three months on Kaitan. Dad had rebuilt a hut they'd found there, thatched the roof with *nipa* palm leaves, lashed together a verandah out of jungle wood. There was a well which gave fresh water; fish in the lagoon; tapioca root—which they boiled and ate like pota-toes—in the forest clearings. 'It's where you began,' Mum once said to Hanna.

'Where I *began*?'

'Where you were conceived.'

Being conceived wasn't something Hanna wanted to think about in detail, but it made the island seem very special—not like a normal place, but *part* of her somehow. 'I want to go there,' she'd tell Mum and Dad, meaning it from the bottom of her heart, nagging at them. 'I *need* to go there.'

But there'd never been enough money. There were bills to pay, the cottage to buy, and Dad's thatching business and Mum's part-time teaching had never left them with enough spare cash to fly them all halfway round the world and back again.

Until the cheque came through the post.

It was from a trust fund Granny and Grandpa had set up for Dad years ago, which he didn't even know he had. It wasn't a big cheque—just enough to replace the central heating in the cottage, and for Dad to get a new van for his work.

And for four return air tickets.

Mum fixed it with the school. Dad fixed it with Charlie who he worked with. Sadie from the village agreed to come in and look after the goats and the chickens and the horse. They all went to the doctor's in Honiton for a series of seriously painful injections.

Then, when everything was finally sorted and the bags were packed, Charlie drove them all to Heathrow in his clapped-out old car, and they got on a Malaysian Airlines 747-400 headed for Kuala Lumpur. They were going to be gone six and a half whole weeks! *They were going to the Island!*

They stopped over in Kuala Lumpur for three days, while Mum visited friends and tried to see her mother and father. The children hated the Malaysian capital. It was hot and smelly, full of traffic jams and tall buildings; and Mum got very upset when her father refused even to open the gate when she went round to his massive house. 'Don't you want to see your grandchildren?' she'd asked him.

'As far as I'm concerned I don't *have* any grandchildren,' he'd replied.

'I hope he rots in Hell,' Dad said, but that started a row with Mum about him not being respectful, and they ended up yelling at each other in the hotel room, which was the worst *ever* start to any holiday.

But it got better.

A whole lot better.

They flew to Borneo—two and a half hours over the bluest seas you could imagine, before dipping down across rainforests and rivers to Kota Kinabalu, the capital of Sabah State. From there they took another plane—much smaller, with noisy propellers—packed with large ladies in bright sarongs and small, snotty-nosed kids. The aircraft stayed very low, following the coastline, skimming across creeks and sandbars and river mouths. There were little tin-roofed villages half-hidden beneath coconut palms; bright painted fishing boats pulled up on the beaches. As the plane passed overhead, children ran out from their houses, waving and jumping. Hanna could almost hear the dogs barking, the cocks crowing . . .

Then, about an hour after they'd taken off, Dad, who was sitting towards the front, suddenly turned and pointed out of the window to his left. 'See?' he said.

Hanna craned her neck across her brother; squinted through the scratched glass. There, way out at sea, was a greeny-purple shape, surrounded by a white necklace of sand.

It was Kaitan!

And beyond it, just visible through the haze, was Ular.

Ned said they looked quite boring, like lumps of floating grass or something, but Hanna could tell he was excited. *She* was excited too—more excited than she'd been since she was a tiny kid. She desperately hoped they'd go closer so she could get a better view—maybe even spot the hut—but they didn't. Instead the plane turned inland, circled over a medium-sized town clustered around a muddy river mouth, and thumped down onto a cracked concrete runway in the middle of a field full of goats. 'This is Tamu,' Mum said. 'Where we get our boat.'

'*If* we get one,' Dad added, wrenching at the backpack jammed between his legs.

Tamu was horrible—disgusting. For a start it was blindingly, searingly hot. Secondly, it smelt of dried fish, which was the nastiest most sick-making stink in the world, though Mum and Dad both seemed to love the smell. The town consisted of several streets of tumbledown shop-houses, a large jetty where fishing boats came to unload their catches, and dozens of ramshackle wooden houses on stilts connected by bendy planks, which stretched almost the whole way across the river.

They spent two days in Tamu. They checked into a scruffy hotel with fans that didn't work and cockroaches in the bathroom, and the children spent their time trailing round after Mum and Dad while they argued with boatmen about the cost of taking them out to the island, and bought rice and mattresses and cooking oil and mosquito nets and a mountain of other stuff from the stinky provision shops.

But then, at last, everything was fixed, everything ticked off on the list; and after a final sweaty night in the hotel they jammed themselves into a couple of ancient taxis and rattled down to the jetty.

The boat that would take them to Kaitan was dark blue, quite large, and looked even older than the taxis. The boatman's name was Ahmad. He was around Dad's age, with dark brown skin and unsmiling eyes. He had an assistant—a boy of fifteen or so with a strange, crooked mouth, who helped to carry all the stuff on board.

And he had passengers.

There were about a dozen of them—mostly women and children—clustered in a tight group in the bows. They were all very thin, with ragged clothes and large staring eyes. One of the women held a baby wrapped tightly in a piece of dirty green cloth.

'Who are they?' Hanna asked, puzzled.

Dad had a short discussion with Ahmad and turned back to her. 'I thought so,' he said. 'They're Bajau.'

'Bajau?'

'Sea Gypsies. They've hitched a lift. I told Ahmad we don't mind. They're going back to their village.'

'What village?'

'They've got a village on the islands.'

'On *our* island?'

Dad grinned. 'No, not on ours. On Ular, the smaller one. I'd forgotten about the Sea Gypsies. They're like land gypsies, except they travel about in boats not caravans. They're very gentle people, very private, and they'll be no trouble. They'll no doubt sell us fish or a chicken or something if we run short of food.'

Hanna tried to hide her disappointment. There was no reason why these people *shouldn't* be living on the islands, of course, or be on their boat,

21

but somehow she'd imagined that the four of them would have them all to themselves, that they were real *deserted* desert islands, not somebody's home.

But even worse than the thought of the Sea Gypsies living on the islands was the way they looked at her and Ned. As the boat swung out into the muddy river, scraped across a shallow sand bar at its mouth, and chugged out into the crystal-clear waters of the Sulu Sea, they squatted back on their heels and fixed them both with blank expressionless stares. Sitting on the wooden bench in front of the cabin, Hanna began to feel like an animal at the zoo.

Ned obviously felt the same. 'Why do they keep looking at us, Mum?' he demanded.

'Because you're unusual.'

'No we're not.'

'To them you are. They don't see many white children.'

Mum fished in her bag and produced a packet of sweets she'd brought from home. She handed it to Ned. 'Try offering them some of these,' she suggested.

Ned took the packet, held it out. 'They're Liquorice Allsorts,' he said loudly, as if they were deaf. '*Liquorice Allsorts*! They're from England!'

There were four Sea Gypsy children besides the

baby: three younger girls and a boy of about Ned's age. The boy had a skin problem—there were pale patches on his arms and neck. For a while nothing happened.

Then, suddenly, the boy stood up and shuffled towards them. '*Makan*,' Mum urged him in Malay. 'Eat!'

He flashed her a quick, uncertain smile and reached for the packet. As he did so a sharp command rang out from the bows and he scurried back to where he'd been crouching.

It was a dead loss. Eventually even Dad couldn't stand being stared at any longer, and they moved round to the back of the boat where there was more privacy. He rolled out a couple of mattresses under the shade awning, and the children lay down. It was a long way to Kaitan, and with the heat, and the gentle swaying of the boat, they were soon asleep.

A change of note from the engine woke Hanna. She groaned, opened her eyes. She was soaked with sweat, seriously thirsty. She was about to ask Mum for some water when she glanced up ahead and scrambled to her feet, thirst forgotten.

They'd arrived!

At first sight it didn't look like an island at

all—just a dense wall of greenery sliding past the boat. Kaitan was so much bigger than she'd expected, so much taller—thick jungle, slashed here and there with the brilliant orange of flowering trees—rising to a jagged point hundreds of metres above her head. Down below, fingers of bare limestone rock stretched out into the sea, and in between them, one after another, were gently curving bays of white coral sand, fringed by coconut trees. A huge black and white sea-eagle flapped lazily along the shoreline; and as if someone had pressed a switch, a shoal of flying fish exploded out of the sea. It was the most beautiful place she'd ever seen!

'Look, Hanna!'

Ned was hanging over the side of the boat, his head almost in the water. She dropped to her knees next to him and stared downwards.

The water was so clear it was almost as if it wasn't there—as if they were flying above a sandy, rocky, moonscape. Beneath them were thousands—no, *millions*—of iridescent squid, jerking along like small, fat space rockets, as they hunted for food.

Mum had spotted them too. 'Well, at least we shan't starve,' she said.

Ned pulled a face. 'I hate squid.'

Mum laughed. 'You'll change your mind.'

'Wanna bet?'

But then it was Dad's turn to get excited. He was pointing up ahead. 'There it is!'

Sticking out beyond the next bay was a strange hollowed-out cliff, curled like a question mark. It was bare except for a few scrubby bushes, and it looked as if it might collapse at any moment. Ned and Hanna recognized it instantly from the pictures in Mum's album. It was Dead Man's Leap, where you held your nose and jumped down, down, into the sparkling waters beneath—if you dared! It was the first thing Dad had promised they'd do when they got to the island. The very first.

Beyond it—just beyond it—was the lagoon. And the hut! To the children it didn't feel as if they were on holiday at all. They felt as if they were coming home.

They were perfect, those first two weeks—utterly, dreamily perfect. Dad fixed up the hut, which was still in surprisingly good condition, and they cleared the well of fallen leaves and branches, so they could wash and get water to boil for drinking. They made rods from bamboo, and caught large numbers of silvery-yellow striped fish from the deep pools near the rocks, which Mum cooked over driftwood fires in the big black cast-iron wok she'd bought in Tamu.

When they weren't fishing, the children spent most of their time throwing themselves off Dead Man's Leap, or floating face down in the lagoon with their snorkels and masks, gazing in wonder at the brilliantly coloured fish and corals. It was the best reef in the whole of Asia, so Dad said, and they well believed him. Sometimes, when Dad came with them, they swam out to the very edge of the reef, to where a steep coral cliff plunged down to the seabed below. There they saw black-tipped reef sharks—completely harmless so Dad said—and huge scary stingrays. Right at the bottom, grazing like cows on the waving seaweed, massive green turtles. Dad promised that when the moon was right, they would go on an expedition to the beaches on the west of the island, where they'd spend the night watching the turtles come up to lay their eggs.

They saw very little of the Sea Gypsies—just the occasional glimpse of a spindly outrigger canoe way out on the ocean. They might have been a million miles away from the rest of the world—in another century even. Hanna half-expected to see Robinson Crusoe in his goatskin cap walking along the beach towards her, or find Man Friday's naked footprints in the sand.

But then, at the beginning of their third week on Kaitan, the helicopter came.

They'd just returned from a driftwood collecting expedition when they saw it. It was dull brown, and was travelling fast and low towards them from the south. It circled the central mountain twice, then slowed to a hover over the lagoon. 'What's that thing doing here?' Hanna demanded, hating the noise its engines made, furious that anybody should even *dare* to come near their island.

Dad squinted up at it, his eyes screwed tight against the glare of the sun. His relaxed expression had disappeared. 'It's army,' he said uncertainly. 'Or maybe police. I can't see the markings.'

'Are they going to land?' Ned asked.

'I don't think so. There's nowhere flat enough.'

'So what are they doing here then?'

'Checking up on us, probably. Seeing what we're up to.'

'Why should they want to do that?'

Dad shrugged. 'God knows.'

'Perhaps they're looking for pirates.'

Hanna said it as a joke, but Dad didn't take it as one. He glanced sharply at her. 'What pirates?'

'There are pirates in the Sulu Sea. It says so in your Borneo book. I've just been reading about them,' she said defensively.

'Are there, Dad?' Ned chimed in. 'Are there really pirates here?'

'They rob ships,' Hanna went on. 'They've got fast boats. And machine guns.'

'Hanna, be quiet!' Mum had joined them. She too had lost her relaxed holiday face. The thump-thump of the rotor blades was like the worst headache you could ever imagine. 'Ned, there are no pirates here!'

'Then where *are* they?' Ned demanded stubbornly.

There was a flash of anger from Dad. 'Hundreds of miles away, Ned. In the Philippines. Up near Mindanao. Now let's drop the subject, OK?'

'OK, Dad.'

Ned knew better than to say any more. So did Hanna. She peered up at the helicopter. It was spooky the way the thing just hovered there, doing nothing. She found herself hoping it would crash into the sea, or blow up or something. Ned obviously felt the same. He raised his hand, pointed a finger, made a banging noise.

'Ned, please!' Mum grabbed his arm, pulled it down. She shot Dad a quick, questioning glance.

She was scared, Hanna could tell. She didn't like Mum being scared. She gave an involuntary shiver. Suddenly the sun didn't seem quite so warm, the sea didn't seem so blue. Suddenly the island didn't feel like home any more.

The feeling stayed with her even after the helicopter had finally veered away and disappeared in the direction it had come from; even after they'd built the fire, boiled the rice; even after Dad had taken out his tin whistle and started playing the little happy tunes he always played when the sun went down.

It still hadn't left her two nights later when the pirates came.

3

Alone

'You said we were going to do something, so *what*?'
Ned was crouched in the shadow of a huge tree
trunk; a small, black blob.

'I haven't decided yet.'

'Well, decide.'

'Give me time! It's hard to think!' Even though
the night was warm, Hanna felt chilled to the
bone, and began to shiver. It was shock, she knew.
She recognized the feeling from the time she'd
been knocked off her bike by a car on Newton Hill.
Then, Mum had given her sweet tea and made her
lie down. This time she didn't need any tea. Or a
lie down. She just needed Mum. And Dad.

Had they really gone? Had they really been
captured? Maybe she'd made a mistake about the
bodies in the boat—the flickering light could have
easily played tricks on her eyes. Maybe they were
lying injured somewhere. Maybe they needed one
of those things you put round people's arms to
stop them bleeding to death . . .

They must go back down to the beach, she

decided, despite what Mum had said about them staying hidden. It was a risk—some of the pirates might have stayed behind and be lying in wait for them—but she'd never forgive herself if Mum and Dad needed her and she wasn't around to help.

She peered out through the trees once more. It was harder to see now—the fire was beginning to die down—but as far as she could tell the bay seemed to be completely deserted. There was no movement, apart from the swaying of the palm trees in the light breeze that had sprung up. She sucked in a deep breath, forced herself to speak as calmly as she could: 'OK, let's go then.'

'Go where?'

'Back down. We need to check things out.'

'But you just said . . . '

'Stay here if you like, I don't care.'

'No way!'

Ned scrambled to his feet. He was terrified of being left alone in the dark, menacing jungle. She found his hand again, gave it a quick squeeze. Her shivering was getting worse, and she hoped he wouldn't notice it. The last thing he needed at this point was a shaking sister. 'Stay close to me,' she said gently, 'and if I tell you to run, just run.'

'Where?'

'Anywhere. Run like anything and hide.'

'OK.' His reply was almost inaudible.

Going down was a lot worse than climbing up. Several times they stumbled and almost fell. Some of the bushes had long hooked thorns which tore at their bare legs. There were ants too, which felt like red hot needles when they bit. But eventually they reached the path, and soon after that, the rattan screens of the well. They paused there for a moment to rub at their stinging skin. Then Hanna motioned Ned to complete silence and led him out, between the spindly palm trunks, onto the beach.

Mum and Dad were gone.

She knew that for certain the moment she saw how smooth the sand was, how there were no fresh footprints anywhere except for the trail leading from the burning hut down to the water's edge, and in the scuffed area where the fight had taken place. There'd been no trick of the light. Mum and Dad really *had* been in the boat, and she must accept the fact. Despite the pressure of Ned's hand in hers, she suddenly felt acutely lonely, and, for the first time, close to tears.

'What's that?'

Ned was pointing at something in the sand close to the water's edge. It was shiny, reflecting back the dancing yellow light of the flames.

They ran down towards it, and Hanna bent and picked it up. The moment she did so, she wished she hadn't. It was Mum's lucky pendant with the

Chinese writing on it, the one Dad had bought her years ago in Singapore, the one she always wore when they were travelling, to keep them safe. It was broken, wrenched from its chain by some violent force, and it was covered in a dark sticky substance. Even without holding it up to the light, Hanna knew instantly what the substance was.

It was blood.

Frantically she plunged it into the water, rubbing and rubbing at it until all the stickiness was gone. Then she stood up again, and turned towards her brother. 'It's Mum's,' she said slowly, unnecessarily, holding it out to him, not caring now that he could see how much her hand was shaking.

'I know.' He made no move to take it.

'It's supposed to be lucky.'

'Well it isn't, is it?'

Hanna stared at the pendant for a moment longer. She had an overwhelming urge to throw it as far from her as she could, way out into the darkness of the bay. But something stopped her. Lucky or not, it was part of Mum. To throw it away would be like throwing Mum herself away, and she couldn't bear the thought of that. Instead she slipped it into the pocket of her shorts, and turned back towards the beach.

They went and sat in the little cave under Dead

Man's Leap. They'd made a sort of bench there from a driftwood plank soon after they'd arrived on the island, so they could sit in the shade when the sun got too hot on the beach. It wasn't very comfortable, but somehow having a solid wall of rock behind them made them feel safer. With no watch, Hanna had no idea how long it was until dawn—it could be an hour, it could be five—and it was getting darker by the minute as the fire died down. 'We should try to sleep,' she said.

'Why?'

'We're going to need all our strength.'

'For what?'

'To rescue Mum and Dad.'

Ned was silent for a long time—so long that Hanna put out a hand to check that he was still there beside her in the blackness. Then he said, 'What if they're dead? What do we do if they're dead?'

She felt as if she had a tight helmet on her head, crushing her brain. They mustn't even *think* such a thing, let alone say it. 'Of course they're not dead!' she snapped.

'How do you know?'

'Because I saw Mum move. Dead people don't move.'

'What about Dad? He wasn't moving.'

'He was unconscious.'

'You don't know that!'

'Yes I do.'

'How? How do you know that?'

Inside she was screaming. *Please stop asking questions!* 'Because they've been kidnapped, stupid,' she heard herself say. 'Nobody kidnaps dead people.'

Kidnapped!

She hadn't even thought about the word before it had passed her lips. But now it had, she felt a sudden, massive rush of relief. Of course that was what had happened! If the pirates were just robbers, they wouldn't have bothered to take Mum and Dad with them. They'd have just stuffed everything they could steal into their boat and left.

That meant Mum and Dad were not just alive, but being looked after! If you were going to ask for a ransom for somebody you'd make sure they were OK otherwise there'd be no way you'd get any money.

Her happiness evaporated as quickly as it had come.

What money?

Kidnappers always wanted thousands of pounds—millions of pounds—before they'd ever let anybody go. Even if the cottage was sold, even if Granny and Grandpa gave them all the money they had, there would still be no way they could raise that amount. And if they couldn't?

She shuddered.

Ned seemed to be sharing her thoughts. He didn't ask any more questions, didn't seem to want any more answers. He just snuggled up close to her. 'Don't worry,' he said softly. 'We'll think of something in the morning. We'll get Mum and Dad back.'

Hanna must have slept, because it was daylight when she next looked up. Ned was gone from her side, and she saw him standing down by the edge of the lagoon staring out to sea. In the purple light of dawn he looked so young, so helpless—nothing like the pain-in-the-neck brother who shared her life at home.

She ran her tongue round her lips. She felt acutely thirsty. She looked around for the bottles of water Mum had given them, but they were nowhere to be seen. They must have dropped them somewhere in the jungle, which was a really stupid thing to have done. There was no way you could drink the well water until it had been boiled for at least fifteen minutes, which would mean lighting a fire, finding the big boiling saucepan . . .

She stood up, stretched painfully, and went to

join her brother. He gave her a tiny, sad smile of welcome. It was a perfect island dawn, the sun pushing up above the rim of the sea, changing the light from purple, to violet then gold. The scruffy old sea-eagle, who Dad had christened Fred, flapped off from his perch high up in the dead tree near the rocks to begin his morning patrol of the beaches. A flock of orange-beaked mynah birds squabbled and tumbled through the low undergrowth. In the transparent waters of the lagoon shoals of tiny blue and yellow fish swirled and pirouetted. It seemed impossible that the events of the night before had really happened. Hanna found herself listening for Mum's call to breakfast. Pancakes, would it be? Or maybe those tapioca fritters that Dad had taught them how to make, with loads and loads of dribbly, yummy honey . . .

Ned said, 'You seen it?'

'Seen what?'

'The hut.'

Hanna shook her head. The smell of burning was still fresh in her nostrils, and she hadn't wanted to look before. But now she turned towards it.

It was gone.

She'd expected *something* to still be there—blackened poles, maybe, or a heap of smouldering embers—but apart from a ring of scorched coconut trees, and a gap in the vegetation, it was as though their lovely, creaky, friendly hut, with its bouncy wooden verandah had never existed. Even the footprints in the sand leading towards it had been smoothed away by the high tide in the night.

It was a spooky feeling, and despite the growing warmth of the sun, Hanna shivered. She turned back to Ned. He was spooked too, she could tell. 'We'd best go and have a look,' she said, uncertainly.

He shook his head violently. 'I want to stay here.'

'Well, you can't. There may be stuff we need lying around. Dad's *parang* or something. If we can find that we can cut the top off a coconut. At least then we can have a drink. I'm dying of thirst, aren't you?'

Ned admitted he was.

'Well, come on then!' Hanna grabbed his hand, hauled him off across the beach.

There really *was* nothing left of the hut—just a flat carpet of white ash. In a matter of weeks new jungle plants would push up through it, spread their leaves, and nobody would know there'd ever been a building there.

But, miraculously, the kitchen was still standing, leaning at a crazy angle, its thatch blackened by smoke. They'd helped Dad build it in a clearing behind the hut during their first few days on the island—just a roof on poles to keep the rain out, with a wooden shelf for saucepans and pots, and a wok-shaped hearth made of rocks.

There, still on the hearth, its lid firmly closed, was the big water-boiling saucepan.

Hanna hurried towards it and lifted the lid. There was water inside! It was only a third full, but there was more than enough for both of them. She grabbed the tin mug from its hook, blew out the ash, dunked it into the pot and drank deeply.

Normally she hated boiled well water—it always tasted of smoke and the remains of whatever food they sometimes cooked in the same pot—but today it was the best drink in the world! Ned took the mug from her and drank too.

The smaller saucepan was on the shelf, next to the wok. It contained cooked rice left over from last night's dinner. Hanna sniffed at it to make sure it was still fresh, then both children scooped up great lumps of it and stuffed it into their mouths.

It was incredible the difference the food and drink made. Hanna felt energy flood back into her body. She made a quick search of the kitchen. There was no more food, but she didn't expect to find any—Mum always kept their stores up in the hut away from the ants and the palm rats, and everything would have been destroyed—but the fishing lines were still there, coiled up on one of the posts, and there were loads of tapioca plants growing wild up behind Dead Man's Leap, so they wouldn't starve. They must get more water from the well and boil it up so it was ready when they needed it. For an agonizing moment she thought there were no matches, but then she found a box on the shelf. The *parang* should be on the shelf too. With the *parang* they could cut open coconuts, cut bamboo, even chop down trees . . .

It wasn't there.

They hunted all round the kitchen, and even scraped away at the ashes of the hut, but the big knife that Dad always kept so clean and sharp was missing. The pirates must have found it and taken it with them. Never mind, they could use something else: maybe Mum's Chinese cleaver, the one she used for cutting up fish. Hanna's mind was racing. There was so much to do, so much to decide.

But first they must fetch water from the well. She grabbed her straw hat, which miraculously was still hanging on one of the nails, and two plastic buckets. She thrust one into Ned's hand. 'Let's get going,' she ordered.

'You sound just like Mum,' her brother complained.

'Any objections?'

He didn't have any.

4

The Face in the Rocks

'We must make a boat,' Ned said.

'Out of what?'

'I don't know. Bamboo or something.'

Early afternoon. They'd spent most of the morning collecting large black rocks and arranging them on the beach to spell out the letters SOS so the police helicopter would know there was something wrong if it came back. That was Ned's idea, he'd seen it on TV. Now they were fishing near Dead Man's Point, dangling their lines into the shoals of reef fish, desperate to catch something. Normally the fish threw themselves at their hooks, but today they didn't seem interested in the pieces of limpet they were using as bait. No fish meant just lumps of boring tapioca for supper, which was not a very cheerful prospect.

Hanna cast her line further out, watched it sink slowly until the hook was almost resting on the nose of a particularly dozy-looking parrot fish. She'd been thinking about Mum and Dad. They'd be back wherever the pirates had come from by now, locked up somewhere, she supposed. She hoped they'd been given something to eat and drink, and were not tied up or anything, or if they were, the ropes weren't too tight. Dad was very clever with knots. Maybe he could get his hands free, untie Mum. Maybe they could both escape, get help. Maybe . . . 'So where would we go if we managed to make this boat?' she demanded.

'Borneo.'

'Borneo's miles away! Anyway, we don't know which direction to go in.'

'West.'

'We haven't got a compass.'

'We look at the sun. See where it goes down.'

'What about at night?'

'We use the stars.'

Hanna stared out, across the reef, to the white line of breakers in the distance. The thought of bobbing around in the dark on some flimsy little raft, way out on the shark-filled ocean, made her stomach tighten with dread. She'd rather wait until Ahmad the boatman finally came back to fetch them in four weeks' time, than do that.

But they had to do something. They couldn't just sit here fishing while Mum and Dad were in deadly danger!

'There's Ular,' she said. 'We could go there.'

When the weather was good you could see Ular—the island where the Sea Gypsies had their village—quite clearly: a low, palm-fringed ridge sticking out of the sea away to the north. It ought to be possible to get there if they had a good enough boat. They'd need to make a sail, of course . . .

Ned snorted. 'Ular? You're not serious?'

'Why not? I'm sure the Sea Gypsies will help us.'

'They'll kidnap us too.'

'Why should they want to do that?'

'Because they're the pirates.'

'Don't be stupid!'

'Well, who else knows we're here?'

Hanna fell silent. He'd got a point. She thought about those people on Ahmad's boat. Dad had said they were harmless, and they certainly *looked* harmless. But you couldn't tell anything from looks, she knew that. All the same, maybe it was a risk they should take. Unless the police helicopter came back, which it probably wouldn't, it was their only alternative. Even the thought of being captured didn't seem too bad if it meant being taken to where Mum and Dad were being held.

But could they really build a boat that would take them all that way? Dad would know what to do. He'd build a brilliant boat. Except there'd be no need to build one if he was here . . .

'Stupid fish! We'll never catch anything!' she snapped, her frustration and unhappiness finally getting the better of her. She jerked her line viciously out of the water. The baited hook whizzed past Ned's nose and slammed into a small tree growing out of the rocks behind her.

'Dumb idiot!' Ned yelled at her. 'You could have blinded me!'

'Well, you shouldn't have been in the way.'

Now she'd have to spend time untangling the stupid thing, when there was so much else to do! But they couldn't afford to lose the hook—they'd only got the two which were on the fishing lines. The others must have got burned up in the fire.

Still fuming, she turned and clambered up the tree. The line had wound itself tightly round its thorny branches, and the hook was dug into the trunk. Even worse, the whole thing was swarming with angry ants!

Gingerly, she began to unwind the line, slapping at the ants as they scurried up her arms. She'd got about half of it free, when something—a slight movement—made her glance sharply up.

Staring at her, through a V-shaped gap in the rocks just above the tree, was a face.

She screamed, jerked back, lost her footing and crashed painfully down onto her left side.

Ned dropped his rod, scrambled over to her. 'What happened?'

Hanna pointed upwards. 'There's somebody up there,' she gasped. 'I saw somebody!'

She pointed at the gap in the rocks.

The face was gone.

Had she imagined it?

No, she hadn't. *She hadn't.*

Ned looked scared stiff. 'Was it one of the pirates?'

She shook her head. 'No, I don't think so.' She was racking her brains. There'd been something familiar about the face. She'd seen that face before . . .

Then it came to her. 'It's that boy from the boat!' she exclaimed. 'The Sea Gypsy boy. The one with the funny skin!'

She scrambled to her feet, the pain from her bruised side forgotten. If that boy was here, he wouldn't be alone. The whole island could be swarming with Sea Gypsies. And if Ned was right, if they *were* the pirates . . .

She glanced wildly around. Because of the high rocks there was no easy way up into the jungle from where they were, except back along the beach. If the pirates were waiting for them there, they'd be captured for sure. There was always the lagoon, of course. Maybe they could take big breaths, swim under water, get round the headland into one of the other bays . . .

'Look!' Ned was pointing along the beach.

Her eyes followed the direction of his finger. It was the boy again! He was now at the bottom of Dead Man's Leap, near the little cave where they'd slept, and seemed to be making no attempt to conceal himself. He hesitated for a moment, then began to run quickly towards them, leaping from rock to rock. Eventually he stopped on a large flat slab of limestone, blocking their way out to both the beach and the sea.

Now they really were trapped!

Hanna was still wondering what they should do, when Ned pushed past her. He climbed up onto the slab, and planted himself in front of the boy. 'What do you want?' he demanded.

There was no response.

Ned inched closer, until their noses were almost touching. He wasn't afraid now, Hanna could tell. For him it was like being back in the playground, dealing with a bit of bother from one of the other kids. 'Well?' he demanded. 'I asked you a question!'

The boy didn't back off. He stood his ground, and continued to stare, eyeball to eyeball. She wondered what would happen if it came to a fight; who would win? Ned was stockier, but the boy looked wiry, and was obviously quite strong.

She was about to tell Ned that there was no point in asking him questions because he didn't know English, when the boy spoke. *'Likis al sat,'* he said slowly.

It was the first time Hanna had heard him speak. His voice was quite deep, and she realized he must be older than she had thought, closer to her age than Ned's, despite his small size.

'We don't know any Malay,' Ned spat back. 'We don't know what you're talking about!'

The boy repeated the words. *'Likis al sat.'*

Then, suddenly, Hanna understood. The boy wasn't speaking Malay at all! He was saying the words Liquorice Allsort! He wanted a sweet, like the one Ned had offered him on the boat.

'No sweets!' Hanna told him. 'We don't have any more sweets.'

A look of disappointment spread across the boy's face. 'Godammit!' he said.

'You understand what we're saying?' Hanna asked, astonished.

He nodded. 'Learn melikan. Anywhere teach me.' He spread his hands towards the beach. 'Dam fire.'

'You saw the fire?' Ned asked.

'See. Big dam fire. Everybody see.'

'Everybody?'

'Everybody in *kampung*.'

47

'That's his village,' Hanna explained to Ned. 'He's talking about his village on Ular Island.'

'I *know* that!' Her brother didn't take his eyes off the boy. 'Are you pirates?' he demanded. 'Was it you lot who kidnapped our mum and dad?'

The boy looked blank. This time he really didn't seem to understand.

A sudden thought crossed Hanna's mind. Maybe the pirates were using him like bait to catch a fish. Maybe he'd been sent to keep them talking while they crept up through the rocks until they were close enough to jump out and grab them.

She glanced around again, her eyes straining to detect the slightest movement. There was none. She turned back to the boy. 'Are you alone?' she demanded.

'Lone?'

'One person? Just you?'

The boy grinned. Despite the ugly white patches on his skin he had a friendly face, with big brown twinkly eyes. 'Sure thing! One dam person! People in *kampung* too dam frighten!'

'Frightened of what?'

'*Saitan.* They think fire come from *saitan.*'

'*Saitan?*'

'Dam bad spirit.'

Hanna was astonished. 'You mean they believe the fire was actually started by *evil spirits*?'

He nodded. 'Many *saitan* here. Many many.' He spread his hands around as if he was introducing a group of friends.

'He's totally screwy,' Ned said to Hanna. 'He's a head-case.' He turned back to the boy. 'Listen, dumbhead, it was *pirates*! Pirates came here in a boat. They set fire to our hut. They kidnapped our mum and dad!'

'Kidnap?'

'You don't understand kidnap?'

The boy looked puzzled.

Ned suddenly grabbed himself by the throat with both hands and mimed being dragged backwards, gasping and struggling. 'I'm being kidnapped,' he shouted. 'Get it? Kidnapped!'

For an instant the boy looked on, astonished. Then suddenly his face split into a huge grin, and he began to laugh. Hanna found herself laughing too. Ned looked so idiotic struggling with himself!

'*It's not funny!*' Ned yelled at her—at both of them.

'Not funny,' the boy repeated, tears streaming down his blotchy brown and white face. 'Not dam funny ha ha! No, sir!'

5

Voyage to Snake Island

The boy's name was Jikiri—Jik for short—and he had a boat. He led the children to it. It was drawn up on the beach in Lizard Bay, a small cove on the other side of Dead Man's Leap, where Ned had once seen a huge monitor lizard sunning itself on one of the rocks. It was a long, thin boat, black with age, carved out of a single tree trunk. It had outriggers—bamboo poles stretched out on either side to stop it turning over and sinking—and a short mast with a blue and white striped sail.

'Dam good boat!' Jik said proudly, patting its curved bow.

'Dam good,' Hanna agreed with him. It was catching, the funny way he spoke. She found herself liking him more and more as the minutes passed.

'Now we go!'

'Go?'

'Go to Ular. Go to my island.'

Hanna's eyes sought Ned's. Was it safe—was it *wise*—to go anywhere with this strange boy? Could this be just another trap they were falling into?

Ned obviously didn't think so. He'd been mad keen on sailing ever since he'd done a weekend course with his school, and the last of his suspicions seemed to have disappeared the moment he laid eyes on the boat. 'Does it go fast?' he asked Jik.

'Dam fast!' Jik told him proudly, and slid the boat easily down into the water. It bobbed gently on the end of its line, looking like a friendly water beetle with its long, stretched-out legs.

Ned scrambled on board, eyed the sail professionally, tugged at a couple of ropes. 'Wicked!' he said. 'Come on, Hanna!'

Hanna glanced back at Dead Man's Leap. Surely they couldn't just *go*, even if it was safe to do so. There were things they needed. Stuff they should take—clothes, passports . . .

But those had all been burnt up.

Water. They needed water!

Jik seemed to read her mind. He pointed to a large earthenware pot in the bow of the boat, made a smacking noise with his lips. 'Drink,' he said.

'Is it boiled?'

'Boiled?'

'You must boil water for fifteen minutes or you'll get sick.'

'Get in, for God's sake!' Ned ordered. 'Or I really *will* have to start calling you Mum!'

Jik was right about his boat. It *was* fast. Ned helped him paddle it out round the point of the island, where they hoisted the sail. There, a brisk southerly breeze sent them skimming across the surface of the waves. Jik called the wind '*habagat*' which meant 'good wind' in the Sea Gypsy language. The two boys seemed to have hit it off immediately, and were soon chatting and laughing and pointing things out to each other. Give them a few weeks and they'd both be able to speak each other's language fluently.

Hanna crouched near the mast and pulled her battered old straw hat down over her ears to stop the wind whipping it away. She was glad Ned had cheered up, but at the same time she was a bit irritated. After what had happened he had no reason to be *this* cheerful.

Despite the cool wind and the sparkling waves, despite the fact that every minute they were getting closer and closer to Ular—where somebody, surely, would help them look for Mum and Dad—the worry she felt in the pit of her stomach refused to go away. The whistling of the wind in the ropes seemed to have exactly the same pitch as that terrible scream they'd heard coming from the beach last night. The hunched shape of the water pot in the bows reminded her of Dad lying at the bottom of the pirates' boat. He'd been so still . . .

She tried to imagine what would happen if Dad and Mum were never found, if they never came back. What then? She'd have to look after Ned, she supposed, until he was grown up—and probably even after that because he was so useless at doing things in the house. She tried to imagine them both back in the cottage, getting ready for school, with no Mum to make sure they'd got their sports kit and their homework books, no Dad singing in the bathroom while the shower water hissed and gushed.

She couldn't. It was utterly impossible. She refused to even think about it.

Except she couldn't stop herself. She just couldn't . . .

'Look!'

Ned was pointing excitedly beyond the bows. A gleaming blue-black shape broke the surface. Then another.

Dolphins!

There was a whole group of them—a pod—shooting through the water, trailing streams of silver bubbles. They were so beautiful they made her want to cry.

'*Lumba lumba*,' Jik said, and mimed eating.

'You *eat* dolphins?' Hanna asked, horrified.

He grinned cheerfully. 'Dam good!'

'You're disgusting,' she said, and turned away.

Did the Sea Gypsies *really* eat dolphins? She supposed they did. After all, they lived from the sea, and presumably ate anything they could catch. She thought about what Dad had told her about them. How they had their own language, their own religion, and had special 'ghost' islands where they buried their dead. Even though the government had tried to get them to live on the mainland, so the children could go to school and the men could find work, they'd refused. Any trouble and they'd simply get into their boats and sail away . . .

Then, quite without warning, Jik began to sing. It was a strange, haunting song, dipping and rising like the sea. Hanna caught the words *'lumba lumba'* repeated over and over again. He was singing to the dolphins! How could you talk about eating something one minute, then sing a song to it the next? Even Ned was awed into silence.

'Wind song,' Jik explained, when his singing finally ended. 'Goddam good song! Make wind blow!' And as if in response, the breeze, which had begun to die away, picked up again and threw the little boat through the water.

Gripping his steering paddle with both hands, Jik pointed the bows towards the palm-lined shores of the island where he lived.

* * *

Mum had once told them that 'Ular' meant 'snake' in Malay, and the island certainly looked like a snake, with a lumpy, jungle-covered head, and a long, low tail of sand and coconut trees which curled itself around a shallow central lagoon. Jik's village almost filled the lagoon—a mass of moored boats and rickety-looking thatched huts on tall stilts, connected by flimsy plank bridges. Blue smoke from cooking fires spiralled up into the evening sky.

There were boats everywhere—tiny dug-outs being punted along by women and children; outriggers like Jik's skimming home with their sails set; and here and there bigger boats crewed by men wearing bright-coloured headcloths, returning from their day's fishing. It was like being in the middle of rush hour.

As Jik's boat nosed in towards the village, Hanna and Ned immediately found themselves the centre of attention. Small kids in even smaller canoes pulled alongside jabbering and pointing. Other children leapt from the platforms of their houses and swam towards them like so many wriggling brown fishes. Women paused in their cooking, put their hands on their hips and stared. The fishermen shouted loud, unfriendly-sounding questions from the decks of their boats as they passed.

Jik seemed totally unfazed. He was loving all the attention, revelling in it as if he'd just won a pop contest or something. Hardly bothering to steer any more, he launched into long complicated-sounding conversations with everybody they passed, pointing in turn at Hanna and Ned, and then back at the distant hump of Kaitan Island. Hanna caught the words *'salusu'* which she'd worked out meant 'pirate', and *'ma-laga'* which meant 'fire'. Even though she hated being stared at and talked about, one thing at least made her feel better: if these *Sea Gypsies* really were the pirates, they'd hardly be asking questions about where the children had come from. They'd know already.

As they approached the village, Jik expertly dropped the sail, grabbed a paddle, and began to steer them down a sort of watery street between two rows of houses. The smell of woodsmoke and cooking fish was stronger now, mixed with another nastier smell, which reminded Hanna of blocked toilets. Women leaning from their house-platforms fired a constant stream of comments at the boat, and at each other. Dogs barked. Babies cried.

Suddenly Jik gave Hanna and Ned a big grin. 'Arrive!' he exclaimed, and slid the boat to a halt beneath one of the houses. He tied it to a wooden upright, leapt onto a nearby ladder and disappeared onto the platform above.

Seconds later his face reappeared, looking down over the edge. Beside him was a row of other small faces, all looking distinctly like Jik. 'Come!' he ordered.

'Come!' echoed all the kids, and burst into hysterical giggles.

Ned seemed to have suddenly lost all his new-found confidence and showed no signs of wanting to get up and go anywhere. Trying to ignore the excited chatter from above, Hanna hauled him to his feet and shoved him upwards. Then, sucking in a deep breath, she followed.

There were at least ten kids on the creaking wooden house-platform, and more were arriving by the second—the older ones dressed in shorts and ragged T-shirts, the younger ones completely naked. One of the smallest, a tiny tot with huge eyes and a bulging brown belly, greeted Hanna with a twinkling fountain of pee that just missed her left hand as she hauled herself up the last rungs of the ladder.

Jik had disappeared, but he emerged from the doorway of the house a moment later. Following him, wiping her wet hands on her sarong, was a woman Jik introduced as his mother. She had creased, leathery skin and wore her hair scraped tightly back from her face. She was not pleased. She directed a few sharp words at her son then marched off along the plank walkway, and was lost from sight among the other houses.

Jik looked rueful. 'She say we must go.'

'Go where?' Ned asked.

'Visit Panglima.'

Every Sea Gypsy village had a Panglima, Hanna remembered Dad saying. He was a sort of chief, and was very important. Jik beckoned them to follow.

It was like being in some weird version of the Pied Piper. First there was Jik. Then, following close behind him, was Ned. After that came Hanna, and behind her, in a long line, chanting and giggling, marched what seemed to be every kid in the village. They wound in and out of the houses, and across alarmingly bendy planks, like an endless wriggling, bouncing snake.

Eventually Jik stopped outside a larger than usual house. He indicated that Ned and Hanna should take off their shoes, and they went inside.

It was more like a shed than a place where people lived. Apart from a few baskets piled against the walls, its single room was completely empty. There was no furniture—not even any mats. Hanna could quite clearly see the sea swishing about through the gaps in the sagging plank floor.

Jik's mother was squatting, talking rapidly to an old, white-haired man who was sitting near the far wall. He was extremely thin, with tired-looking watery eyes, and was wearing only a pair of ragged shorts. When he moved, Hanna noticed that his hands shook.

The three children stood respectfully in the middle of the floor while the conversation continued. Jik's mother did most of the talking, occasionally turning to point in the direction of Kaitan Island. The Panglima, Hanna noticed, seemed to be getting more and more worried by what she was telling him. He kept repeating a single word over and over again. *'Triti. Triti.'* Hanna tried to ask Jik what it meant, but he shushed her into silence.

After a few minutes, two younger men, who she'd seen mending fish traps on the house platform outside, came in through a back entrance and stood next to the Panglima. Hanna began to feel as if she and Ned were on trial for something, waiting for the verdict from a judge. Behind them, the village children crowded the open doorway, whispering and shuffling, clearly awed by what was going on.

Eventually the old man seemed to make up his mind. For the first time since they'd arrived he stared directly at the children. *'Katoh!'* he said.

Jik looked stunned. He turned to Hanna and Ned. 'He say you must leave here!'

'Leave?'

'Go back to Kaitan.'

'But we can't do that!' Hanna exclaimed, horrified. 'We can't go back there! We need help! Our mum and dad have been kidnapped. Doesn't he understand?'

'*Katoh!*' The Panglima spoke again, this time with more force. He turned to the two men beside him—his sons, Hanna guessed—and made a quick gesture. They crossed quickly over to the children. The taller of the two, who had a stupid, brutal face, gripped Hanna's arm painfully. The other man grabbed Ned. Jik started to protest, but was silenced by a sharp command from his mother.

The village kids scattered in alarm as Hanna and Ned were marched outside. A fishing boat was moored next to the platform, bobbing gently on the rising tide. The children were dumped unceremoniously into it, and the two men jumped in after them. The taller man held them, while his companion bent to fiddle with an ancient black engine. It coughed once, but refused to start.

He cursed, and was about to try again when a strange, cracked shout from above made him freeze.

The shout came again; louder, sharper. This time it was the taller man's turn to react. He let go of the children and dropped to his knees in the bottom of the boat, cowering like a terrified dog.

Hanna and Ned peered upwards in alarm. A weird, stooped figure was standing on the edge of the platform, staring down at them. It was a woman—an old, old woman—with sunken cheeks and a deeply lined face. She wore a stained yellow headcloth, with strings of red coral beads round her neck, and was dressed in a bizarre assortment of green and yellow rags.

But it was not her clothes that were so alarming. It was her mouth.

Her toothless gums, which were moving slowly from side to side like a cow chewing its cud, seemed to be dripping with fresh blood!

6

The Woman Who Could See Through Mountains

The old woman made a quick movement with her claw-like hands, indicating that the children should climb back up to the platform.

Ned shook his head. 'No way am I going up there,' he gasped, pressing back against Hanna.

But then a familiar figure appeared next to the woman. It was Jik! Far from being scared, his face was once more split by a huge grin. 'No dam problem!' he called cheerfully down to them. 'This Manai Liha, and if she say you can stay, you stay. Come come!'

Hanna and Ned hesitated for a moment, but since the old woman didn't look as if she was about to sink her fangs into Jik's neck, they decided the risk was worth it, and clambered back up to the platform. The Panglima's sons got up to follow them, but a sharp word from Manai Liha sent them once more grovelling back into their boat. Seconds later the engine started, and they sped away into the lagoon.

The old woman hurled a loud shout of contempt

in their direction, then turned and shuffled swiftly into the Panglima's house. The children followed her, not wanting to miss a moment of what might happen next.

It was like one of those school assemblies when a group of kids gets hauled up in front of the Head for doing something really serious. Manai Liha planted herself a couple of metres away from the Panglima and Jik's mum, opened her blood-stained mouth, and let out a torrent of abuse. For a short while the Panglima tried to defend him-self—Hanna heard him use the word *triti* again several times—but in the end he was forced into silence. Jik's mum sat with her head bowed as blobs of red-coloured spittle showered down on top of her.

'What's she saying?' Hanna whispered to Jik.

'She say you are guest of the Bajau people. She say they must make you welcome. She say you are in trouble and need help.' He giggled. 'She say it would be better to have a chicken for a Panglima than him!'

Then, as suddenly as she had begun, Manai Liha stopped. She turned to the children, gave them a bloody, toothless grin, and whispered a few quiet words to Jik. He nodded, and stood aside. She shuffled out into the evening sunshine, along the plank walkway, and was gone.

There was a short, stunned silence, broken only by the sound of the Panglima muttering unhappily to himself under his breath. Then Jik's mum stood up, wiped at her face with the corner of her sarong, and spoke briefly to Jik.

He turned to the children. 'My mother say we go to my house, eat food. She say you are now dam guest. Later, when it is time, we visit Manai Liha who will search for your mum and dad.'

Hanna's heart gave a lurch. Had she heard Jik right? 'You're telling me she'll *search* for them? How can she possibly search for them? Are they somewhere on this island?'

Jik shook his head indignantly. 'Not here!'

'Then what on earth are you talking about? She's an old woman. It'll be dark soon.'

Jik gave a mysterious smile. 'Manai Liha not need *light* for search.'

Hanna *had* to know. She *had* to find out. 'Why doesn't she need a light to search for Mum and Dad? Go on, Jik, tell me!'

They were back at Jik's house now, sitting on the platform, their faces stained orange by the setting sun. Jik's mum was cooking something on a smoky wood fire in the small kitchen. His brothers and sisters—all six of them—were crouched giggling by the hut wall, watching every move they made.

'Yeah, tell us, Jik!' Ned urged. 'You can't just say stuff like that and make out it's no big deal.'

Jik hesitated, searching for the right words. 'She not need light because . . . *because she is magic woman.*'

Ned's eyes widened. 'You mean she's a witch? Is that why everybody's so scared of her?'

Jik didn't understand the word witch. Manai Liha was an *umboh*, he explained, which meant that she cured people when they were ill, and helped people when they were in trouble. She could talk to the *saitan*—the evil spirits that lived everywhere—and make them go away. Sometimes she would take a *saitan* into her own body if it was being particularly troublesome. She was the most powerful *umboh* in the whole of the Sulu Sea. Wherever the pirates had hidden Mum and Dad, she would find them. She could see every-where—inside mountains, under the sea, even inside people's heads—and she didn't need a light for that.

Ned whistled. 'Cool! And what about her red mouth? Does she really drink blood?'

'Blood?' For an instant, Jik looked puzzled. Then he burst into loud laughter. 'That not blood! That betel nut. Every old people chew dam betel nut!'

He got up, went inside the house, and returned moments later with a small cloth bag. He placed it carefully on the wooden platform and opened it up. Inside was a sharp knife, a few leaves, a shrivelled brown nut and a small bamboo tube full of white powder. He spread out one of the leaves, carefully carved a few shavings from the nut onto it, tapped out some powder, then rolled up the leaf into a sort of miniature parcel which he popped into his mouth. He chewed at it for a moment or two, and sure enough, what looked like blood started to spurt between his lips.

He grinned, pointed at another of the leaves. 'You try?'

Hanna shook her head. It looked like some sort of dangerous drug, and that was the last thing they needed. 'No thank you! And nor will Ned,' she said firmly.

Jik shrugged, chewed some more, then spat the contents of his mouth over the edge of the platform into the sea below. 'No sweat,' he said, wiping his lips with the back of his hand. 'Anyway, food come soon. Much more tasty than goddam betel nut.'

They ate in the main room of Jik's house. Like at the Panglima's, there was no furniture, just a mat on which the family squatted in a tight circle. The food was served on a battered tin tray, and consisted of a mound of soggy tapioca with a few grey boiled fish draped on top. Everybody ate with their hands, even the baby, scooping the porridge-like tapioca into their mouths in great sloppy dollops, and sucking loudly at the fish bones. Tasty was the last word Hanna would have used to describe it—sick-making would have been more accurate—and if she hadn't been so ravenously hungry, she would have refused to eat. As it was, she managed to force quite a lot down her throat, washed down with lukewarm water from a plastic jug. She assumed the water had been boiled for fifteen minutes, but didn't like to ask.

Ned ate a huge amount and belched loudly at the end, which made the younger kids scream with laughter. Even Jik's mum managed a sort of smile. She was less hostile now, Hanna sensed, but she still seemed very worried. Maybe it was something to do with this *triti* that the Panglima had kept going on about. Hanna wondered where Jik's father was. There was no sign that anybody else was living in the house.

When the meal was finished, Hanna glanced expectantly at Jik, but he shook his head. It was still too early to visit Manai Liha, he told her. Her magic wouldn't work until the *saitan* came out of their hiding places after midnight.

To pass the time, he lit a kerosene lamp and

they sat and talked, while the younger children played a complicated-looking game with a coconut shell and some small stones. Hanna asked Jik a question that had been puzzling her since they'd first met—how he'd managed to learn English when nobody else on the island seemed to speak a word of it. He grinned. 'I tell you already. Learn melikan from anywhere.'

'What on earth's melikan?' Ned demanded.

'Melikan! From goddam Melika! You wait!' He got up, went over to a bag hanging on one of the walls. He took out a tattered envelope, and brought it over. It was addressed to Jikiri, care of somebody called Father Reyes in Tamu, and it had two American stamps on it. He tapped at them with his finger. 'See! Goddam Melika!'

The penny dropped. He meant America! As far as Jik was concerned he spoke *American*, not English! He carefully opened the envelope and slid out a photograph. He handed it to Ned. Hanna peered over his shoulder to see.

It was a picture of Jik in his boat with a white woman. She looked about thirty, with a friendly, open face and cropped blonde hair. She was wearing a sarong, a pair of rope sandals, and a battered straw hat a bit like Hanna's.

Ned turned the picture over. There was a message written on the back. It read: '*To Jik. In memory of all the great times we had together! Love and kisses, Annie.'*

And there was an address:

Dr Annie Weir
Department of South-East Asian Studies
Baltimore State University
Baltimore
Maryland
USA

'This woman stayed here?' Hanna asked.

Jik nodded. 'One whole year in *kampung*. Ask many questions about Sea Gypsies. I help her. Show her many things. She write book.'

'And she taught you to speak Melikan?'

'Annie Weir teach me dam good!'

So it wasn't *anywhere*, but *Annie Weir* who'd taught him English! Another puzzle solved.

Jik took back the photograph, stared at it wistfully for a moment or two, then slipped it back into its envelope and replaced it in his bag. 'Annie Weir find *triti*,' he said conversationally, as he returned to the mat.

The mysterious *triti* again! What on earth could it be? The way the Panglima had kept on referring to it, it had to be something pretty important, something sacred to the Sea Gypsies no doubt. Hanna could imagine Dr Annie Weir, trowel in hand, gradually scraping away the earth from some massive stone statue, a bit like those ones on Easter Island. The sacred *triti* of the Sea Gypsies. She could imagine everybody falling down on their hands and knees and worshipping it. 'Can we see it?' she asked.

'See what?'

'This *triti*. Are we allowed to see it?'

Jik shook his head. 'In Tamu.'

'But that's miles away! Is it some sort of statue?'

Jik looked puzzled. 'Statue?'

'A carving?' Hanna groped for the right expression. 'An . . . *idol*.'

Jik seemed even more confused. These were obviously words that Dr Annie Weir hadn't taught him. Hanna had a couple more goes at getting him to understand, then gave up. It didn't matter anyway. They were going to visit Manai Liha, the woman who could see through mountains. If she really could do magic, if she really could tell them where Mum and Dad were, it would be the most brilliant thing ever. Better than any stupid *triti*— whatever that was!

7
Voices

The children didn't go anywhere—at least not for what seemed like an eternity. Jik stayed right where he was, squatting comfortably on the mat, asking question after question. He wanted to know *everything* about their life in England—every tiniest detail: what their house was like; how many other brothers and sisters they had; what kind of nets they used for fishing. When Hanna told him they didn't have any other brothers and sisters, he plainly didn't believe her—though he believed Ned even less when he said they didn't need nets because their fish came in small boxes from the supermarket in Honiton, and were called fish fingers. 'Fish not have goddam finger,' Jik said crossly. 'Not have goddam toe neither!'

The younger kids finished their game and slumped against each other sleepily. Jik's mum squatted next to them. She opened the betel nut bag, wrapped up a slice of nut and some of the white powder and began to chew. The moon came up, and sent a long, rippling shaft of light across the surface of the lagoon. Mosquitoes whined and danced, and the children slapped at their exposed legs and arms. Hanna hoped that the pills they'd been taking were still working well enough for them not to get malaria or anything nasty. She worried about things like pills now, and clean water. Before, she'd never given them a moment's thought.

It must have been well past midnight before Jik finally pulled himself to his feet and went to the door. He glanced up at the sky, turned back to his mother and said something in a low voice. She continued to chew for a moment or two. Then she nodded, directed a glob of red spittle through a crack in the floorboards, and spoke directly to Hanna.

'My mother say it is time to go,' Jik translated, picking up the kerosene lamp. 'She say all good fortune be with you. She say the *saitan* know everything, if only they choose to speak.' Hanna gave the thin, tired-looking woman a smile of thanks. It was not returned.

What followed was one of the weirdest, scariest walks Hanna and Ned could ever remember. During the day, negotiating the sagging, swaying planks between the houses was tricky enough; but now, following the dancing light from Jik's lamp, with the rising tide swishing and swilling beneath them, it was like taking part in a suicidal high-wire act. Hanna wondered what would happen if she fell—if she'd ever be able to find a ladder, or if she'd have to swim all the way to the shore between the slimy, smelly, barnacle-encrusted posts of the houses above. It didn't bear thinking about.

She hadn't realized the village was so big, or that it stretched so far along the shores of the lagoon. But eventually the houses began to thin out, and finally stopped altogether. All that remained now was a single rickety walkway, supported on thin, bent poles, that seemed to continue on for ever into the blackness of the bay.

'She lives out *here*?' Hanna asked disbelievingly, as she caught up with the two boys.

'Manai Liha live in boat,' Jik explained. 'Now follow please, and no dam talk.'

Silently, the children tiptoed along the buckled, twisted planks. The sounds of the village—the barking of dogs, the clunking of boats against their moorings, the gentle singing of mothers trying to lull their babies to sleep—gradually faded, to be replaced by a new noise: a low, insistent muttering, like somebody grumbling to themselves. Hanna felt a prickle of fear. What if Manai Liha wasn't a magic woman after all? What if she was just plain mad? How safe would they be, stuck out on a boat with her in the middle of nowhere?

Suddenly Jik put up a hand, and stopped. The walkway had ended in a small, broken-down jetty. Ned and Hanna crept up next to him and stared down.

The muttering was coming from what, at first sight, looked like a mound of floating garbage. Lengths of dead palm branch, old pieces of woven floor-mat, even a few scraps of ripped sail, had been heaped higgledy-piggledy onto a sagging bamboo frame. It was a roof—of sorts—and just visible beneath it was the narrow outline of a boat. It was about eight metres long, with a raised bow, and a flat open platform at the back. It looked as if the tiniest wave would sink it instantly.

Jik dropped to his knees; called the old woman's name.

For a while the muttering continued. Then there was a loud cough, what sounded like a tin can being rattled, and a cracked voice rose up through the ramshackle roof: '*Mari.*'

'She say come.'

There was no ladder, just a single palm trunk with notches cut out of it. Jik scrambled down it like a monkey. Ned and Hanna followed more carefully. There was a powerful stench of dried fish, rotting wood, and what could only be unwashed human flesh. The doorway to the interior of the boat was low, spiked with sharp palm branches. The children peered through it apprehensively.

Manai Liha was squatting in the bows. She was still wearing her strange green and yellow rags, but she'd taken off her headcloth and her white hair fell in a loose pigtail down her back. Her mouth gleamed red with fresh betel juice. In front of her, on a tray, was half a coconut shell, a bottle of what looked like pale yellow oil, and a thick, sausage-shaped bundle about a foot long, wrapped in a dirty green cloth. Apart from a battered cooking pot stacked in one corner, and a flickering kerosene lamp, the rest of the interior was bare. Hanna and Ned felt quite relieved. They'd been half-expecting to see dried lizards hanging from the ceiling, or maybe even a couple of shrunken human heads.

The old woman nodded a greeting and beckoned them in. She motioned them to sit down opposite her. Then she lit a match and dropped it into the coconut shell. A curl of grey smoke began to spiral upwards. There was a strong smell of incense, like joss-sticks in a Chinese temple.

She peered closely at the smoke, moving her hands round it and through it, as though feeling its shape. After a while she looked up at the children. *'Maraiau!'* she said, and her lips split into a blood-red smile.

Jik translated in an awestruck voice: 'She say magic good. Very good.'

She reached out, and took the sausage-shaped bundle from the tray. She placed it on her lap and began to unwrap it with extreme care. Hanna craned forwards to see, her heart thumping painfully. Whatever was inside had to be *seriously* spooky.

It was two lengths of wood, black with age, crudely carved into the shapes of a man and a woman. They had small white cowrie shells for eyes, and what looked like tufts of real human hair sticking out of their heads. Manai Liha held them up in front of her and began to speak to them rapidly in a strange, sing-song language, from time to time twisting them to face the children. Every time she did so, Hanna felt a weird tingling sensation in her skin, as though the carvings were radiating some sort of invisible electric current.

Eventually the old woman glanced up at the children again. '*Amah*,' she said softly, holding up the male figure. She held up the female: '*Inah*.'

'She say they are your father and mother,' Jik whispered. 'She say, do you have a thing belong your mother and father?'

'*A thing?* What sort of thing?' Hanna asked, her mouth dry with apprehension.

'Any dam thing!'

She was about to say no, when she remembered: *Mum's lucky pendant!* She scrabbled in her shorts, praying that it was still there. She found it scrunched up in a piece of paper at the bottom of her left pocket, untangled it, and held it out to the old woman. Manai Liha took it, and draped it carefully round the neck of the female carving.

'Father?' Jik asked.

Hanna shook her head in despair. 'I've got nothing of Dad's.'

But Ned was wriggling as if he'd been stung by a bee. 'I've got something, I think!'

He began to frantically haul stuff out of his pockets—shells, pieces of coral, a penknife, a roll of tangled fishing line. Several small coins clattered into the bilges of the boat. 'Got it!' he yelled excitedly. 'I've got it!'

He thrust a dirty green piece of towelling at the old woman. It was a Nike sweatband, one of the ones Dad used to keep his hair back from his face when he was chopping wood or digging tapioca.

She grabbed it from Ned's hand and wound it swiftly round the male carving's head, like a sort of turban. Then she took the bottle, poured a little of its contents into her cupped hand, and rubbed it onto the statues.

'What's that stuff?' Ned whispered to Jik.

'*Lanah*—oil of coconut. Make *Amah*, *Inah* come alive.'

Ned's eyes widened. 'You mean it's going to turn those things into Mum and Dad? *For real?*'

But Jik didn't have time to answer. Manai Liha suddenly clutched the carvings tightly to her chest, and with her body hunched over them, began to sway backwards and forwards, chanting loudly in the same weird sing-song language she'd used earlier.

For a time—for a long time—nothing happened. The light from the kerosene lamp flickered and danced. The boat bumped gently against its mooring posts. The old woman carried on chanting and swaying. It was as though she was opening herself out, waiting to receive something . . .

Then, just as Hanna was starting to wonder whether this whole thing might be a stupid waste of time, and they should go back to Jik's house, Manai Liha gave a sudden harsh grunt. It was as if somebody had kicked her hard in the stomach.

It was followed almost instantly by a second, even louder grunt which sent her sprawling back against one of the bamboo roof supports.

The kerosene lamp went out.

'I don't like this . . . !'

In the sudden, intense blackness, Hanna just had time to register Ned's terrified voice when she too was violently thrust sideways. It felt as if the whole boat had been invaded by a crowd of jostling bodies—hot, muscular, eager—trampling everything in their path in their urgency to get inside.

Manai Liha was no longer chanting. She was shouting—screaming—at something—at some-body—close to her.

There were more grunts, more thumps. And fresh sounds—howls, hoots, and snarls. The boat began to rock violently from side to side, water sloshing in over the bilges. Something hard clat-tered painfully against Hanna's legs. Parts of the roof were coming loose, cascading down into the inky waters of the lagoon . . .

And then, quite clearly, through the appalling cacophony, Hanna heard a voice.

A familiar voice.

'Hanna?' the voice said. 'Ned?'

It was Mum!

Before she could respond, Dad's voice, his big, booming voice, cut in over the top. 'Hi, kids!'

'Mum!' Hanna heard herself screaming. 'Dad!'

She was aware of Ned yelling beside her. Was he hearing their voices too?

'Are you OK?' Hanna screamed, her voice crack-ing under the strain. 'Where are you? Tell us where you are? We need to find you . . . !'

But if there was a reply, she didn't hear it. Something new was happening—something even more violent, even more terrifying.

A great noise, like the beating of heavy drums, began to pound at her ears. A blinding white light—the most intense, dazzling light she had ever seen—lit up the interior of the ancient boat. In an instant, a mighty wind had sprung up out of nowhere and turned into a raging hurricane.

There was no way such a tiny craft could survive a wind like this!

The jumble of branches and leaves that formed its flimsy roof was sucked up swirling into the air. Huge waves began to crash on board, tipping it violently onto its side. There was the sound of cracking wood. '*Mum!*' Hanna was still screaming, not wanting to believe what was happening. '*Dad!*'

'*We go!*'

Somebody was dragging at her shirt. It was Jik, his terrified face sheet-white in the blinding light.

'*We go now!*'

Ned, she could see, had already launched himself at the bucking jetty outside. Urged on by Jik, Hanna followed, grasping at the slippery notched pole, hauling herself painfully upwards.

As she reached the top she glanced down. The now roofless boat was sinking fast. Jik was knee-deep in water, frantically hauling at Manai Liha, trying to get her to stand up, save herself; but the old woman was resisting, beating at him with her arms. In desperation he turned, found a knife from somewhere, began to saw at the mooring ropes that held the craft to the jetty.

Stretched tight with the immense force of the wind, the ropes snapped, and the stricken boat slewed violently away, beyond the edges of the light, into the darkness of the bay . . .

'Come on, Hanna!'

Now it was Ned's turn to pull at her. She twisted in his direction and gasped in horror.

The whole of the rickety walkway that joined the jetty to the shore was starting to collapse, its flimsy support posts buckling, planks jerking loose, crashing down into the pounding surf below.

Desperately they began to race along it, leaping the jagged, yawning gaps as they appeared. The noise, the light, the hurricane seemed to be following them, getting stronger all the time.

And then, suddenly, there were other lights too, and a new, even louder noise . . .

Hanna glanced wildly towards the village. Two massive black boats, with searchlights mounted on their roofs, were screaming in across the bay, throwing up immense bow waves as they came. As she watched they slewed to a stop next to the outermost houses, and their crew began to scramble up the ladders and onto the platforms. They were wearing uniforms, and were carrying semi-automatic rifles. The boats had the word *POLIS* written in big letters along their sides.

'STOP! STAY WHERE YOU ARE!'

A voice—harsh, deafening—boomed down at them.

Terrified, the children skidded to a halt, craned their necks upwards. Hovering directly above them was a menacing black shape, the violent down-draught from its massive rotors hammering at the flimsy planks on which they stood.

It was a helicopter!

No wonder it had seemed as if the hurricane was following them! It was this same savage downdraught that had ripped the roof off Manai Liha's boat, filled it with water, sent it lurching away, sinking, into the blackness of the lagoon!

And now, abseiling down towards them, was a black-uniformed figure.

The man landed lightly on the planking beside them, grabbed Ned and started to buckle him into a harness.

They were being rescued!

But it wasn't them the helicopter should be res-cuing, it was Jik and Manai Liha!

Hanna clutched at the man's arm, pointing out

into the bay. 'You've got to help!' she screamed above the thrashing of the rotors. 'There's a boat out there! It's sinking! There's a boy on it, and an old woman. She's too old to swim! They'll drown if you don't save them!'

But the winchman either couldn't or wouldn't understand. He gave a quick signal, and he and Ned were suddenly jerked upwards out of her grasp.

She peered around frantically to see if she could spot Jik or Manai Liha, but there was just darkness and lashing waves. There was no way their broken-down, leaky old boat could survive for long in this. The helicopter man had to listen! He had to do something!

Ned was almost up to the helicopter now, looking small and scared, with the man's arms tight around him. Hands reached out and hauled him on board. The man swung out again; dropped rapidly downwards.

'Did you hear what I said? There are people out there! They're drowning!' Hanna screamed at him, as he reached her.

He didn't even look in the direction she was pointing. Instead he gripped her by the waist, pulled her towards him. She fought with him, but he was too strong. She felt the snap of the harness around her body, the crushing force of an arm around her neck. Then the walkway dropped away beneath her, and she was dangling in space.

In the instant before she was jerked into the helicopter, Hanna glanced down at the village below. In the glare of the searchlights it looked like a scene from a war film. Desperate battles going on—people wrestling with the policemen, others hurling themselves into the sea, trying to escape. Villagers were lined up against the hut walls, guns pointed at their chests. More were being dragged to join them. She spotted Jik's house. His mother was struggling frantically with somebody in the open doorway. She could imagine the terror of the kids inside, their screams . . .

And Jik, what about Jik?

She peered wildly out, beyond the village, into the darkness of the lagoon.

No boat disturbed its glistening, inky surface.

8

Strange Landing

Hanna kept on trying to tell them about Jik, even while she was being strapped into her seat, even while the helicopter was tipping forwards and gathering speed away from the island, but nobody wanted to listen or understand. It was as if she no longer had a voice, as if nothing she could say or do mattered any more.

As they swept on, past the V-shaped bulk of Kaitan, past its familiar headlands and bays, and out towards the open sea, she tried to put the vision she had of Jik and the old woman, locked in a desperate last struggle as the black waters of the lagoon closed above their heads, out of her mind. She failed. Drowning must be the worst way to die, she thought. The very worst . . .

She glanced up at Ned who was sitting opposite. Like her, he was flanked by a pair of black-uniformed crewmen with guns clasped between their knees. He'd always wanted a ride in a helicopter—ever since he'd been tiny—but this was different. It was as though they'd been captured, not rescued. It was as though they were being taken somewhere to be interrogated, tortured, shot. She felt confused, scared, and suddenly very tired. Judging by Ned's pinched white face, he felt the same.

She caught his eye, forced a smile onto her lips, but he didn't respond. He looked so young, so lost, in the cramped, dimly lit cabin. She wondered how much more he could take before he broke up completely. She must stay strong for him, she realized, and not give in to her own despair. Now Mum and Dad were gone, she was all he'd got.

The journey that had taken them almost a day by boat on the way out, took them a fraction of the time on the way back. The helicopter flew fast and low, close to the surface of the waves, and it seemed only minutes before the scattered lights of Tamu were racing towards them. Peering over the pilot's shoulder, Hanna could see the river mouth with its moored boats, the scruffy streets of the main town, and the airport with a small plane parked on its runway. But instead of landing there as she'd expected, they roared past and climbed almost vertically up the face of a jungle-clad ridge, before banking, and dropping down onto a circular helipad ringed with high-powered floodlights.

It was only when the rotors had finally stopped turning, when they were finally unstrapped from their seats and led down the ladder to the ground, that the children had a chance to see where they had landed.

When they did, their eyes widened in astonishment.

Stretching away from the helipad was a smooth green lawn, bordered on one side by flowering shrubs that scented the night air, and on the other by white marble statues of Greek gods and goddesses.

Beyond the lawn was a line of fountains, dancing and sparkling in the dazzling light.

And beyond the fountains was one of the most beautiful houses they had ever seen.

It was long and low, with white walls, and a wide verandah running along its entire length. Exquisite crystal chandeliers gleamed through its arched windows, their light reflected in massive gilt-framed mirrors. In the centre of the building, a pair of carved wooden doors was thrown open to reveal a marble-columned hall adorned with tapestries and expensive looking paintings.

It looked more like a palace than a house, and hurrying down its broad white steps towards them was a woman who could quite easily have been a queen.

She was about Mum's age—and in some ways looked a little bit like Mum, with the same high cheekbones and beautiful almond-shaped eyes. But there the resemblance ended.

She was dressed in fold upon fold of deep blue floaty silk. Her jet-black hair was gathered into soft swirls around her perfect, oval face. Diamonds flashed and glinted at her neck and on her ears.

The two policemen who had escorted Hanna and Ned off the helicopter drew themselves smartly to attention as she approached. She ignored them and stretched out her hands to the children. 'Thank God you're OK! I was so worried for you,' she said in a high, anxious voice. 'When I heard what had happened I said to the Datuk we must send the chopper immediately and get those kids back here. You've not been harmed in any way?'

The two children shook their heads numbly.

'Well, at least there's that to be thankful for. You probably don't realize how much danger you were in with those dreadful people. It was highly irresponsible of your parents taking you to those islands without a permit. Come! You must be so tired and hungry!'

She looped her arms around the children's shoulders and shepherded them towards the house. Behind them they heard the helicopter engines start up again. The huge machine lifted off, hovered for a second or two over the helipad, then headed swiftly back in the direction of the islands. The floodlights dimmed and went out.

'My name is Datin Viana,' she told them as they walked. 'Though most people just refer to me as the Datin. My husband, Datuk Kamal, is District Administrator. *Datuk* and *Datin* are like your *Lord* and *Lady* in England. And of course I know your names. You're Hanna and you're Ned.'

'How do you know all this?' Hanna managed to ask, stumbling in her exhaustion.

The Datin smiled. 'Because it is our business to know. It's my husband's job to keep tabs on everything that happens in the Tamu area. When we learnt that there was an unauthorized family out on Kaitan we were horrified. Unfortunately, before we could get to you, they did.'

'Who's *they*?'

'The pirates, of course. The Sea Gypsies.'

'But they're not pirates!' Ned exclaimed. 'They rescued us!'

The Datin smiled down at him condescendingly. 'No, Ned, you've got it all wrong. *We* rescued you. I only hope we're in time to rescue your mother and father too.'

The children's hopes suddenly soared. 'You know what's happened to them?' Hanna asked.

The Datin shook her head. 'Not yet. But we shall find out, believe me.'

They'd reached the house now, and were climbing the steps up to the main entrance. A white-uniformed manservant came out; stood respectfully to one side as they went in. The children gasped as the chill of air-conditioning replaced the damp heat of the garden. 'Please, wait here for one moment,' the Datin said, and disappeared through a pair of large double doors.

Shivering in the sudden cold, the children stared nervously around them. It really *was* like being in a palace. Slender columns soared up to an intricately plastered ceiling above their heads. Paintings and sculptures glowed in their own individual spotlights. There were cabinets full of valuable looking Chinese vases. At the top of the wide mahogany staircase that led to the floor above was a full-length portrait of the Datin wearing some sort of official robes. Hanna felt Ned edge closer to her. She put an arm round him protectively. The black and white marble floor felt chilly beneath her bare feet.

Seconds later the doors opened again, and the Datin beckoned them through.

The children found themselves in a lavishly furnished sitting room. There were Chinese silk carpets on the floor, antique cabinets and chairs arranged against the walls. In the centre of the room three large white sofas were grouped round a low table. On the table were boxes of delicious-looking chocolates and a number of empty glasses. Some kind of party had obviously recently taken place.

Two men of about Dad's age, both wearing white tuxedos and both smoking fat cigars, were standing near the tall windows, deep in conversation. One of them was a European, his sandy hair trimmed close to his scalp, with the hard, anonymous face of a successful international businessman. The other was browner-skinned, smaller—Chinese, or possibly Filipino—with thinning hair, and one of those beak-like mouths that seemed to have too many teeth in them. He wore a heavy gold watch on his left wrist, and had a large jade ring on the third finger of his right hand. He reminded Hanna of a well-dressed crocodile.

He passed a final remark to his companion, then strode across to greet them. As Hanna had already guessed, crocodile-man was the Datuk. She wondered how somebody so ugly could possibly be married to such a beautiful woman as the Datin. He gave them a brief, tight smile. 'Well,' he said smoothly, 'our two castaways! You look like you could both use a bath and a square meal! You like chocolates?' He picked up a box from the table, held it out. 'Herr Krull brought them all the way from Switzerland for us. They're delicious.'

'They are pralines, the speciality of my home town,' Herr Krull said. He sounded like a Nazi in a war film.

Ned took one, put it in his mouth, but Hanna refused hers. The last thing she needed right now was a chocolate. Her eyes were watering with the Datuk's cigar smoke and an acute need for sleep. 'The Datin told me you were going to get our mum and dad back,' she said bluntly.

'I said we would find out what's *happened* to them,' the Datin put in.

'Isn't that the same thing?'

The Datuk replaced the box of chocolates on the table; turned slowly back to face her. 'No, young lady, it is not.'

'Why not?'

'Because we are dealing with thieves and murderers, Hanna—people who have no under-standing of civilized behaviour, of the difference between right and wrong. Sea Gypsies have always been pirates, and always will be. They're capable of any outrage. And until we've captured and interrogated those who are responsible for this crime, it would be better not to build your hopes too high.'

'But they're *not* pirates!' Hanna protested. 'I know they're not!'

'And how exactly do you know that?'

Hanna racked her tired brain, trying to find the right words. How could she explain about Manai Liha, about the kindness they'd been shown? In the end she said, limply, 'I just know, that's all.'

'Well, believe me, young lady, I know differently.'

Now it was Ned's turn, 'So why did Jik come and rescue us then, if he is a pirate?' he demanded.

The Datuk turned to him sharply. 'Jik?'

Warning bells rang somewhere deep inside Hanna's head. It was a mistake to mention any names, she sensed. 'Just a boy,' she put in hastily. 'He sailed over to Kaitan in his boat to find us.'

'And why do you think he did that?' the Datuk enquired.

'Because he saw the fire when the pirates burnt our hut,' Ned said.

'Because he was *sent* to find you, to trick you, to get you to go with him to his island so you could be captured too.'

'But we *weren't* captured!' Hanna protested. 'The Panglima tried to send us back again! He didn't want us there!'

The Datuk's eyes hardened. He was obviously not used to being challenged, especially by a couple of children. 'Well, we shall soon find out the truth. I've put all the forces of law and order I can spare on to this case, and believe me, they are very highly trained and equipped. Now I have things I need to discuss with Herr Krull in private.' He glanced up at the Datin. 'Darling, I think it's way past these children's bedtime, wouldn't you agree?'

'Way past!'

Before the children could say any more, the Datin had taken their arms and ushered them back into the hall. As the door clicked shut behind them, Hanna heard the warble of a phone, and the sharp bark of the Datuk's voice issuing orders into it in Malay.

9

A Million Miles
from Home

Her name was Sitti, and she seemed to materialize out of thin air when the Datin clapped her hands. She was tiny, wearing a red checked sarong, with her hair scraped up into a tight bun on top of her head. She had big, friendly brown eyes and looked no more than a year or two older than Hanna. She would be their personal servant during their stay, the Datin said, and they were to ask her for anything they needed—anything at all. She would show them to their room. The Datin then wished them goodnight and told them she was sure there would be good news about their parents in the morning, and that they were to try to get a good night's sleep. With a final smile she disappeared back into the sitting room to rejoin her husband and his guest.

'Please, to come,' Sitti said, in a soft, almost musical voice, and led the children through a series of rooms each one more sumptuously furnished than the last. Eventually they climbed a short flight of stairs which led to a richly carved balcony overlooking a central courtyard filled with brightly coloured flowers and shrubs. Three doors led off the balcony. Sitti opened the middle one. 'Your room,' she said, standing back respectfully to allow the children to enter.

After so many days on the island, after everything they'd been through, it was like stepping through a doorway into heaven. Two comfortable beds were waiting for them, their covers turned down. There was a table spread with plates of food under woven rattan dish covers, and through a rear door they glimpsed a marble-tiled bathroom with fluffy white towels.

There were clean clothes laid out on the bed—shorts and T-shirts that looked exactly the right size, and several colourful sarongs. It was as if the Datuk and Datin had *known* that they were coming, and had had time to get everything completely prepared.

'You eat now?' Sitti asked. 'Or take bath first?'

'Eat,' replied Ned quickly. 'I'm starving!'

Hanna suddenly felt hungry too. It seemed hours since she'd forced herself to swallow those few soggy mouthfuls of tapioca and fish in Jik's house.

The servant girl led them to the table; lifted the rattan covers. There was fried rice with eggs, delicious-looking barbecued chicken, satay with peanut sauce, and slices of mango and papaya for afters. There were cans of Coke to drink. 'You like ice?' Sitti asked.

Ice! It was the one thing they'd really missed on Kaitan and now there was a whole silver bucket of the stuff gleaming on a side table! They nodded, and Sitti clinked some cubes into a couple of tall glasses. She filled them to the brim with Coke and placed them next to the children's plates. 'Now I go,' she announced. She pointed at the button on the wall. 'When you want me, ring bell, I come.' She brought her hands together, smiled. *'Selamat malam.'*

'*Selamat malam*,' the children replied.

The door closed behind her.

Selamat malam. That was Mum's special phrase! Ever since they could remember she'd always said goodnight to them in Malay. Hanna was reminded suddenly, painfully, of her own little bedroom in the cottage at home; of the touch of Mum's lips on her forehead; the creak of her feet on the stairs as she tiptoed down to rejoin Dad in the living room.

Home.

It seemed a million miles away suddenly—a million million miles. And no room, in no palace, however luxurious it might be, could ever make up for that.

She glanced at Ned. His eyes were shiny with

tears. He was obviously sharing her thoughts. 'They'll be fine,' she whispered. 'I *know* they will be.'

He shook his head miserably. 'No you don't. You don't know that.'

'Yes I do.'

'Prove it then.'

Hanna sucked in a deep breath. Should she tell him why she was so certain? Would he think she was mad? There was only one way to find out. 'I heard them,' she said quietly.

Ned stiffened. 'You *heard* them?'

'On Manai Liha's boat. They were calling out to us. Calling our names . . .'

Hanna stopped. Her brother was staring at her. He was no longer crying, and judging by his expression he obviously didn't think she was mad. After what seemed like an eternity he said: 'I think I heard them too. Dad was shouting "Hi, kids!"'

Hanna felt a sudden surge of joy. If they'd both heard the same thing, they *couldn't* have imagined it! 'Dad's always shouting!' she exclaimed.

'He needs a volume control, Mum always says!'

So Manai Liha *had* made those statues talk! 'That means they're still alive!' she exclaimed. 'If only that stupid helicopter hadn't come we'd know where they are by now!'

But Ned's expression had changed. The spark of

hope that had lit up his tired eyes was fading. 'If it *was* them,' he said quietly. 'There was so much noise. It was so difficult to hear. Maybe it was somebody else shouting. Maybe it was Jik. Or the man from the helicopter. Maybe we just *wanted* it to be Mum and Dad.'

'But I did hear them! I know I did . . . '

Hanna broke off. Ned was right. There was no point in fooling herself. What she'd heard—what they'd both *thought* they'd heard—didn't prove anything. For it to prove something it would mean *really* believing in magic, which was crazy. Only young kids believed in that sort of stuff. No, Mum and Dad had been kidnapped. They were being held somewhere. There'd be a ransom demand from the kidnappers some time soon. That was how things worked in the real world, in the grown-up world.

All the same, it was hard not to believe that *something* strange had happened on Manai Liha's boat, something that couldn't just be explained away . . .

Now they'd never know for sure. The old woman was dead. And Jik too. Nobody could have survived in that pounding sea. Nobody.

Again Ned read her thoughts. He spoke bitterly: 'That helicopter could have rescued them. I know it could have.'

'The man wouldn't listen. I tried to tell him . . . '

'Maybe he didn't understand English.'

'He understood . . . ' Hanna stopped. Ned was shaking, trembling like someone with hypothermia. 'You'd better have a warm bath,' she said. 'You're cold.'

'No I'm not. This is the tropics.'

'Well, we should eat something.'

'I'm not hungry.'

Hanna glanced at the table. The food, which had seemed so delicious a few moments before, now seemed to be made of plastic, not edible at all. Exhaustion and despair threatened to overwhelm her. She felt herself sway suddenly, and gripped at a chair for support. 'Perhaps we'd better lie down for a while,' she said. 'Maybe we'll feel hungry later.'

'Maybe.'

The two children stumbled across to the beds, and, not bothering to undress, threw themselves face down onto the silken sheets.

They were asleep instantly.

10
Foreboding

Hanna opened her eyes. Points of brilliant white light were dancing above her head, diving and swooping across a wide ceiling where two fans lazily turned. For a moment—for a long moment—she had no idea where she was. 'Ned?' she called out uncertainly.

'I thought you'd never wake up.'

She turned her head towards the sound. Her brother was standing next to a window, a green sarong looped around his waist. His hair was spiky with wetness. 'Come and look at this,' he said.

Memory returned, slashing at her like a knife. She forced herself to her feet and made her way across to him. It was only then that she understood what the dancing points of light on the ceiling were. They were reflections from the waters of a large swimming pool that occupied the whole of a U-shaped courtyard at the rear of the house. A man in a white jacket was sweeping the tiles around the edge of the pool, pushing aside rattan sun loungers and low tables as he did so. Dazzling yellow birds tumbled and squawked in the purple bougainvillea which cascaded down the brilliant white walls on every side. It was breathtakingly beautiful. 'How good does that look?' asked Ned enviously.

For an instant Hanna shared his yearning. It would be blissful to take a running dive into the pool and forget everything in the cool rush of water against her skin. But then reality kicked back in. 'We're not on holiday,' she snapped. 'This is not a hotel. We've got to find Mum and Dad.'

She regretted her tone of voice the moment she spoke. Ned seemed to shrink back inside his own skin. 'I haven't forgotten,' he said quietly. 'Please believe me, Hanna, I haven't.'

'I know you haven't,' she said quickly, desperate to heal the hurt she'd caused. 'How could either of us ever forget?'

Someone must have come into the room while they were asleep, because the untouched food from the night before had been cleared away, and break-fast things were arranged on the table. Cereal, fruit, hard-boiled eggs, and *nasi lemak*—banana leaves piled high with fragrant coconut rice, cool slices of cucumber, and fiery hot sambal curry.

This time there was no doubt about their appetites, and the children ate until they thought they were going to burst. Afterwards, Hanna took a long, cool shower in the bathroom that was still ankle-deep in water from Ned's earlier attempts to clean himself.

Feeling fresher, and full of new energy, she went back into the bedroom, and put on the clothes that had been laid out for her. As she got dressed she couldn't help noticing the brand names stitched into their seams: Calvin Klein, Ralph Lauren, DKNY. At home Mum got their clothes from Matalan, or if they were *really* unlucky, from the charity shops in Yeovil. Ned, who had abandoned his sarong for tastefully coordinated T-shirt and shorts, looked like one of those flash kids in the clothes catalogues they sometimes got sent in the post.

Hanna was attempting to brush out the tangles in her damp hair when a gentle knock and the sound of the door opening made her turn. It was Sitti.

Hanna smiled at her, but the servant girl's face was expressionless. 'You come,' she said. It was an order, not a request. Filled with a sudden foreboding, the children followed her out.

This time they didn't cross the inner courtyard, but turned left into a long anonymous corridor. Eventually they came to a tall wooden door. Sitti knocked and stood back respectfully.

A murmur of conversation, just audible from inside, broke off, and moments later the door was opened by the Datin. She was dressed casually in elegantly tailored shorts and an open-necked top. She waved Sitti away, and turned to the children. 'You slept well?'

They told her they had.

'Good. Please come in.'

They found themselves in a high-ceilinged office, with large windows overlooking the helipad at the front of the house. On the walls were signed photographs of the Malaysian King and Queen and other dignitaries. A massive, intricately carved desk occupied one corner of the room. Standing in front of it was the Datuk and a plump, pink-faced man in business clothes. Despite the chill of the air-conditioning, his shirt, Hanna noticed, was transparent with sweat.

The Datuk wished them good morning, and introduced his companion. 'This is Mr Henderson, children. He's the British Consul. He's come along to see what he can do to help.'

Mr Henderson shook hands. His skin was damp, clammy, like a recently landed fish. He seemed highly nervous, constantly glancing sideways at the Datuk as if seeking his support or approval. 'I'm so sorry,' he said limply.

'We're all sorry,' the Datin added in a sympathetic voice. 'So very very sorry . . .'

Mr Henderson was about to say more when Ned cut in. 'What's a consul?'

'I represent Her Majesty's Government here in Tamu.'

'Like an ambassador?' Hanna asked, trying to hide the physical revulsion she felt.

Mr Henderson gave a short, self-conscious laugh. 'Hardly as grand as that. But I am an honorary member of the Diplomatic Service.'

'So you can get us some money then?' Ned's voice was hard, challenging.

A look of alarm spread over the Consul's face. 'Money?'

'To pay the ransom. Our mum and dad have been kidnapped. We need lots of money. Millions of pounds. You must tell the government to send it to us straight away.'

A bead of sweat trickled down the side of the diplomat's nose. 'I don't think . . . ' he began.

The Datuk didn't allow him to finish. He stepped between them and pointed to a pair of richly upholstered chairs. 'Children, please sit down. There is something very important we need to say to you.'

Hanna's foreboding intensified. She could hear the blood pounding in her ears. 'We'd rather stand,' she said firmly.

'Very well. I have to tell you that overnight we've had fresh information about your parents.'

'Information?'

'Not the best information, I'm afraid.'

'They're hurt. We know that. We saw blood . . . '

A long silence. A very long silence. Hanna felt Ned's hand steal into hers. She gripped it tightly. Outside the window a cicada made a noise like an electric drill, then stopped.

It was the Datin who spoke finally. She drew in a deep breath. 'Hanna. Ned. I'm afraid that your mother and father are dead.'

11
Without Trace

'*No they're not.*'

Hanna said it quietly at first. But then, as if everybody in the room had suddenly become deaf, she screamed it at the top of her voice. '*No they're not! They're not dead! You're lying to us!*'

Ned joined in, tears exploding from his eyes. '*They're not dead! Liar! Liar!*'

The Datin's face hardened. 'Why should I lie to you, Hanna? What reason could I possibly have? We've caught the men who did it. They've confessed.'

'Well you've made a mistake, because Mum and Dad aren't dead. I saw Mum move. She was tied up. She was wriggling.'

'Yeah and I saw it too,' Ned added through his sobs. 'They've been kidnapped! You're just trying to save money . . . '

It was at that precise moment that Hanna *knew*—beyond any doubt whatsoever—that Mum and Dad really were alive. Up until then she'd been wishing—hoping against hope—that they were OK. But now she knew it with complete certainty. How she came to know it—or why—she couldn't say. There was no blinding flash of light, no voices speaking to her like they had—or hadn't—done in Manai Liha's sinking boat. Just a calm, quiet knowledge.

She felt a new strength, a new ability to face up to whatever challenges lay ahead. Somehow, some way, she'd find out where they were. Somehow she'd get them back, however long it took, whatever it cost.

She glanced sideways at Ned, who she could see was building himself up for a fresh outburst. 'It's OK,' she whispered. 'Stay cool. Let me deal with this.'

She turned back to the Datuk, to the Crocodile Man. The dislike she'd felt when she'd first met him was now hardening into a cold, irrational hatred. 'So where are they, then?' she demanded. 'If they're dead, where are their bodies? Show them to us.'

The Datuk's lips parted. 'That's not possible.'

'And why not?'

'Hanna, this is not England.' It was the Datin. She spoke slowly, and with exaggerated clarity, as if addressing somebody with learning difficulties.

'I know that.'

'Bodies . . . disappear without trace. In the jungle there are wild animals . . . '

'But they're not in the jungle. They've never been in the jungle!'

' . . . and in the sea, there are sharks.'

'You're telling us that Mum and Dad were thrown into the sea?'

The Datuk again: 'That is our information. They were killed and thrown overboard.'

A strangled sob from Ned. Hanna clutched at him, held him to her.

'Why? Why would the pirates do that?'

'To dispose of the evidence. They are utterly ruthless. Human life means nothing to them.'

'You must accept that what we are telling you is the truth,' the Datin said. 'We understand what you must be feeling, what you must be going through.'

'No you don't,' Hanna shot back fiercely. 'It's never happened to you! You don't understand.'

It was the fat consul's turn now: 'Hanna, we've contacted your next of kin.'

Next of kin? What a strange phrase. For an instant Hanna struggled to understand what he was saying to her. 'What next of kin?' she demanded.

'Your grandparents.'

'You've told Granny and Grandpa?'

Mr Henderson dabbed at his forehead with a folded handkerchief. 'They have been . . . ah . . . informed. They will arrive here as soon as possible.'

'But Granny's got bad legs,' Ned protested. 'She can't fly. She can't even walk very well.'

'Nevertheless, I believe she will be accompanying your grandfather.'

'And naturally, in the meantime, you must stay here with us,' the Datin put in. 'Sitti will look after you. You may use the pool. And if you feel the need to see somebody—a priest maybe . . . '

A priest? What had a priest got to do with it? People only needed priests when somebody had died.

And nobody had died.

NOBODY HAD!

'I don't believe in God,' Hanna said angrily.

'Nor do I,' chorused Ned through his tears.

There was an awkward silence. The fat consul shifted his weight from one foot to the other like a small boy who needed the toilet. The Datin nervously brushed away a lock of hair that had fallen over her eyes. Only the Datuk seemed completely in control of the situation.

He moved forwards and dropped onto his haunches in front of the children. He cleared his throat. 'Hanna, Ned, I'm afraid there is a painful duty that I need you to perform—if you feel you are up to it, of course.'

Hanna eyed him with suspicion. 'What duty?'

'I need you to formally identify your parents' attackers.'

110

'But they've confessed. You said.'

'It will help us a great deal. It will make doubly certain that these ruffians get the justice they deserve. I realize it was dark when the attack took place, but something may just jog your memory.'

'I remember it clearly,' Hanna said coldly. 'Every second of it. How could I ever forget?'

The Datuk looked relieved. Stood up. 'Then it should be no problem.'

'Hanging is too good for them!' the Datin exclaimed suddenly, emotionally. 'Far too good for them.'

Ned's eyes widened. 'They'll be *hung*?'

The Datuk nodded. 'If they are found guilty. Piracy and murder are both crimes that carry the death penalty here in Malaysia.'

12

Predators

An identity parade was fixed for late afternoon at Police Headquarters. In the meantime, the Datin suggested, perhaps they might like to swim. She sent a colourful selection of swimsuits up to the children's room, but they ignored them. Instead, they closed the shutters against the blinding tropical sun and lay in semi-darkness on their beds.

They talked for a long time about what had happened during the last few days, and what they were going to do next. Hanna told Ned about her conviction that Mum and Dad were still alive, despite everything the Datuk and Datin had said, and to her surprise he told her that he was convinced of it too. 'It was when they started talking about sharks,' he said. 'That was when I knew it couldn't be true. No shark could possibly find Dad tasty.'

They both laughed at that, and laughing made them feel better. Anyway, it was impossible to contemplate the alternative.

It was what to do next that was the problem. With nobody to help them, how could they even *start* their search? Maybe they'd pick up a clue at the identity parade—something the police knew, but didn't think was significant. Even though she was dreading coming face to face with the captured men, it was their best and only hope of getting fresh information.

'Will they really hang them?' Ned asked.

Hanna nodded. 'If they're guilty. I remember Dad saying how they still execute quite a lot of people in Malaysia.'

'So it all depends on us.'

Hanna turned towards her brother, puzzled, alarmed. 'What do you mean?'

'If we say they're the pirates, they'll get hung. If we say they aren't, they won't.'

'Don't be stupid!'

'I'm not being stupid.'

Hanna knew he wasn't. Suddenly the full consequences of what they'd done by agreeing to attend an identity parade became clear. If the men they were shown really *were* the attackers, could she bring herself to condemn them to death with a nod of her head—despite what they'd done to Mum and Dad?

OK, they'd already confessed. But as the Datuk had implied, with only their confessions

113

to go on, there was a chance they'd get off. But not if she and Ned positively identified them. It would be the final nail in their coffins—quite literally.

Could she live with that? Could she really?

The children slept for a while during the main heat of the day, and when they woke they nibbled at some slices of mango and papaya left over from breakfast. They were talking about Granny and Grandpa—what would happen when they arrived, how upset they must be feeling—when there was a knock at the door. It was the Datin. The car was waiting to take them to Police Headquarters. They must leave immediately.

She seemed ill at ease. Worried. 'You *must* accept that what I've told you this morning is the truth,' she said, as the children sorted out a pair of trainers each from a row lined up outside their door.

Hanna glanced up at her. 'Accept that Mum and Dad are dead? Never!'

'Pretending it hasn't happened will only make the hurt worse when you eventually have to face up to reality.'

'We're not pretending *anything*!' Ned snapped back fiercely. 'We *know*.'

The Datin shook her head wearily. 'In that case I am at a complete loss to know what to say to you. So is the Datuk. I can only hope that your grandparents will have more success when they come to collect you.'

'They're *collecting* us?'

'They'll be arriving tomorrow morning. Mr Henderson is arranging temporary passports so that you can travel back with them.'

'We're not going anywhere! Not without Mum and Dad!'

'Hanna, please! Keep your voice down. I have a bad headache. Of course you'll go back with your grandparents. They're your closest relatives and they're legally responsible for you. Now kindly follow me or you'll be very late. The Datuk has been at Police Headquarters for more than an hour now making sure that everything is properly set up for the identity parade, and he doesn't like to be kept waiting.'

A large white Mercedes was drawn up at the main entrance. Its uniformed driver saluted smartly and opened the rear door. 'Ibrahim here will take you into town,' the Datin explained. 'I have a prior engagement so I cannot come with you. Afterwards, I hope you will eat with us. Just a simple family meal.'

'We're not your family,' Ned told her coldly.

It was a short drive through the dusty streets to the Police Headquarters. It was a squat, ugly building, its white walls streaked with black mould. A forest of antennae sprouted from its flat roof. It was surrounded by a tall metal fence topped with razor wire. As they approached the main gate an armed sentry stepped forward to open it, and they sped through. There was something sinister about the building, with its heavily barred windows and ancient, rusting air-conditioning units. Hanna gave an involuntary shiver as they drew up outside. She could imagine going inside and never, ever coming out again.

A young policeman was waiting for them. 'Please, to come,' he said, and ushered them through a pair of thick metal doors into a scruffy reception area. Two more policemen, seated behind a desk, watched blank-faced as the children were led past and up a short flight of stairs.

At the top were a number of glass-fronted offices, some occupied, most empty. Yellowing *Wanted* notices were sellotaped to the walls. There was a strong smell of fried noodles and some sort of chemical—lavatory cleaner maybe.

'Ah, children, you've arrived.' The Datuk strode towards them, lips drawn back into what was presumably intended to be a reassuring smile. He was closely followed by a man who was almost his exact physical opposite: short stocky legs, barrel chest, a broad, flat face with flared, pig-like nostrils. There was a gold crown on the shoulder tabs of his police shirt. 'This is Superintendent Lazarus,' the Datuk said. 'My right hand man here in Tamu. You've got a lot to thank him for. He masterminded your rescue yesterday evening.'

The policeman nodded curtly. There was no smile. He seemed anxious to get the proceedings over with as soon as possible. They followed him into a large, bare room with heavy steel bars in the windows. A drooping ceiling fan turned slowly—uselessly—overhead. He slipped a radio from a holder on his belt, and spoke quickly into it in Malay. His voice was deep, heavily accented. He then turned to the children: 'Neither of you have attended an identity parade before?'

They shook their heads.

'It is very simple. We will show you some prisoners. We will then ask you some questions. That is all.'

'You don't want us to point at them?' Ned asked, puzzled.

'Point?'

'To tell you which one is guilty. Like they do on TV.'

'This is not TV, Ned,' the Datuk put in sharply. 'They are *all* guilty. We merely want you to confirm that what we already know about them is correct.'

'And if it isn't?' Hanna challenged. 'If your information isn't correct, what then?'

'Oh, it's correct, Hanna,' the Datuk said quietly. 'One hundred per cent correct. Wouldn't you agree, Superintendent?'

The policeman nodded slowly, his narrow eyes locked onto Hanna's, like a predator onto its prey.

13

Face to Face

There were three prisoners—just three—barefooted, dressed in stained jumpsuits, each one handcuffed to a burly policeman. A fourth policeman followed them into the room and took up position in front of the door. He was holding a squat sub-machine gun and looked as if he knew how to use it. The Superintendent grunted an order and the captives were lined up in front of the children.

'I'm afraid they're a bit of a mess,' the Datuk said, as if apologizing for a set of naughty boys. 'They put up quite a fight when we tried to arrest them. I hope you don't find the sight of them too disturbing.'

Hanna clutched at Ned. 'We're OK,' she just managed to say.

'In which case, take a good, hard look.'

The prisoners were not like human beings, they were more like pieces of meat. They had been sav-agely beaten, their faces split and bloodied, the flesh around their eyes blackened and puffed. Two of them were young—early twenties maybe—one quite tall, the other shorter. The third man was much older, with silver hair, painfully thin. There was a strong smell of human excrement and blood.

'Go closer,' the Superintendent ordered. 'They can't hurt you. They're securely fastened as you can see.' To prove his point, he went up to one of the prisoners and jerked at his handcuffs, causing a howl of pain.

Her heart beating wildly, Hanna led Ned a few feet forwards. She forced herself to examine the men, one by one. Had she seen them before? There was something vaguely familiar about them, but their faces were so injured, so swollen and distorted, it was impossible to tell. Desperately she tried to recall in detail what the attackers on Kaitan had looked like. She could see them clearly in her mind's eye—brown skin, flat noses—but then everybody looked a bit like that around here. Could she have picked these men out even if they hadn't been beaten up? She wasn't sure. If only there was something special to look out for—a tattoo maybe, or a scar.

'Well?'

She turned back to the Datuk. 'It's too difficult. It was dark. It might have been them, I don't know.'

'I'm afraid *might* is not good enough, Hanna. You must be absolutely certain.'

'Well I'm not.'

'And how about you, Ned?'

'He's the same as me,' Hanna said.

'Let him answer for himself.'

But Ned didn't answer—at least not straight away. He freed himself from Hanna's hand and approached the swaying, bloodied men. One of them, the prisoner on the left, made a strange gasping noise as Ned came near, as if he was trying to say something. He was silenced by a sharp command from the Superintendent. Hanna could see the men's eyes now, bloodshot, terrified. You wouldn't treat an animal in this way, she found herself thinking. If it was a cat or a dog you'd take it to the . . .

'I know who they are,' Ned announced suddenly, loudly. 'It's the Panglima and his two sons. From Ular.'

Was it possible? Hanna peered closely at the old man in the middle. He was near to collapse, she saw, still on his feet only because his escort was supporting most of his weight. His right ear had been hit with something hard and was a mess of gristle and blood, and his left eye was closed—but it *was* him. She was certain of it now Ned had pointed him out. And the two men on either side of him were his two sons with their brutal, stupid faces, who'd tried to throw them off the island.

121

'Have we struck gold?' the Datuk enquired, making no attempt to disguise the satisfaction in his voice.

Hanna turned back to him. 'If you mean can we identify these men, yes we can.'

'They tried to get rid of us. They tried to put us in a boat. If it hadn't been for—' Ned began.

And stopped.

He shot Hanna a glance. He too seemed to sense that there should be no further mention of Manai Liha or Jik.

The Datuk completed the sentence for him. 'If it hadn't been for the Superintendent and his men rescuing you, I have no doubt that you would be dead by now. These men are known criminals. They are the leaders of the gang which mounted the cowardly attack on you and your parents.'

'But he's too old,' Ned said indignantly, indicating the Panglima. 'There's no way he could have been one of the pirates.'

'He was the mastermind, Ned. The evil genius behind it all.'

The idea that the Panglima—who'd been terrified of an old woman—could be an evil genius was so preposterous that Hanna nearly burst out laughing.

And as for his stupid sons . . .

She peered at them again. Could *they* have been part of the raid though?

It was possible. Definitely possible. They were young enough, and certainly nasty enough. Now was the chance to find out for sure. 'I need an interpreter,' she said urgently.

'A what?' The Datuk sounded incredulous.

'An interpreter. Somebody who can speak the Sea Gypsy language. I need to ask these men some questions.'

The Datuk exchanged glances with the Superintendent. 'We have already questioned them,' the policeman said curtly. 'This is an identity parade. You are here to confirm their identities. Nothing more.'

'But if we're not allowed to talk to them, how can we confirm it really was them?'

The Superintendent issued another sharp command, and the prisoners were half-marched, half-dragged out of the room. The door slammed shut behind them. 'The parade is concluded,' he announced. He turned, picked up a sheet of paper from a side table. 'Now you must sign this.'

'What is it?' Hanna asked, furious.

'A statement that you have identified these men as the pirates who attacked you on Kaitan Island.'

'We're not signing that!'

The Datuk came up close to Hanna. Very close. 'And why not? You plainly know who those men are.'

'We may know who they are, but it doesn't mean they did it. I could have found out for certain if you'd just let me talk to them.'

'There was no need. We already know they did it.'

'Well I *don't* know—and I won't sign anything that says I do!'

'Nor will I,' Ned added. 'And you won't make me!'

The Datuk sighed deeply. 'You really are the most tiresome children. Superintendent, Exhibit A, if you please.'

The policeman produced a small padded envelope from his pocket. He handed it to the Datuk who opened the flap and slid something out. 'I presume you can identify *this*,' he said.

Hanna's heart lurched.

Nestling in the palm of his hand was her iPod!

There could be no mistake. Her name, which she'd neatly scratched onto the metal case, was clearly visible. 'Where did you get that?' she gasped.

'It was found in the pirates' possession when they were arrested. No doubt they were intending to sell it when they could find a buyer.'

She reached out to take it, but the Datuk shook his head. 'I'm sorry, Hanna, it is needed as evidence. There are fingerprints. It will be returned to you once this case is over.' He handed the iPod to the Superintendent who slipped it back into its envelope. 'Now, please, I would be grateful if you would sign this statement so we can get on with the rest of our day.'

The Datuk was offering her a pen. She took it numbly. The statement was written in Malay and there was no translation.

She should say something, she knew. She should tell them that whatever these men had done, hanging was wrong and she wouldn't agree to it. She should tell them that whatever the evidence said, they *couldn't* be guilty because Mum and Dad were still alive!

She opened her mouth, but no words came out.

She no longer felt brave. She just felt tired, and helpless. She glanced at Ned. All the fight seemed to have left him too. If they refused to sign, this nightmare would just go on and on. She didn't know how much more either of them could take.

Hating herself, she grabbed the paper and scribbled her name. Ned added his beneath hers. It was an open and shut case, the Datuk told them. The trial would take place as soon as possible. And now if there was nothing more . . .

'There were six of them,' Hanna said, suddenly remembering. 'There were *six* pirates. What happened to the other four?'

The Superintendent's voice was cold: 'They were killed. They tried to resist arrest. Regrettably, these things happen.' He said a curt goodbye and disappeared through a side door.

The Datuk smiled at the children. He seemed pleased with himself. 'Well, I thought that went very well, didn't you? Now you know the truth you must try to put this all behind you. Make a fresh start.'

Hanna was close to tears. What fresh start? There could be no fresh start without Mum and Dad! There could be no future if they weren't around. She took Ned's hand and, followed by the Datuk, she stumbled downstairs and out across the lobby to the main entrance.

The photographers were waiting.

There were maybe half a dozen of them, all locals, one with a television camera, surging forwards as the children emerged into the twilight. There were reporters too, thrusting microphones at them, gabbling questions in a mixture of English and Malay.

Trembling with shock, blinded by the camera flashes, the children turned and tried to go back inside. The Datuk blocked their way. 'It's OK,' he said in a reassuring voice. 'They have my permission to be here. Your story is big news.'

'Well we don't want it to be!' Hanna snapped. 'It's got nothing to do with anybody else.'

'I'm afraid it has,' the Datuk replied. 'I have told these people that you will allow photographs, but will not answer any questions. I shall issue a statement to them later containing everything they need to know about your case. Now please, turn and face the cameras. Just for a moment.'

He spoke sharply in Malay to the reporters, who obediently lowered their microphones. 'Well, children? We're waiting.'

The tears were coming now, hot and fast. Hanna reached up to wipe away the wetness from her cheeks, but the Datuk stopped her. 'You look fine,' he said. 'Just fine. Now please, turn around.'

It seemed easier, suddenly, to do what she was told. Gripping Ned's hand tightly, she swung to face the lights.

Their ordeal was over in less than a minute. With his hands on their shoulders, the Datuk turned the children to the right, to the left, then finally to the centre, before abruptly ordering the cameramen to stop.

As if on cue, the white Mercedes drew up. Hanna and Ned were ushered into the back; the Datuk slid in next to the driver. 'There are tissues on the shelf,' he told them in a satisfied voice, as they accelerated smoothly away through the compound gates and headed back towards the house.

14

A Very Posh Prison

They ate in the dining room. It was a long, rectangular room lined with gilt-framed mirrors which made it seem even bigger than it really was. The chairs and table were made from polished rosewood which gleamed like silk in the light from half a dozen chandeliers.

Places had been set for them at the far end, the Datuk at the head of the table, the Datin on his right. The children sat opposite. A small army of white-uniformed servants hovered in attendance. It was like having supper at Buckingham Palace.

The food was delicious—soup made from real tomatoes, delicately roasted chicken, with triple chocolate ice cream for pudding. Their chef had trained in England, the Datin explained, and had suggested that familiar food might make everybody feel better.

It certainly seemed to make the Datuk and Datin feel better. The tension the children had sensed in them earlier seemed to have disappeared entirely now. 'You were so brave,' the Datin insisted. 'So very brave. I'm not sure I could have done what you did—certainly not at your age. Those dreadful men didn't threaten you in any way?'

'There was no chance of that,' the Datuk said, smiling. 'Not with the Superintendent around.'

'He's such a wonderful man,' the Datin exclaimed. 'I don't know what my husband would do without him!'

The Datin became increasingly chatty as the meal went on. She asked the children about their home, their school, their favourite subjects.

Hanna struggled to answer. It was as hard to reply as it was to swallow the food which, despite its delicious taste, seemed to stick in her throat. She didn't want to talk about home. Or school. Or anything that reminded her of the life they'd once had and would never have again.

Never?

No, not *never*. That word was totally banned!

One mystery was solved though—where the clothes they were wearing had come from. Hanna noticed some framed photographs on a side-table and, trying to change the subject, asked about them.

The Datin asked a servant to fetch them, and spread them in front of the children. 'Benny and Mia,' she said proudly. 'Our son and daughter.

They're a little older than you—Mia is fifteen, and Benny is twelve. Luckily their things seem to fit you extremely well.'

Ned asked where they were.

'In the States. They're at school there. We shall be joining them for a holiday once this dreadful pirate business is finally cleared up. It will be such a relief to get away.'

Hanna hated the children in the pictures instantly. They looked so smug, so self-satisfied. The boy was the spitting image of the Datuk—the same crocodile mouth with too many teeth—the girl more like her mother, only much less beautiful. They'd been photographed standing in front of various famous sights around the world: the Golden Gate Bridge in San Francisco; the Eiffel Tower; what had to be the Taj Mahal in India. They'd probably flown there first class *and* been able to order anything they liked from hotel room service too!

When the meal was over, the Datuk wished the children goodnight, and went to his study. He had important work to do, the Datin explained, and there were never enough hours in the day. Now, perhaps, they might like to watch a film—or if they wished she could take them on a tour of the house and grounds.

Hanna was about to say that a film would be

fine, when Ned opted for the tour. He was keen on history, he told the Datin.

Hanna stared at her brother in amazement. He *hated* history, she knew that for certain. He always had. In fact he hated every single subject at school, except for sport—and he only liked *that* because of the football.

The Datin was delighted at Ned's decision. 'My Benny's a history buff too,' she exclaimed. 'He can recite all the names of the Presidents of the United States from George Washington right through to the present day!'

Disliking the nauseous-sounding brat even more, Hanna had no option but to follow as the Datin looped an arm round Ned's shoulders and steered him onto the terrace outside.

The house was known as the *Istana*, which meant 'Palace' in Malay, the Datin explained, and had originally been built for one of the directors of the British North Borneo Company more than a hundred years ago. It had been extended since then, of course, and much improved. The North Borneo Company had been set up to administer what was then a jungle-clad wilderness, and to put an end to piracy.

'You mean there were pirates around here even then?' Ned asked.

'There have always been pirates. And the

Bajau—the Sea Gypsies—were the very worst. They were cut-throats and killers—just like they are today.'

'So this North Borneo Company obviously didn't manage to put an end to them then?'

The Datin shook her head sadly. 'I wish they had, Ned. I really wish they had—for all our sakes.'

It was surprisingly pleasant walking through the grounds in the cool of the evening. There were statues and fountains galore, and besides the swimming pool there were floodlit tennis courts, and even a quad-bike track which the Datin told them had been built at Benny's special request.

And there was the wall.

Hanna had noticed the wall when they'd been driven out through the main gates on their way to Police Headquarters earlier, but she hadn't realized that it encircled the whole house. It was painted brilliant white, three or four metres high, topped with vicious steel spikes. Security lights and cameras were mounted at strategic intervals along it. It made the whole place seem like a fortress—or a very posh prison.

She asked about it.

The Datin shrugged. 'These are lawless times, Hanna. There are people—bad people—who envy what my husband and I have achieved here. We have to take precautions.'

There was something quite sinister about the Datin's words. Hanna shivered despite the heat.

After that they went inside.

It seemed impossible that one house could be so big. Luxurious room followed luxurious room. There was a full-sized cinema with a massive plasma screen that descended at the touch of a button; a gym gleaming with up-to-date and obviously little-used equipment; a sauna and plunge pool. It was so unfair, Hanna found herself thinking, that some people should have so much, and others should have so little. Take Jik and his family . . .

Jik.

Just the thought of him caused her actual physical pain. Despite everything she'd learnt at Police Headquarters, she still found it difficult to believe that any of the Sea Gypsies had been involved in the attack on Mum and Dad. If they had been, Jik would surely have known about it, and would surely have told them.

Unless he was a liar. A very good liar.

But why should he have bothered to lie? What reason could he possibly have had? It didn't make sense.

But then, how to account for the iPod . . . ?

They went back onto the landing and stopped in front of their bedroom door. The Datin opened it and peered in. She nodded, satisfied. 'I see Sitti has been in and turned down the beds for you. Now I suggest you have an early night. You've got a long journey ahead of you tomorrow. Your grandparents will be arriving mid-morning, and you're booked out on the afternoon flight to Kota Kinabalu.'

Hanna stared at her in horror. 'You mean we're leaving straight away?'

'Of course. Now that you have so bravely identified the criminals who have attacked you, what reason could there be for you to stay any longer? There are too many painful memories here.'

'But we can't . . . '

'The arrangements have been made,' the Datin said firmly. 'I'm afraid you have no choice. Now I wish you both a very good night!'

She turned and strode away.

The children waited until she had crossed the courtyard below and disappeared into the main house before they went into their room. As she closed the door behind them, Hanna gave full vent to her fury. 'We're not going!' she yelled at Ned. 'She can't make us!'

To her surprise, Ned didn't seem angry at all. 'Stay cool,' he said calmly. 'We don't have to go anywhere.'

'But we don't have a choice! The Datin said . . . '

'You think Granny and Grandpa are going to

agree to go home the moment they get here? *No way!* They'll want to find out what's happened to Mum and Dad as much as we do. They'll insist on staying right here. You know what Grandpa's like when he gets going.'

Hanna did. He was just like Dad—stubborn, headstrong, tough—with an even louder shout. He'd been in the army, in the Special Forces, and though he was now quite old, he could probably still put up a serious fight if he had to. Ned was right. There was no way Grandpa would ever agree to being bossed about by anybody—except for Granny, and *that* was only because he loved her so much.

She felt a sudden warm, happy feeling. It would be so wonderful to see them both again, not to feel so alone. They'd bring money with them—they were bound to. Even though Granny would probably have to stay behind because of her legs, Grandpa could hire a boat and the three of them could go out to the islands and ask questions.

And not stop asking them until they got some answers.

Ned said, 'That's why I said I was interested in history.'

Hanna was puzzled. 'Pardon?'

'When the Datin asked us. Because of Grandpa coming. I was doing a recce, checking out the lie of the land, like Grandpa says you always should do before an operation.'

'What operation?'

'Operation Getting Mum and Dad Back. The more we know about everything there is to know, the better. True or not?'

'True.'

Hanna looked at her brother with new respect. He was growing up fast. He was no longer the little brat who made her life a misery. In the course of just a few days he'd become . . . a friend.

Together they'd do it. She was sure of that—especially now Granny and Grandpa were on their way!

15
Strangers

The warm feeling was still with Hanna when she woke the next morning. In just two or three hours' time she'd be seeing those two smiley, wrinkly, loving faces again. She wondered who she'd hug first—Granny or Grandpa? Not that it mattered, so long as it was a big, long, loving, squidgy sort of hug.

After they'd eaten the breakfast that Sitti brought them, Ned proposed that they should go for a swim, and this time Hanna agreed. It would make the minutes till Granny and Grandpa arrived pass quicker, and the pool, sparkling in the morning sunshine, looked *so* inviting. She selected a red Calvin Klein bikini, while Ned opted for a massive pair of yellow boardies. Grabbing towels they raced down the stairs and flung themselves into the water.

It was blissful! Hanna swam lengths, plunging and surfacing, imagining herself to be one of the sleek black dolphins she'd seen from Jik's boat, whilst Ned dive-bombed her from every conceivable angle. 'Granny and Grandpa are coming!' he was singing at the top of his voice. 'They are coming, they're coming today!' His happiness was so infectious that Hanna found herself joining in.

They were still singing an hour later when they heard the wheels of the Mercedes crunching to a halt on the gravel at the front of the house. 'It's them!' Ned yelled. 'It's gotta be! Come on, let's get changed!'

They scrambled out of the water and, hardly stopping to dry themselves, charged upstairs. They were frantically hauling on their clothes when Sitti's gentle knock came at the door. 'Grandparent arrive,' she announced solemnly.

'Just one grandparent?' Hanna asked anxiously.

'Two grandparent. One woman grandparent, one man grandparent.'

'That's brilliant! We'll be right down! They're in the sitting room?'

Sitti nodded.

'No need to take us, we know the way!'

They didn't stop to dry their hair—or to comb it—they just ran straight down, trailing streams of drips. The huge double doors of the sitting room were closed, but they didn't bother to knock. Ned shoved them open. 'Granny! Grandpa!' he was yelling. 'Granny . . . '

The words froze on his lips.

Granny and Grandpa were not there.

The Datuk and Datin were standing next to the tall windows. With them was Mr Henderson the British Consul.

And two complete strangers.

No, not *quite* complete. After a moment's confusion, Hanna recognized them from the pictures in Mum's album, from the brief glimpse she'd had of them through the barred gates of their house at the beginning of the holiday.

They were Mum's parents—the old, sour-faced Chinese couple who'd never forgiven her for marrying a white man, who'd told her that as far as they were concerned, they had *no* grandchildren.

'Where's Granny and Grandpa?' Ned demanded. 'I thought you said they were coming!'

The Datin's face hardened. 'These are your grandparents, Ned. They've come all the way from Kuala Lumpur specially to fetch you. You might at least greet them politely.'

Mr Henderson scanned a sheaf of papers he was holding. 'Mr and Mrs Wing are clearly named as your next of kin here in Malaysia,' he said uncomfortably. 'They *are* your mother's parents, or am I mistaken?'

'But we don't *know* them!' Hanna exploded. 'They wouldn't even open their gate when we went to see them! Where are our English grandparents? Why aren't they here?'

The fat consul flicked desperately through his papers. 'I'm afraid I can't find a reference to any English grandparents.'

'Mr and Mrs Bailey. Eric and Jean. Seven Bradavon Close, Winchester, Hampshire. Our dad's mum and dad.'

'No, I've got no record of them.'

'So they don't even know what's happened?'

'Presumably not. Of course I will make arrangements for them to be informed. This is most unfortunate—' Mr Henderson broke off. He was sweating heavily once again. He had a sour, unwashed smell.

Hanna planted herself in front of him. 'I want you to phone them now! Right this minute! I want to talk to them.'

'I don't think that will serve any immediate purpose.' It was the Datuk. There was an edge to his voice.

Hanna swung towards him. 'Yes it will. Grandpa'll get on a plane and come straight out here. We need him to help us.'

'To do what?'

'To find our mum and dad, of course. What else do you think?'

'Hanna, they're dead. I thought you'd finally begun to accept that.'

'They aren't! We know they aren't!'

It was like a bad dream. A nightmare. Any

minute now she'd wake up and Granny and Grandpa would be here. Any minute now their familiar arms would be stretching out for her, welcoming, soothing . . .

Ned crept up beside her, found her hand. She fought to stay calm, but it was impossible.

She turned back to the consul. 'Are you deaf?' she shouted. 'I want to talk to my granny and grandpa! Now!'

'*Stop that!*'

The command was harsh, heavily accented. Shocked, Hanna twisted towards its source.

It was her Chinese grandfather, his face distorted with fury. 'Show respect! You will not speak to your elders in this way! Datuk, I apologize for these children. They are like wild animals. They have been wrongly brought up!'

It was Ned's turn to react with rage. 'No we haven't! Don't you dare say that about our mum and dad!'

'I said be quiet!'

For a moment, Hanna thought Ned was going to run at the old man, smash at him with his fists. Desperately she clung on to his hand, hauled him back to her.

The Datin stepped between them. 'Hanna, Ned, please, this isn't getting us anywhere.'

'We don't need to *get* anywhere,' Hanna retorted.

'We're staying right here until our proper granny and grandpa arrive!'

The Datin's eyes sought her husband's. His lips tightened. 'That's not possible,' he snapped.

'Why not? You've got plenty of room. More than enough.'

'It's not possible because it would be against the law. Mr and Mrs Wing are now your legal guardians. You must return to Kuala Lumpur with them. You have no choice.'

'Yes we do!'

'No you don't. And if necessary I shall contact the police to make sure that you obey.'

There was a tense silence, broken only by the distant clatter of plates. Eventually the consul swallowed loudly and said, 'I will arrange for somebody from the British High Commission to visit you once you get to Kuala Lumpur. No doubt arrangements can be made for your return to England in due course, if that is . . . er . . . deemed to be desirable.'

Deemed to be desirable! What on earth was this fat idiot talking about? Hanna was about to ask him to repeat himself in plain English when the Datin once more intervened. 'I've ordered an early lunch so that there is plenty of time for you all to catch the plane,' she said brightly. 'I suggest we go in and eat now.'

'I'm not hungry!' Ned yelled at her.

'Well, I'm sure Mr and Mrs Wing are. They had a very early start this morning. Now please, everybody calm down and come through into the dining room.'

It was a highly uncomfortable meal, served buffet-style. The adults, clustered at one end of the long table, spoke mostly in Malay, casting frequent searching glances at the children, who had positioned their plates as far away from them as possible. The old Chinese couple were obviously very much in awe of the Datuk and Datin, and nodded vigorously in agreement at everything that was said. It was almost as if they were getting their orders about what to do next.

Hanna wondered what they were thinking, feeling. Mum was their daughter after all, and they must have only just been told that she was dead. Yet there was no sign of grief on their mask-like faces. Was it possible to hate your own daughter *that* much? Mum had always changed the subject when she and Ned had asked about them, and all that Dad would ever say was that they were a couple of evil old so-and-so's. The thought of being with them for even a single day filled her with utter dread.

Ned put down his fork. 'I can't eat this stuff,' he declared.

'Nor can I.'

Hanna looked desperately across at her brother. They *had* to find a way out of this, but it was impossible to plan anything without being overheard. Perhaps they could pretend there was a bomb on the plane or something when they got to the airport: stop it taking off. Perhaps . . .

Then Ned smiled.

The smile was so slight that somebody who didn't know him as well as Hanna did would probably not have spotted it. But it *was* a smile. He said, 'I'm thirsty. How about you?'

Hanna was about to tell him she wasn't particularly thirsty when Ned grabbed a bottle of mineral water and filled her glass to the brim. He then filled his own, drained it in a series of loud gulps, filled it again, and drained that. 'Drink up,' he said cheerfully. Then under his breath he whispered, 'Trust me.'

Even a week earlier, Hanna wouldn't have trusted her brother with *anything*. But now she did. Totally.

Unable to work out what he had in mind, she drank up as instructed, and when the meal was over the pair of them meekly followed the adults back into the sitting room.

There were several last-minute things to be done—papers to be signed by the Chinese grandparents, tickets and travel documents to be handed over and checked. The consul, who had stuffed himself with two massive plates of curry at lunch, seemed happier now, more relaxed—as did the Datuk and Datin. Not long now, they were obviously thinking; soon they would be rid of these dreadful children and life could get back to normal again.

When everything was completed, the Datin presented each of them with a small metal dish engraved with a picture of the Istana. 'Something to remember us by,' she said with a smile. 'I hope we'll meet again in happier times.'

'I hope so too,' replied Ned politely. *Too* politely.

It was time to go.

Ibrahim was waiting outside with the Mercedes, doors open, engine running. They climbed in, Grandfather in the front, Grandmother and the children in the back. The doors were closed and they drew smoothly away. Before they turned the corner, Hanna glanced back at the house. The Datuk and Datin were standing together on the steps watching them go. The Datin raised her hand and waved. Hanna didn't wave back.

Even though the airport was close to the Istana as the crow—or the helicopter—flies, it was much further by car. The road was narrow and rutted, climbing up the steep ridge that separated the two in a series of sharp U-bends. It wasn't jungle that covered the ridge, Hanna saw, but rubber trees, their trunks slashed with diagonal cuts, fresh white sap dribbling down into small coconut shell cups.

Not that she had much time to notice what was going on outside. Their grandfather was talking to them from the front seat—not turning his head, not making eye-contact, not inviting any kind of response—just talking. It was as if he was giving a speech he'd prepared earlier. 'We have decided that you will remain with us in Kuala Lumpur,' he announced to the windscreen. 'This will involve us in much problems and expense, but it is our duty. In return you will learn to speak Mandarin, and you will learn Chinese customs. You will show humility, obedience, and respect to your elders at all times. If you fail to do this, you will be punished.'

'You can't punish us!' Hanna exclaimed, horrified. 'You've got no right!'

'I have total right! If you do not show humility you will be whipped!'

'You must be jok—'

She never finished her reply. Their grandmother, who until now hadn't uttered a single word in the children's presence, let out a sudden loud exclamation in Chinese. A large patch of wet was spreading towards her from where Ned was sitting. '*I need to pee!*' Ned began to shout at the top of his voice, bouncing violently up and down. *I need to pee! I can't stop myself!*

Hanna stared at him in amazement. Was he *really* peeing his pants? Whether he was or not it was a brilliant idea! 'Stop the car!' she yelled. 'My brother's got a weak bladder. He can't help himself. He's got weak bowels too!' she added for good measure.

Ibrahim glanced over his shoulder, saw what was happening, cursed loudly in Malay and swerved the Mercedes to a halt at the side of the road. He clicked off the central locking which up to now had imprisoned them in the car and Hanna flung open the door. She scrambled out, closely followed by her brother. 'Run!' Ned was screaming. 'Run like hell!'

16

On the Run

Which way?

Hanna scarcely had time to formulate the question in her head before Ned's actions answered it. He veered to the left and plunged downhill, back towards the Istana. Was he crazy? They'd only just managed to escape from the place!

She tried to ask him what he was doing, but he was already too far ahead to hear. As she swung to follow him she risked a quick glance back. Ibrahim had started to give chase, but stopped, out of breath. He was frantically keying numbers into a mobile phone. There was a scared look on his face.

Ned was running faster and faster now, dodging the scarred tree trunks, leaping the crumbling termite nests which littered the plantation floor. Ahead of him the red-tiled rooftops of the Istana were getting closer. 'Ned!' Hanna hissed desperately as she fought to catch up.

Then, quite suddenly, he stopped. Taken by surprise, Hanna crashed into him, and the two of them went sprawling. 'What on earth are you doing?' she demanded as they scrambled back to their feet.

Ned ignored her. He was peering back the way they had come. A spur of fern-covered rock now hid the car from view. 'Lost them!' he said triumphantly. 'Now all we've got to do is find a good place to get back up the hill again.'

'But we've only just come down it!' Hanna protested, her chest heaving. 'Are you totally loopy?'

Ned grinned. 'Not loopy but brilliant. When they come looking for us they'll think we've gone all the way down, but we won't have. We'll be back up there on top. Cunning or what?'

'Not bad,' Hanna was forced to admit.

'So what are we waiting for?'

They followed a narrow path for a while until they came to a place where a small stream cascaded down through a rocky V-shaped gully. Then they turned and began to haul themselves upwards.

It was Hanna's idea to use the boulders of the stream as a sort of staircase up the hill. People in films were always wading up rivers to put trackers and dogs off the scent. That way they left no footprints, nothing to show which direction they'd gone.

It was easier said than done. The rocks were

slippery and sharp, and the water had etched out the occasional unexpectedly deep pool. Within minutes they were completely drenched.

As they climbed higher, the stream got smaller and smaller, and finally became a damp trickle. They were close to the ridgeline now, and when they reached it they instinctively turned north, away from the Istana and the town. It was vital to find somewhere safe where they could hide up and decide what to do next.

But there was nowhere. The rubber trees marched onwards in unwavering lines, and with hardly any undergrowth beneath them, any pursuer would be able to spot the children a mile away.

They slowed to a walk. It seemed pointless to run, and anyway it would just attract attention. They should just keep going steadily, put as much distance between themselves and civilization as possible.

Something—a landslip it looked like—had knocked down several trees just below the crest of the ridge, and as they emerged into the open space that had been created, they paused to take in the view.

The airport and the town were visible away to the right. And beyond them, vivid blue, dotted here and there with fishing boats, was the sea.

Ned spotted it first, a familiar triangular shape far away on the horizon. It was difficult to see clearly, because of a violet-coloured haze that was obscuring the line between the sea and the sky, but there could be no mistake.

It was Kaitan!

Hanna found herself close to tears. It was so good to see the island again. Somewhere out there—*somewhere*—Mum and Dad were being held prisoner, waiting to be rescued. She had a crazy feeling that if she had a powerful enough telescope she might even be able to spot them on a beach somewhere.

But it was so far away! How on earth would they ever reach it again?

'We must get a boat,' Ned said quietly, in answer to her question. 'Steal one if necessary.'

'We can't *steal*!'

'If we've got no money what else can we do? This is life and death we're talking about. Stealing stuff is allowed.'

Hanna was about to say it was still wrong, when the words dried on her lips. *Heading towards them, out of the sun, was a helicopter.*

She saw it before she heard it, sweeping towards them along the ridge. Cursing their stupidity in leaving the shelter of the trees, she grabbed Ned, and they dashed for cover.

They were too late. As the machine passed overhead they were still at least fifty metres from safety.

For an instant Hanna thought they hadn't been spotted, but then it circled and made a second swoop. This time it stopped just above them. She could see the pilot talking into his radio, no doubt giving their position to somebody on the ground.

There was no point in staying where they were and waiting to be captured. 'Keep going!' she yelled to Ned above the roar of the engine.

Within seconds they were back in the trees, heading for higher ground. If they ran far enough and fast enough, she was thinking, they might just manage to give it the slip. Eventually it would run out of fuel, be forced to turn back . . .

Ned was fitter than she was—quite a lot fitter, Hanna discovered, and soon her breath was coming in painful gasps. She wanted to stop—*needed* to stop—but she wouldn't allow herself to. She tried to imagine she was in some sort of race. An Olympic final maybe. Or the London Marathon . . .

Surely the stupid helicopter would give up soon!

It didn't. It stayed with them whichever way they turned, the downdraught from its rotors battering the treetops. How could the pilot be so certain of where they were going? He must have eyes like an eagle.

Then she realized: there must be some kind of spotting device on board—something that could pick up a person's body heat through dense undergrowth. If she was right, it meant they could *never* escape. Wherever they ran, wherever they hid, the helicopter would still be able to spot them. The Datuk and his nasty policeman friend were probably already checking coordinates, getting ready to move in . . .

She was about to tell Ned to slow down, to stop wasting his breath, when something hit her face.

It was a splash of water. It felt far too big to be a raindrop.

There was a second splash.

And a third.

It *was* rain! She glanced up between the branches. The violet-coloured haze which had obscured Kaitan earlier had swallowed up the whole sky. A massive tropical storm was heading their way.

As if in confirmation, a shaft of lightning hissed down into the valley below, followed almost instantly by a deafening crack of thunder. The raindrops were coming faster now, whipping at her face as she ran. Ned, who was racing ahead of her, glanced back. 'Don't stop!' he yelled. 'Keep going!'

She kept going.

But not for long.

The storm hurled itself against the ridge,

wrenching at the trees, threatening to rip them bodily from the earth. Lightning no longer came in isolated bolts, but shot continuously across the sky in a barrage of searing white light. It was like every fire hose on the planet had been turned on her at maximum force. Stinging, lashing water filled her eyes, her mouth, her ears. It seemed to be drilling through her skull, through her skin and bone, into the very centre of her brain.

She tried to spot Ned, but it was impossible to see anything. For a short while she staggered on, then she dropped to the ground and hid her head in her arms as the earth was churned into liquid mud around her. It seemed impossible that the trees could stay upright in this; impossible that she wouldn't be sucked up into the sky with them, whirled higher and higher until she disappeared for ever . . .

As suddenly as it had started, it was over.

Thunder still cracked, lightning still flashed, but the storm had passed onwards, heading north up the coast.

As the wind dropped, Hanna pulled herself to her feet, wiping at her mud-caked face, peering upwards through the dripping leaves.

The helicopter was gone! It must have veered away, raced for safety as the storm had struck.

She turned to share the good news with Ned.

But he wasn't there.

It took her a while to register the fact, to fully comprehend that her brother had disappeared. At first she thought he must have gone on ahead, somehow carried on running despite the storm—but that would have been totally impossible, even for him.

What in God's name had happened?

Had he been struck by lightning? Or just as bad, crushed by a falling tree?

Her heart pounding, she began to run, frantically calling out his name. It was impossible for a person to disappear, she was telling herself, to just vanish from the face of the earth . . .

Then she saw him. Or rather she saw his shirt, a streak of red wrapped round the base of a tree trunk way down below her on the western side of the ridge. He must have tripped, fallen, rolled over and over down the precipitous slope, unable to stop himself until he slammed into the tree. There was no movement, no sound.

Screaming his name, she half slid, half tumbled down towards him in a shower of fallen leaves and twigs.

Please be OK, Ned! Please don't be hurt. Please don't be . . .

She could see his face now, see the blood coating it. It was the same colour, the *exact* same colour as his shirt. There was too much blood. Far too much blood . . .

'Ned! It's me! Are you OK?'

Then she was with him, cradling his head in her hands. His eyes were closed. Blood was oozing from a wide cut just below his hairline. You shouldn't move people when they were hurt, she was thinking, they might have internal injuries. Suddenly she found herself wishing the helicopter would come back again. She could signal to it, get Ned winched to safety, get him to hospital. She couldn't bear it if he was badly hurt. Not on top of everything else. She'd go mad. She'd go totally mental.

Why oh why had they tried to escape? Why oh why had they been so stupid as to think they could get Mum and Dad back all by themselves?

Then Ned groaned, stirred.

His eyes flicked open.

'Thank God!' Hanna gasped, bursting into tears. 'Thank God! Are you all right?'

His voice was slurred. 'I don't remember. Where . . . '

'You fell. You've hit a tree. You've been unconscious. I must get help.'

'Help?'

'Hospital. You must go to hospital.'

'No!' Ned jerked upright, as though he had been hit by a powerful electric shock. He scrambled to his feet, eyes blazing, his bleeding scalp ignored. He was speaking quite clearly now—shouting. 'No way do I go to a hospital! We've got to get Mum and Dad back, remember? I'm perfectly *OK*.'

'Your skull might be fractured.'

'Well it's not! We've come this far. We're not stopping now!'

17

The Hideout

Apart from the cut, Ned really did seem to be OK—either that, or he was just being brave. Hanna made him move his arms and legs, stretching each one in turn to check if it hurt. When he told her they didn't, and when he told her his chest didn't hurt either when he took deep breaths, she decided it was safe to go on.

But where to?

One thing was certain, they must get away from the rubber trees as soon as possible. There was no cover, and the helicopter could be back any minute now.

A narrow path—no doubt used by people on the rubber estate—zigzagged down towards the valley floor. It was their only option, so they took it. At first Hanna tried to help Ned, to support him as he walked, but he shook her off irritably. He was OK, he insisted. Totally fine. Eventually she was forced to believe him.

After a while, the rubber trees ended. They were replaced by chest-high scrub—thorny bushes and clumps of tall spear-leaved grass interlaced with the clinging tendrils of pitcher plants. It was like clambering through tangled barbed wire. Their progress slowed almost to a halt. Every movement they made showered them with rainwater and tiny crawling insects. The sun came out, beating down relentlessly on their exposed heads.

But it wasn't the heat or the insects that bothered Hanna most. It was the noise.

It was as though a thousand demented cows had all started mooing at once! The noise was so deafening, so relentless, that she wondered if her eardrums might burst.

What in God's name could it be?

It was Ned who solved the mystery. He was wading through the scrub ahead of her when he suddenly stopped and pointed downwards.

There, nestling at the base of a bush, in a muddy pool of rainwater, was the biggest frog she had ever seen.

For a long moment Hanna stared at the frog, and the frog stared back. Then, apparently without taking a breath, it inflated its chest to the size of a party balloon and mooed like a cow.

It was a *bullfrog*—it had to be! Hanna remembered Mum telling her how they always came out after heavy rain, and how they were really good to eat if they were skinned and stir-fried.

'Cool,' mouthed Ned, thrilled by his discovery.

'Cool,' Hanna mouthed back, and pushed past him. This was not the time or place to stand around admiring wildlife.

Soon after that they found a track. It was little more than a V-shaped slash through the vegetation, but the going became easier. With their bare legs bleeding from countless pricks and scratches, they followed where it led. The mooing of the bullfrogs continued, joined now by the brain-lancing drill of cicadas as they dried their wings in the sunshine.

And then, unexpectedly, there was a new noise. A different sort of farmyard noise—a loud grunting. Hanna's eyes met Ned's. Was there such a thing as a *pig-frog*? Mum had never mentioned one of *those*.

They turned a corner and nearly collided with a low thatched shed. A chorus of squeals from inside left them in no doubt as to what it was.

A pigsty!

Trying to ignore the smell, and the swarms of angry flies buzzing around her head, Hanna stared at the building. It was perfect, she suddenly realized. All they had to do was go inside, and if the helicopter came back—*when* it came back—all its stupid heat sensor would pick up would be a shed-load of sweating pigs! No way would it be able to tell that two of the pigs were human.

It took her some time to convince Ned that it was essential to actually go *inside* the reeking hut, but eventually, reluctantly, he agreed.

Gingerly, they edged round the walls until they came to a rickety wooden door. To Hanna's puzzlement it wasn't bolted in any way, just pulled shut. Surely the pigs must be able to push it open and escape?

She levered it ajar, and peered cautiously inside. It took her a moment or two to adjust to the darkness, but then she saw why there was no need for bolts. The pigs—there were six of them in all— were squashed into small iron cages, scarcely larger than themselves. They were matted with filth, their skins rubbed raw against the bars that imprisoned them. It was more like a torture chamber than a pigsty. 'You poor things!' Hanna said, her eyes filling with tears.

She turned to Ned. He must be as horrified as she was. But he wasn't looking at the pigs. He was staring up at the sky. 'Get inside!' he yelled suddenly, and shoved her hard in the back.

He jerked the door shut behind them just in time.

The helicopter was on top of them almost instantly, the roar of its engines making the pigs squeal with terror. The children held their breaths as the huge machine thundered overhead, turned and made a second pass.

Had they been spotted?

For a moment it seemed as if they had, but then it swung away and headed up the valley, apparently satisfied that there were just pigs in the building below.

It had been a close thing—*too close*. How much longer would it be before their luck ran out?

Hanna's eyes were becoming accustomed to the gloom now. The pig cages, she saw, occupied only half the hut. Behind them, stacked almost to the roof, were large numbers of empty rattan baskets.

There was a gap between the baskets and the rear wall which was just wide enough for them to squeeze into and get out of sight of the door in case somebody came in. She pointed it out to Ned, who nodded. He was feeling as exhausted as she was, she realized, and the cut on his head must surely be hurting him. They needed to rest for a while, get some strength back. One of the pigs snorted softly—a large white sow. She glanced down at it and their eyes met. It looked so desperately sad in its cruel iron prison. 'We'll get help for you,' she said to it gently. 'As soon as we've got the chance. That's a promise.'

They found a couple of sacks and spread them out behind the baskets to form a sort of mattress. It didn't look very comfortable, but it would have to do. They were about to lie down when Ned suddenly pulled off his shirt. Even though it was quite muddy from the storm, it was still too bright, he told Hanna. If anybody came in they'd spot it straight away. She should take hers off too. White was even brighter than red.

'But I can't go topless,' she protested.

'You don't have to. We'll dunk them in there.' He pointed to a muddy puddle near the pig cages.

'But that's full of pig wee!'

'Got a better idea?'

She hadn't. Reluctantly, she wriggled out of her shirt, and dropped it into the reeking puddle. Ned added his own on top. 'Stamp on them!' he ordered. 'Make sure they're completely soaked.'

Holding her nose, she did so.

Ned fished them out, stained and dripping, and handed Hanna's shirt back to her. 'Now put it back on.'

Easing the stinking garment back on over her head was one of the worst things she'd ever had to do in her life. At Ned's insistence she smeared more mud on her shorts, and onto her bare arms and legs. He walked round her twice, inspecting her from all angles before announcing that she would do. Then he began to slap mud on his own body. 'How do I look?' he asked finally, as he pulled his stained shirt back over his head.

Hanna took a couple of paces back and examined

her brother critically. He was transformed. With his filthy skin and spiky black hair he looked like some kind of street urchin—no, better than that, he looked like . . . a *Sea Gypsy*! He could easily pass as Jik's brother.

She told him, and he grinned broadly. 'You're not so bad yourself,' he said. 'Apart from the pong.'

Normally she'd have said something—done something—about a remark like that, but she felt too tired. She squeezed herself behind the baskets and slumped down onto the sacks. Ned followed. Judging by the angle of the sun through a crack in the wall it was still quite a while before dusk. Within minutes they were both sound asleep.

18
A Totally Wicked Plan

Hanna woke with a start. She was conscious of two things—a burning thirst, and a loud squeaking noise. At first she thought the squeaking was from the pigs, but then the noise ceased suddenly and the door to the sty was wrenched open.

She felt Ned stir beside her and clapped a hand over his mouth. He struggled for an instant, but then stopped. Fully awake now, he understood the need for silence as well as she did.

Their hearts thumping, the children peered out between the baskets. Silhouetted in the doorway was a man. He was short, with bowed legs, and was wearing a wide-brimmed hat. He was gripping the handles of an ancient wooden wheelbarrow, which he pushed inside the hut. It was the squeaking of its wheel which had woken Hanna.

There was a chorus of grunts as he emptied the barrow's contents into the pig cages, followed by a loud slosh of water as he refilled their drinking troughs from a tank in the far corner. Then he picked up the handles of the barrow again and headed towards where the children were crouched. Terrified, they shrank back against the rough walls of the hut.

His face was clearly visible now. He was Dad's age—maybe a little older—with badly pockmarked skin, and small, puffy eyes. He was muttering to himself in Chinese—his voice harsh, complaining. He grabbed a pile of baskets and dumped them in his barrow. Then he reached for a second stack. Hanna and Ned were completely exposed now. One glance in their direction and he would spot them for sure . . .

But he didn't look.

Incredibly, amazingly, he didn't look!

Instead, still muttering loudly, he turned and heaved the laden barrow out of the shed. The door thumped shut behind him. The squeaking of the wheel slowly died away.

It was a long time before the children dared to speak, before they were convinced he was really gone. Then Ned said, 'How about thanking me then?'

'For what?'

'For making you cover yourself with gunge. There's no way that bloke wouldn't have seen us otherwise. Am I brilliant or just plain wonderful?'

'You're total rubbish,' Hanna told him, but she

didn't mean it. She'd have hugged him if he wasn't so filthy.

She began to rearrange the baskets, sliding fresh stacks across to conceal their hiding place. Suddenly she stopped, turned to Ned. 'Remember when we went to the market with Mum and Dad to buy all that stuff before we went to Kaitan? There were loads of baskets just like these. They all had vegetables in them.'

'So?'

Her brain was racing. The man who kept the pigs obviously grew vegetables too. He was almost certainly harvesting them right now, filling the baskets he'd just collected ready to take to market early tomorrow morning. He *had* to be going to Tamu—it was the only town big enough to have a market for hundreds of miles. She remembered the market clearly: a huge, smelly, open-sided shed full of stalls selling fruit and vegetables, meat and fish, chillies and rice.

It was next to the harbour.

And the harbour was full of fishing boats— hundreds of them, big and small. Boats that could take them to Kaitan. Boats that could take them to Mum and Dad!

The farmer must have some sort of lorry to transport his vegetables. If they could get on board it without being seen, they'd get a free ride into town!

Ned's eyes flashed with excitement when Hanna told him her plan. 'Wicked!' he breathed. 'Totally wicked! Then we just grab a boat and go!'

Hanna had a strong feeling that whatever happened would be a good deal more complicated than that, but she nodded. 'When it's dark we'll go and check it out.'

The final hours the children spent in the stifling, stinking pigsty were the worst of all. As dusk fell every insect in Borneo seemed to zoom in to where they sat, and they were soon slapping desperately at their exposed skin. Rats began to rustle and squeal in the gathering gloom, fighting over spare scraps from the pigs' meal.

It was so difficult with no watch to estimate how much time had passed. Even though Ned was keen to get going the moment the sun had set, Hanna knew it would be foolish to do anything until after midnight. Only then could they be reasonably certain that the farmer—and anybody else who might be living nearby—would be in bed and asleep.

Eventually, after what seemed a lifetime, she stood up, went to the door and peered through. The moon was high in the sky, so several hours *must* have gone by. Surely it was safe to leave now?

She felt Ned push up beside her enquiringly. After a moment's hesitation she took his hand. Together they slipped outside.

The moon was bright—almost too bright—throwing pools of dense shadow beneath trees and bushes. A broad, well-worn path led away from the door of the sty through the scrub. They began to tiptoe cautiously along it. In the distance a dog barked once, twice.

After a while the path curved sharply to the left and the scrub disappeared. They found themselves on the edge of a small field. It was completely bare—except for what looked like a lot of large footballs.

The children stopped, puzzled. Then Ned exclaimed: 'Watermelons!'

Hanna bent and picked one up. It was smooth and heavy, still warm to the touch from the day's sunshine. Ned was right. It *was* a watermelon, a big fat melon full of delicious water!

It took them a long time to saw through the tough outer skin with Ned's penknife, but eventually they were able to tear it apart and bury their parched lips in its sweet, juicy interior.

It was bliss! Ned cut open a second melon. They ate that too, and started a third.

Finally they could eat no more. Ned belched loudly and giggled. 'Stop it!' Hanna ordered sharply, once more conscious of her surroundings. As if in response, the dog began to bark again, more loudly.

On the far side of the melon patch was another field, this time planted with rows of leafy vegetables. Here and there bare patches indicated where the produce had been harvested.

As they threaded their way cautiously between the rows, the barking continued. Suddenly Hanna felt Ned's hand on her arm, and stopped. He was pointing up ahead.

Just visible through a dense clump of banana trees, was a house. It looked more like a shed, with a corrugated iron roof and a single small window. Chained up outside it was a large dog.

The animal had heard them—smelt them too, no doubt—and was charging backwards and forwards at the end of its leash.

There was a sudden, gruff shout and a light flicked on inside the house. Terrified of being seen, the children flung themselves flat between the rows of vegetables. Seconds later the door opened and the farmer appeared. He was wearing shorts and a baggy white singlet.

He took a step or two outside, and peered intently around. For one horrible, stomach-churning moment it looked as if he was going to let the dog off its chain. But then, apparently satisfied that the disturbance was not serious, he turned and went inside again. The dog quietened down.

'Did you see what I saw?' Ned whispered excitedly.

Hanna had. The glow from the open doorway had lit up an ancient pick-up truck parked in the deep shadows next to the house. It was fully loaded. If her theory was right it was their taxi into town!

But how to get to it? The slightest movement would set the dog barking once more. They'd just have to make a dash for it, she decided—hope they could reach it, get themselves on board and get hidden before the farmer came out to investigate again.

There was just one problem.

One *big* problem.

The dog was chained up directly in front of it!

Hanna tried to estimate the distance. There looked to be just enough room to get past it without being bitten. *Just*. She glanced at her brother. His eyes were gleaming in the moonlight. He was up for anything. Unlike her, he seemed to thrive on danger. 'Should we try?' she asked.

He nodded.

She took a deep breath. It was now or never. '*OK go!*' she hissed urgently. '*Go go go!*'

They reached the edge of the field in an instant,

hurling themselves over a low gate. The dog, as if unable to believe its eyes, cowered back against the house for a moment or two, snarling, then launched itself into the attack.

It was too late. Its jaws snapped shut millimetres from Hanna's legs. Instantly its head jerked back and its feet skidded from under it as the slack in its chain ran out and the collar tightened round its neck. Choking, snarling, it wrestled to free itself, but the chain held . . .

The children dived for the truck, colliding painfully with it in the darkness. Its back part was made of wood—crudely-sawn slats, bolted together. They scrambled on board.

The baskets were covered with banana leaves, to stop the vegetables from wilting when the sun came up. They burrowed frantically beneath them, trying to make enough space to hide themselves . . .

They did it—just.

The lights in the house flicked on again. There were more shouts—a woman's voice joining in this time. The door burst open and the farmer came out. He was holding a torch in one hand and a heavy stick in the other. Peering between the slats of the truck, trying to control their heaving breath, the children watched him sweep the area around the house with the torch's powerful beam, paying particular attention to the vegetable field—the very place where they'd been hiding just seconds ago!

He seemed nervous, jumpy. There were no tigers in Borneo, Hanna knew—but were there leopards? Was that what he feared was lurking in his fields? The thought of a leopard made her shiver. Supposing—just supposing there'd been one watching them, stalking them, when they'd left the pigsty . . .

The dog, jerking at the end of its chain, was going crazy now—not just barking but howling dementedly. The woman in the house continued to shout. The farmer, apparently satisfied that there was nothing hiding in the front of the yard, turned his attention to the truck.

He shuffled swiftly towards it and directed his torch underneath. His face was inches away from Hanna's now. She could hear the wheezing of his breath, smell the taint of tobacco smoke. She felt Ned tense beside her. If either of them so much as sneezed . . .

There was no way they were going to get caught by this horrible man, she decided. Surprise was the best form of attack. She'd leap out at him, try to hit him in the chest with both feet. If she was lucky he'd be knocked flying and there'd be time for them to escape . . .

But there was no need for luck. After a moment

or two the farmer turned away satisfied. He directed a shout at the house, then raised his stick and walked quickly across to the dog.

The children didn't see what happened next, and they were glad. There was a series of loud blows. The dog's barking turned into agonized yelps, and then into pathetic whimpers.

Finally there was silence.

The door of the house slammed shut. The light in the window flicked off.

Now all they had to do was wait for dawn.

19

Taxi to Tamu

Dawn was a long time coming. The agonizing cramps that gripped Hanna's scrunched up legs, and the vital importance of staying silent made sleep impossible. Even the slightest cough or snore might set the dog barking again, and that was too big a risk to take.

Ned was awake too. She could just make out his face, pale in the reflected moonlight, his eyes blank with fatigue. He must be even more uncomfortable than she was, she thought, his knees tight to his chest, his back pressed against the sharp rattan of the baskets. The cut on his forehead stood out as a vivid black line. It should be bathed, she knew, maybe even stitched, otherwise it was certain to become infected. She marvelled at how her normally vocal brother hadn't referred to it once since the accident happened.

Thoughts whirled through her tired brain. Could they *really* hope to find Mum and Dad on their own? Even if they got to the harbour without being caught, neither of them knew how to drive a motor boat, and she doubted whether Ned was skilful enough to sail an outrigger all the way to the islands.

And even if he was, even if they somehow managed to get there without being spotted, what then? Without Jik to translate for them they couldn't even communicate with the Sea Gypsies, let alone ask them for help.

Besides, if the Panglima and his two sons really were responsible for the pirate attack, the whole of Ular must be involved too. They'd probably end up dead. The Datin's words came back to her clearly: the Bajau were cut-throats and killers. Always had been . . .

And yet . . . and yet . . .

And yet what? It was so difficult to think clearly, so difficult to make the right decisions. Things that had seemed so certain when they were discussing them back at the Istana now didn't seem certain at all. It was exhaustion no doubt. Despair.

No, not despair! She must never admit to despair. That way they really would be lost!

Despite her determination not to, she must have slept, because she didn't hear the farmer and his wife until the doors of the truck were jerked open. It was early dawn, the sky bathed in a cold pink light. Peering between the baskets, the children saw the woman for the first time. She was painfully thin, with a pinched, weather-beaten face and tightly frizzed hair. She climbed up beside her husband and the doors slammed shut. The engine coughed into life and they lurched out of the farmyard.

The discomfort Hanna and Ned had suffered during the night got rapidly worse as the truck pitched and yawed along the rutted laterite road. The vegetable baskets seemed to take on a life of their own, sliding and twisting. Only by using all their strength were they able to stop themselves being badly squashed.

They were travelling through an oil palm plantation now—endless stumpy trees with tattered, drooping crowns. Here and there bunches of golden palm nuts were stacked at the roadside awaiting collection. They passed a truck driving fast in the opposite direction. Peering through the slats, they could just make out the word 'POLIS' written on its side. Its back was open and inside were several sleepy-looking men in uniform. The sight made the children smile. If it was a search-party sent by the Datuk, it was in for a long, hot, useless day!

The oil palms ended on the outskirts of Tamu, and they began to pass through a shanty town— row upon row of crude shelters constructed from scraps of plywood and plastic. Small children with protruding bellies stood ankle-deep in mud from the previous day's storm. Women carrying buckets of water on their heads squelched past on semi-submerged duckboards. As the truck slowed at a junction, Hanna overheard a shouted conversation between two of the women. Their language sounded familiar, and after a moment's puzzlement she realized: they were Sea Gypsies!

What on earth were they doing here, so far from their beautiful islands?

Beyond the shanty town the streets became more familiar, with rows of scruffy shop-houses and workshops. There was a strong smell of dried fish and river mud. Hanna felt her stomach knot. Only a few more minutes and they'd be there.

Then what?

This was the moment she'd been dreading. With so many people about, how could they hope to get out of the truck without being seen?

They'd just have to make a run for it, she decided. Try not to get caught . . .

They were bumping along the quayside now, past lines of brightly painted fishing boats just returned from sea. Baskets of fish and prawns were being swung ashore. A man with an axe was splitting up huge blocks of ice. Moments later the truck lurched to a halt and its engine cut.

The children peered cautiously out. They were

at the back of the market, parked in a row of similar trucks. All around them people were rushing to and fro, some of them carrying boxes, others pushing laden barrows. There was a new smell now, competing with the odour of fish and mud—the delicious scent of frying food. Hanna's mouth began to water. Apart from the melons, they'd eaten nothing for nearly twenty-four hours, she realized. She was starving!

The farmer and his wife got out of the truck. Were they going to start unloading straight away? Hanna craned her neck, but from where she was hiding it was impossible to tell.

Ned, who had a much better view of what was going on, reassured her. 'They've gone to eat,' he whispered. 'There are food stalls. Loads of them.'

More trucks were pulling up all the time. Many of them had passengers riding in their backs—stout, cheerful women with shopping baskets, clambering awkwardly out, chattering at the tops of their voices as they did so. Watching them, Hanna suddenly realized that getting out of the truck without attracting attention was going to be no problem. *Everybody* was getting out of trucks. All she and Ned had to do was make sure the farmer and his wife weren't looking in their direction when they did it.

She told Ned, who gave her a quick thumbs up

before resuming his inspection of the food stalls. He began to describe what was being eaten, licking his lips as he did so: 'Fried eggs . . . omelette . . . satay . . . chicken curry . . . '

Then he stopped. 'They've turned their backs!' he hissed urgently. 'They're talking to somebody. Come on!'

He jumped to his feet, vaulted over the side and dropped to the ground. Hanna followed, narrowly missing an old woman who was shuffling between the parked trucks. She muttered angrily, but didn't stop. There was no reaction from the farmer and his wife.

They'd done it!

Her elation was short lived. She felt suddenly acutely self-conscious, aware of her mud-stained shirt, her filthy face and hands. Ned had inherited enough of Mum's Chinese features to pass as a local—but had she?

She needn't have worried. As they squeezed between the parked trucks into the main market hall it was as though they were both invisible. The farmer and his wife didn't even glance up as they passed, and a man pushing a barrow loaded with pineapples slammed straight into them without stopping.

The food stalls were crowded with people—market traders, shoppers—some chatting, some reading newspapers, everyone eating. An Indian man with a protruding belly was making *roti canai*—delicious flaky pastry pancakes—whirling the dough through the air before folding it over and slapping it onto the griddle in front of him.

The children stopped to watch him, their mouths watering. As the golden-brown *rotis* were cooked he stacked them one on top of the other at the corner of his griddle. It was so tempting to reach out and grab one . . .

Hanna was just thinking how useful money was—how *essential* it was—how not being able to get enough to eat must be the very worst thing in the world, when something caught her eye.

It was a newspaper, left by a customer on one of the tables next to the *roti* stall. It was heavily stained with curry, but the picture on its front page leapt out at her. *It was of her and Ned standing on the steps of the police station, with the Datuk posed between them!* The headline was a single word set in huge type. It was in Malay, but its meaning was crystal clear. '*TRAGEDI!*' it screamed. The tears trickling down her cheeks were clearly visible.

Alarmed, she looked around. Several people were flicking through copies of the same newspaper as they ate. Any moment somebody would surely glance up, spot them, and put two and two together. They must get out of the market as soon as possible. It was far too dangerous . . .

'*Berhenti!* Stop!'

A sudden loud shout and the crash of a table being overturned made her spin in terror. She expected to see a squad of policemen rushing towards her.

Instead she saw Ned. He was clutching a fistful of *rotis* in one hand, and indicating frantically with the other that they should run like hell.

Had he gone mad? Had he gone totally crazy?

He was clear of the tables now, hurtling between the market stalls. Baskets of yams and cucumbers went flying. Horrified, Hanna rushed after him.

There were more shouts. Another loud crash. The *roti* man was giving chase, his face distorted with rage, his huge belly vibrating with the effort. A banana seller stuck out a foot to trip Hanna as she went past, but she hurdled it with ease and sped on after her fleeing brother.

He was heading towards the far side of the market. Through the hall's open sides Hanna could see the glint of sunlight on the slow-moving waters of the harbour. She could kill him, she was thinking— and she probably would if they ever got out of this without being caught!

Fruit and vegetables gave way to meat. Chickens squawked as they were being hauled out of plastic crates to be slaughtered. Mutton sellers in bloodstained singlets were hacking at dripping sheep carcasses with huge cleavers. The floor became wet with blood, slippery with guts. The *roti* man was tiring now, his breath coming in loud gasps. Suddenly there was an agonized yell as his feet skidded from under him and he crashed down onto his outsize bottom. There was loud laughter from the mutton sellers.

Glancing back, Hanna saw to her immense relief that nobody was looking in their direction any more—nobody could care less about a fistful of *rotis* stolen by a couple of street kids. It had been good entertainment, something to liven up a boring morning.

The chase was over.

Or it would have been if only Ned had realized it.

Still running at top speed he dodged round an empty pile of chicken crates and disappeared into the bright sunshine outside. Hanna opened her mouth to yell at him to stop, but checked herself just in time. It was vital that nobody heard her shouting in English. Instead, growing angrier by the minute, she forced herself to follow him.

He was heading for the harbour, but his route to it was blocked by a tall chain-link fence. He swung to the left, running alongside it, searching for an opening. He was slowing a little now, giving her a chance to catch up. She'd almost succeeded when the fence suddenly curved sharply away from the market buildings and ended at a pair of stout double gates. The gates were wide open, and without pausing or looking back, Ned dashed straight through them.

It was only when she'd reached the gates herself that Hanna realized how stupid he'd been. Attached to a post was a notice in Malay. She couldn't understand what it said, but the picture that went with it was crystal clear. It was of a running man being shot in the back by somebody in uniform. This was obviously some kind of police or army compound—somewhere where intruders would be killed on sight.

Ned couldn't have seen the notice—or if he had, its meaning hadn't registered. He'd come to a halt fifty metres or so inside the compound, and was leaning against a pile of oil drums, getting his breath back. The *rotis* were still firmly clutched in his hand, and he waved them cheerily at Hanna.

She gestured frantically at him to come out, but he either couldn't or wouldn't understand her. He carried on waving the *rotis*, licking his lips exaggeratedly. There was no alternative: she would have to go inside and fetch him out—by force, if necessary.

Glancing quickly round to check that nobody

was watching, she dashed through the gates towards him.

He was grinning as she reached him, still holding out the *rotis*. 'I've got two each,' he said triumphantly, 'and they're still hot. Dee-licious!'

Hanna ignored the food. She had to stop herself punching him on the nose. 'Are you crazy?' she hissed. 'Are you completely mad? First you steal those things, then you come in here! Do you know what this place is? It's somewhere where they shoot you if you go inside it. There's a notice . . . '

'I saw it,' Ned said unconcernedly.

'You *saw* it?'

'I figured if they'd left the gates wide open, it couldn't be that serious. Anyway, nobody's shot us yet.'

'I would!' Hanna exploded. 'If I had a gun I'd shoot you! You stupid, stupid idiot! I'll never trust you again! Never! Now come with me!'

She grabbed at his arm; jerked him towards the gates.

Then she froze.

There was an empty guard post at the entrance to the compound. Sauntering back towards it was a policeman. He was carrying a packet of fried noodles in one hand.

In his other, he held a semi-automatic rifle.

20

Stowaways

The children were trapped, and this time there was nowhere to hide. Scarcely daring to breathe, they edged round the stack of oil drums until they were out of sight of the guard—but now anybody approaching from the opposite direction would be able to see them clearly. Ned's bluster had evaporated. He was close to tears. 'I'm sorry, Hanna,' he whispered. 'I'm really really sorry. I didn't think.'

'Well, it's about time you did think,' she retorted bitterly, wondering if she would ever be able to forgive him, if he would ever properly grow up.

Now what?

She glanced around. To her intense relief, apart from the policeman on the gate, the compound appeared to be deserted. It was about the size of a football pitch, ringed with tall fencing, which ran down to the river's edge. Moored on one side of a double jetty was a police patrol boat. It had a powerful searchlight mounted on its wheelhouse roof, and what looked like a large machine gun underneath a cover on its front deck. The sight of it made Hanna shiver. It had to be one of those two evil-looking boats she'd seen screaming towards the Sea Gypsy village on that terrible night Jik and Manai Liha had drowned. Its twin was no doubt out on patrol somewhere—maybe even still at Ular.

She forced herself to concentrate on the area around the jetty. Could they use the river to escape? Was it possible to swim to safety?

It was, but they'd be spotted by the guard before they got anywhere near the water. They'd have to wait until it was dark, and that was *hours* from now.

She was still trying desperately to work out what to do, when she heard the sound of engines. She peered apprehensively round the edge of the oil drums. Speeding into the compound was a convoy of vehicles. In the lead was a police car, its lights flashing. Behind it were two covered trucks and an unmarked van. A second police car brought up the rear.

The vehicles pulled to a halt close to the water's edge, and a familiar figure eased himself out of the leading car. It was Superintendent Lazarus, his uniform stretched tight over his burly chest, his pig-eyes concealed behind aviator sunglasses.

Hanna ducked swiftly from sight. Had somebody spotted them and reported them to the police?

It was possible. But surely they wouldn't need lorries to arrest a couple of kids!

She risked a second look. As she watched, the doors of the van were flung open, and half a dozen armed policemen climbed out. The Superintendent barked a series of orders and they began to fan out around the jetty. One of them headed straight towards where she and Ned were hiding.

It was impossible they wouldn't be seen this time! There was nowhere left to go, and there was no point in trying to run—unless they wanted a bullet in their backs.

Hanna sucked in a deep breath, gave Ned what she hoped was a reassuring smile, and waited for the inevitable.

It didn't happen.

The policeman suddenly stopped and turned. He was staring intently out towards the harbour entrance. The other policemen were also staring in the same direction.

A boat was creeping slowly in over the bar, turning towards the unoccupied berth on the jetty. It was so overloaded with passengers it was a miracle it was still afloat. Fortunately the sea was flat calm—even a medium-sized wave would have swamped it instantly.

Mooring ropes were caught and secured. Its engine cut.

The Superintendent shouted loudly at the boat in Malay. After a moment's hesitation, its passengers started to climb ashore and head for the trucks.

Knowing they might be spotted at any moment, Hanna and Ned strained to get a good look at the arrivals. They were women and children for the most part; painfully thin, dressed in tattered rags. Many of the women were clutching babies, and all were struggling with large bundles of possessions. There were a few elderly men who glared angrily at the police as they passed. If it hadn't been for the guns, Hanna sensed, they might have launched a full-frontal attack.

Then she saw Jik's mother.

She'd been below decks, and was one of the last to leave the boat. She had her children with her—the youngest clasped to her waist. With her free hand she was half-lifting, half-dragging a large bundle tied in an old sarong. Jik's oldest sister was trying to help, but the load was too heavy for them. Hanna looked desperately for Jik, but he was nowhere to be seen.

The Superintendent issued a quick, impatient order, and one of the policemen stepped forward. He picked up the bundle and threw it into the nearest truck. Then he aimed a vicious kick at Jik's mother. She staggered, almost dropped the toddler. Hands reached out to haul her on board, and she half-climbed, half-fell into the vehicle. The children followed, their small faces pale with fear.

Hanna felt a surge of worry. Could *she* be responsible for what was happening here—*she and Ned?* When they'd signed that statement at Police Headquarters, had it meant the whole village would be found guilty of kidnapping Mum and Dad—not just the Panglima and his two sons?

Surely they couldn't *all* be involved!

Even if they were, why was everybody being brought to the mainland—even the children? They couldn't all be put in prison. She remembered the shanty-town they'd passed through on the way to Tamu. Those women were Sea Gypsies. Had the same thing happened to them? Had they been forced to leave the islands too?

Nothing that any of them might have done could possibly deserve treatment like this!

The last of the Sea Gypsies was finally crammed into the trucks. The armed policemen returned to their van. Engines roared into life. Led by the second police car, the convoy turned and jolted through the gates.

The Superintendent remained behind, watching impassively as everybody left. Then he crossed swiftly to the boat and banged on the glass of the wheelhouse. Moments later the boatman emerged.

It was Ahmad, Hanna realized with a shock—the man who'd taken them out to Kaitan what seemed like a lifetime ago. And this was the very same boat!

There was a brief conversation. The Superintendent produced a wad of banknotes from his back pocket, peeled off several and passed them over. Then he turned and looked out to sea, pointing at his watch as he did so.

Hanna's heart leapt. If she understood what was happening correctly, Ahmad was being ordered to make another trip out to Ular as soon as possible to bring back more villagers.

There'd never be a better opportunity to hitch a ride. Somehow they had to get on board his boat and stow away without being seen!

The two men spoke for a short while longer, then the Superintendent got into his car and sped away. Soon afterwards Ahmad also left, heading for the market. The guard closed the gate behind him.

Ned's eyes gleamed with excitement when Hanna explained her plan. But how were they going to succeed? The guard's face was clearly visible through the window of his little hut. The slightest movement would instantly attract his attention. They'd be captured straight away—or worse, shot without any questions being asked . . .

Long minutes ticked by. The boat bobbed gently on its moorings. It was so close they could almost touch it. It would be unbearable if it left for the islands without them!

There was a sudden, urgent nudge from Ned. He was pointing at the guard. He'd obviously got fed up with staring out of the window, and had opened a newspaper. Something inside had caught his attention, and his face was completely hidden by the pages.

It was the moment they'd been waiting for . . .

They raced for the boat, leapt onto the deck. One of the hatches was open and they plunged down through it. They waited for shouts, the sound of running feet, but none came.

They'd done it!

As her eyes adjusted to the gloom at the bottom of the ladder, Hanna turned triumphantly to Ned, and grinned.

Except it wasn't Ned she was grinning at.

Ned was behind her. Whoever was standing next to her was taller. Much taller . . .

She glanced round wildly, but there was no escape.

The man was holding a spanner, swinging it slowly from side to side. Hanna shrank back against the hull of the boat. As she did so, a shaft of sunlight streaming through the open hatchway lit up his face.

It was Ahmad's assistant—the youth with the crooked mouth who'd helped with their luggage when they'd first gone out to the islands. She'd forgotten about him completely.

Far from being menacing, he seemed as nervous as she was!

It was Hanna who broke the silence. 'Please don't call the guard,' she said desperately. 'We're looking for our mum and dad. If you call the guard we'll never find them.'

The youth made no reply. He peered at her closely, then switched his stare to Ned. Did he recognize them? Hanna couldn't be sure.

She carried on talking in English, though she was convinced he didn't understand what she was saying. 'They've been kidnapped. We're trying to find them. We need to search for clues. We want to go to Ular . . . '

A look of puzzlement spread over the youth's face. He opened his mouth as if to say something, then closed it again slowly. He sucked in a deep, anguished breath.

Was something the matter with him? He hadn't spoken a single word to anybody on that first journey out to the islands with Mum and Dad, Hanna recalled. It was Ahmad who'd done all the talking. Come to that, she didn't even know his name.

She forced a bright expression onto her face. 'OK then, forget Ular! Can you get us to Kaitan? We'd ask Ahmad but we don't trust him. We trust you . . . ' She was gabbling now, but she couldn't help herself. One shout and the guard would come running and it would all be over.

Then the youth spoke—or at least, attempted to. His mouth contorted into a series of alarming shapes as his tongue and lips desperately tried to form words.

All that emerged was a series of animal-like grunts.

Then the truth dawned on Hanna. He couldn't talk! That meant he couldn't tell Ahmad they were on board, even if he wanted to!

She glanced urgently at Ned. Could they use hand gestures to communicate with him? She was about to suggest it, when they heard voices. There was a creak as the compound gates were swung open.

Ahmad was returning!

The sound seemed to make up the youth's mind for him. The puzzled look disappeared from his face. He went quickly to the bows and wrenched open a small door. Behind it was a cramped storage locker. In the dim light Hanna could just make out an anchor and chain, several coils of rope, and a jumble of white polystyrene boxes. It smelt strongly of fish. He pushed the children inside.

In the brief instant before he closed the door he pointed at his chest. *'Bow-wow!'* he said proudly. *'Bow-wow! Bow-wow!'*

21
Cliffhanger

The darkness was total. There was not even the faintest gleam of light around the locker door. It was like being buried alive.

'What does he mean by *bow-wow*?' Ned whispered as they groped around for somewhere to sit. 'Does he think he's a dog?'

'Of course not!' Hanna retorted.

'Then what?'

Even if she'd known what to tell him in reply, she had no opportunity. Feet thumped onto the deck above their heads and descended heavily down the ladder.

Ahmad was back on board and he was not happy. He shouted at the youth who grunted apprehensively. He was obviously being blamed for something he'd failed to do when he'd been left in charge of the boat. There was the sound of a blow landing, a yelp of pain which reminded Hanna of the noise the farmer's dog had made when it was being beaten. She wondered what Ahmad would do to them if he suddenly felt the need for a spare anchor or a coil of rope and opened the door . . .

For a long time they went nowhere. Judging by the noises filtering through to them, the engine needed adjustment, and there was refuelling to be done. As the sun rose higher, the heat in the tiny, airless locker became almost unbearable.

Then, finally, there was a shout from Ahmad, and the engine vibrated into life. The mooring ropes were freed and the boat swung out into the stream.

It got mercifully cooler as they crossed the bar and picked up speed into the open sea. Hanna felt Ned stir beside her. Something soft and crumbly was being pressed into her hand. To her astonishment she realized it was a *roti*. He must have been clutching them all this time! 'I know they're stolen, but they still taste nice,' he whispered uncertainly.

She was about to scold him again—tell him that she couldn't—*wouldn't*—eat them under any circumstances, when a thought occurred to her. It was a silly thought, and she didn't really believe it, but it was impossible to ignore: if it hadn't been for these stupid *rotis*, they'd never have gone inside the police compound in the first place, and they'd certainly never have got on board Ahmad's boat.

Maybe they were lucky *rotis*. Maybe if they ate them they'd be swallowing all that luck, taking it inside themselves. Maybe they'd become lucky too!

She took a big bite. Then another. She could almost feel the luck spreading inside her with each mouthful. 'We're coming!' she whispered. 'We're coming, Mum! We're coming, Dad!'

She had to stop herself from shouting it out loud.

After she'd finished eating, she adjusted the coil of rope she was sitting on to make herself as comfortable as possible, and closed her eyes. She was thinking about Mum and Dad—about how much in love they were. Sometimes, back home, when she went into the kitchen without warning, she'd catch the pair of them kissing. Ned called it gross, because they were too old to do stuff like that—but she didn't think it was gross at all. It was just lovely and cosy and comforting. She prayed that wherever they were, whatever had happened to them, they still had each other to hug and hold on to.

As the boat surged out into the long, slow swell of the Sulu Sea, its gentle movement felt like the rocking of a baby's cradle. Ned leaned against her and rested his head on her shoulder. After a while he slept.

Hanna slept too.

For a minute. For ten minutes. For half an hour . . .
Then the door jerked open.

Trembling with shock, blinking in the sudden light, they peered fearfully out. To their relief it wasn't Ahmad, but the youth. He was smiling his strange, crooked smile, and holding out a plastic bottle of drinking water.

They took the water gratefully and smiled back at him. Why was he being so nice to them, Hanna wondered? He was risking big trouble from Ahmad if he got found out . . .

Then the penny dropped. 'Are you a *Bajau*?' she whispered.

He nodded enthusiastically. '*Bow-wow! Bow-wow!*'

She glanced triumphantly at Ned. Bow-wow was nothing to do with dogs—it was just his way of pronouncing the word *Bajau*! He was telling them he was a Sea Gypsy and that was why he wanted to help them. He was almost certainly from Ular, so he'd know all about what had happened to Mum and Dad. He obviously felt sorry for them, and maybe—just maybe—he knew something important, something that could *really* make a difference.

But he couldn't speak, so there was no way of finding out. It was so frustrating! It occurred to Hanna that this was why Ahmad had employed him in the first place—because he couldn't give away any secrets. He must really hate his boss for what he was doing to the islanders . . .

An angry shout from above. The youth gave a rueful grin and closed the door. Once more blackness descended.

Sleep was impossible after that. They drank the water, guzzling it greedily until the bottle was almost empty. Hanna tried to use some of it to bathe the cut on Ned's head, but it was too difficult in the darkness, and she kept hurting him. Eventually she gave up and they settled down to talk.

Not bothering to whisper any more because of the thunder of the engine, they discussed everything that had happened since they'd escaped from the Chinese grandparents. It had been an extraordinary twenty-four hours—exhausting, terrifying. For the first time, Hanna was able to ask Ned the question that had been intriguing her ever since they'd managed to escape: *had he really peed on the back seat of the Mercedes?*

He'd intended to, he told her—that was why he'd drunk all that water when they were having lunch—but when the time came, he'd been so tense he hadn't been able to squeeze anything out. Luckily he'd brought a spare bottle of water with him and had hidden it upside down under his shirt. He'd just unscrewed the top and started yelling.

'You should have seen the old woman's face!' Hanna said, spluttering with laughter.

'And the old man's!'

'And Ibrahim's!'

After that they talked about the islands. Hanna hoped that somehow the youth would manage to put them ashore on Kaitan—though how he'd be able to do that without Ahmad knowing about it was another matter. On Kaitan they could hide until it was safe, then comb the beach for clues. There had to be something they'd missed on that first terrible day—something the pirates had dropped, maybe, or even a footprint. A footprint would be a clue if it matched up with the person who'd made it.

'What happens if we *don't* find any clues?' Ned asked. 'It's been a long time since it happened.'

'Then we go to Ular and look for clues there.'

'How do we get to Ular?'

'How should I know?' Hanna replied crossly. 'We'll get there somehow. Something will turn up. It always does. Nothing's going to stop us now—true or not?'

'True,' Ned answered. But he didn't sound quite so convinced any more.

The voyage seemed to go on for ever. But eventually, at long last, the engine note changed and the boat began to slow down.

There was a swift patter of feet on the hatch ladder and the door opened. The youth beckoned them out urgently, pressing a finger to his lips to indicate that they should be silent. As they emerged blinking into the bright evening sunshine, the children saw why. Ahmad was lying underneath the shade awning on the rear deck. He was fast asleep, snoring rhythmically. The boat, which had slowed almost to a standstill, was apparently steering itself.

Soaring out of the water, just a short distance away, was an island.

The youth led them to the side, made a swimming motion with his hands. They'd have no problem reaching the shore if they swam steadily, they saw.

There was just one problem.

It was the *wrong* island.

It wasn't Kaitain. Or Ular. It was some other island—one they hadn't seen before—with steep limestone cliffs and boulder-strewn beaches. Where on earth could it be?

After a moment of panic, Hanna realized this must be the other side of Kaitan, the side Dad had promised he'd take them to one day to see the turtles lay their eggs; the side that pointed out to the open sea.

Why on earth had the boy brought them here? Had he forgotten where their hut had been? Had he forgotten about Dead Man's Leap and the lagoon?

It wasn't possible. There had to be a reason, but there was no way he could tell them what it was. They just had to trust him.

The children smiled their thanks, and after a quick glance at Ahmad to make sure he was still sleeping, slipped overboard. The youth went swiftly to the wheelhouse, opened the throttle, and the boat surged rapidly away. Within a few minutes it was lost from sight.

There was a strong current running, and for a few horrible moments the children thought it was going to carry them out to sea. Instead, it swept them into a small rocky cove surrounded by tall cliffs. It occurred to her as they scrambled ashore having hardly swum a stroke that the youth had known exactly where the sea would take them when he'd dropped them off.

It was wonderful to be cool again after so many hours of heat and sweat. There was a deep pool amongst the rocks—not much bigger than a large bath—and the children stripped to their underwear and jumped into it, washing themselves all over, getting rid of the last of the smelly pigsty mud that had served them so well.

At last Hanna was able to take a good look at the cut on Ned's head. It was a long, shallow wound—more a slice than a deep gash—and despite everything it was beginning to heal. It would leave a thin scar—nothing more. She bathed it carefully in fresh sea water which she knew was good for cuts. It must have stung, but Ned said nothing.

After that they washed out their clothes and trainers, and not waiting for them to dry, slipped them back on. It was time to decide what to do next.

One thing was crystal clear—they couldn't stay where they were. It would be dark soon, and the tide was rising fast. Before long their tiny cove would be under water. They had somehow to find a way up the cliffs before night fell.

The cliffs looked even taller than they had done from the boat—smooth rock faces rising vertically from the beach, dotted here and there with spindly bushes. Even a professional climber would think twice before tackling them head-on. There had to be an easier way up.

Ned eventually spotted it at the far corner of the cove—a narrow ledge leading diagonally upwards from a pile of fallen rocks. If they pressed themselves flat to the cliff wall they could maybe—just maybe—edge their way up it.

Hanna went first, wishing she had suckers attached to her hands and feet, not daring to look down at the jagged rocks below. Ned followed, arms and legs outstretched like some new species of spider. Inch by inch they pushed themselves upwards.

It got harder as they got higher, the rock wall bulging alarmingly out over the ledge in some places, forcing them to grope desperately for hand-holds as they swung themselves round.

Ned had the worst of it, his face constantly bombarded by earth and stones dislodged by Hanna's feet. Eventually, after a sharp sliver of rock had landed painfully close to his left eye, he stopped and announced he'd go no further until she'd reached the top.

Feeling suddenly exposed and lonely without him close by, Hanna pushed herself onwards. She was now only a few feet from the top, but she could have been a mile. A mass of small trees and bushes grew out from the cliff edge, their roots exposed where the topsoil had fallen away. They looked like gnarled brown hands signalling to her to go no further. Somehow she'd have to get past them if she was ever going to make it to safety.

Now it was no longer solid rock she was climbing on, but soft earth that slid away alarmingly under her feet. She slowed to a halt, examining the tangled roots closely, trying to work out which of them was strong enough to bear her weight if she used it to pull herself the last few feet.

It was impossible to tell for certain—even some

of the bigger pieces came away in her hand when she jerked at them. Eventually she selected a sinewy rope-like root dangling down from a large tree growing close to the edge.

Whispering a silent prayer, she grabbed it and began to haul herself up.

She realized instantly, sickeningly, that she'd made the wrong choice. There was a tearing noise above her head and loose earth began to shower down onto her. She felt the root begin to give way.

She was falling!

Then a hand reached out and grabbed hers.

It was a small hand, but very strong. For an instant she swung out into space, but then her scrabbling feet managed to get a grip, and she was dragged to the top where she lay gasping with shock and terror.

'Dam close thing,' a voice said cheerfully.

Hanna opened her eyes and looked up.

Grinning down at her was Jik!

22
Back from the Dead

Hanna felt as if she was dreaming. 'You're alive!' she exclaimed, pushing herself upright. 'We thought you'd drowned.'

Jik chuckled. 'No dam way! Float like goddam coconut, swim to shore no problem.'

'But what about Manai Liha? What about her boat?'

He hesitated. His eyes flickered with sadness. 'I think . . . she go visit *Tuhan*.'

'*Tuhan?*'

'God. *Bajau* god.'

'You mean she's dead?'

He nodded. 'Dam stupid old woman! I try to save her, but she fight fight . . . ' He stopped. A tear trickled down his cheek.

Hanna put out a hand and took his. He'd lost weight since she'd seen him last, and there were dark hollows round his eyes. She felt an over-whelming sense of gratitude—no, more than that, *love*—towards this funny undersized boy with the bad skin. He'd saved her life. Without him she'd even now be lying crushed on the rocks beneath.

She was about to question him further when an irritated shout rose up from the cliff below. She'd forgotten all about poor Ned! 'We're coming!' she yelled. 'Just stay where you are!'

'Brilliant!' was her brother's first word, as they hauled him the last few feet to the top of the cliff. And he kept repeating it over and over again. *'It's brilliant you're alive, Jik! Just brilliant!'*

'He saved my life,' Hanna told him.

'That's *brilliant* too,' Ned added, though he wasn't really paying attention. He was too busy giving Jik high fives and leaping about madly.

It really was brilliant to have Jik alive and well and with them again. But what had happened to him since that terrible night on Ular?

Eventually the boys calmed down sufficiently for Hanna to ask. Jik's brows creased. 'Many bad thing happen,' he said quietly. 'Many *many* bad thing!'

After he'd swum ashore from Manai Liha's sinking boat, he told them, he'd hidden in the jungle, narrowly avoiding capture by the police who were combing Ular, searching for anybody who'd escaped from the village. Many men had been arrested, including the Panglima and his two sons, who hadn't been heard of since. The police had stayed on Ular for two days, and it was only when they'd finally gone that he'd dared to venture back to the village.

He'd found his mother and brothers and sisters huddled in the wrecked remains of their house. They were unhurt, but very frightened. He'd wanted to stay with them, but his mother had told him to go. There were no men left in the village—not even boys of Jik's age—and he was in danger of being arrested and taken away if the police returned.

So he'd found a boat and come to Kaitan, sailing by night so he wouldn't be seen. Kaitan was much bigger than Ular, with high mountains. There were many places to hide. He'd been out searching for fruit in the jungle when he'd spotted Ahmad's boat heading towards the island. He'd seen it slow down close to the little bay and the two children slip overboard and swim to the shore. He'd recognized them even from a distance, and had hurried to the cliff-top to meet them.

'Just in time to save my life,' Hanna said.

'*Dam brilliant!*' agreed Jik modestly. Thanks to Ned a new word had obviously entered his vocabulary.

Then Hanna and Ned told him their story. 'Goddam polis!' Jik spat, when he heard about his family being driven away.

He was trembling with fury. It was the first time the children had ever seen him angry, but they totally understood why. Losing Mum and Dad had made them feel like that too.

After a while Jik glanced up at the sky. He seemed anxious, restless; as if he should be somewhere else. 'Night come soon,' he announced. 'We go.'

'Where to?' Hanna asked.

He didn't reply. Instead he set off swiftly between the trees.

Desperate not to be left behind, the children scrambled after him. There was a loud whooshing noise as hundreds of fruit bats, disturbed in their evening feed, took off into the gathering dusk. Where on earth was he taking them? Judging by the direction, he was heading for the central mountain. Was he intending to go right to the top?

After a while the vegetation began to thin and there was an occasional glimpse of the sea far below. A sea eagle, yelping like a dog, circled on the evening up-draughts. Fireflies darted and flickered in the undergrowth.

They'd just skirted a large outcrop of rock when they saw the man. He was straddling the path in front of them. He was about Dad's height, dressed in ragged combat gear. In his right hand he held a vicious-looking *parang*.

A noise behind them made the children spin round. A second armed man was blocking their retreat. Hanna glanced wildly at Jik, expecting him to try to escape, but he didn't. Instead he stopped, and waited meekly as the first man strode down towards him.

The man was furious, and let fly a stream of abuse. For one horrible moment Hanna thought he was going to hit Jik. He was speaking in Bajau, but his meaning was clear: she and Ned were not welcome on the island. Jik should not have brought them here.

Hanna felt a stab of fear. Were they in danger? Jik was pleading now, pointing back towards the sea, obviously explaining how they'd come to be with him.

Eventually—after what seemed like an eternity—the man began to relax. He glanced at his companion who shrugged. The crisis had passed. Jik turned to the children. 'My father very dam mad . . . ' he began.

Hanna stared at him in amazement. 'This man's your *father*?'

'Every dam kid have father!'

'Yes I know but . . . '

Ever since that first night on Ular she'd wondered about Jik's father. He'd never mentioned him, and she'd been too polite to ask. She'd assumed he was dead—drowned in a storm at sea or something. She peered at the man. Now Jik had told her, the family resemblance was obvious. He had the same broad, open face; the same shining eyes—except in his case they were shining with anger, not laughter.

'My father say to me he does not want you here. No dam children are allowed. There is big war.'

'What big war?' Hanna asked, alarmed.

'Soon. Soon there will be one. He say you must go away. Right now.'

Ned thrust himself forward. 'That's stupid!' he said angrily. 'How can we go away? This is an island. We've got no boat. Are we supposed to swim?'

Jik's look of misery deepened. He translated what Ned had just said.

His father sighed exasperatedly. He had a lengthy conversation with his companion. Then he spoke curtly to his son, turned, and climbed away swiftly up the mountainside.

'He say OK, you can stay,' Jik told the children in a relieved voice. 'But only for short time. And you must never tell about this dam place or many people will be killed. You understand?'

The children nodded. They felt a growing sense of unreality. Was there *really* going to be a war? If so, who would be fighting whom? It was like something on the news; something that happened somewhere else, to other people . . .

212

They had no opportunity to question Jik further—
he was already gone, scrambling after his father.
They set off in pursuit.

After a while the trees stopped and there were
just jumbled boulders. Leaping from rock to rock in
the gathering darkness, the children followed Jik
round the summit of the mountain. It was exhausting and dangerous. One slip and there'd be broken
bones for sure.

Then Jik vanished.

One moment he was ahead, waving to them;
the next moment he was gone. It was as if the earth
had opened up and swallowed him. Alarmed, mystified, the children stumbled onwards.

They didn't see the entrance to the cave until Jik
stuck his head out of it and grinned. It was a narrow gash in the rock wall, completely hidden by a
protruding lip of limestone and a curtain of trailing creepers. Unless you knew exactly where it was
there was no way you would ever spot it.

They climbed up to it and slipped apprehensively inside. How big the cave was and how far it
extended inside the mountain was impossible to
tell. The gloom of its interior was illuminated only
by a dim kerosene lamp and the embers of a
smoky fire on which a large cooking pot was bubbling. Crouched around the fire, smoking ciga-
rettes, were ten or twelve men, Jik's father amongst

them. Their conversation ceased abruptly as the children came in.

Hanna recognized some of them. They were the fishermen who'd fired unfriendly questions at Jik when he'd first brought her and Ned to Ular in his little boat. They looked even more unfriendly now, their deeply tanned faces made sinister by the flickering firelight.

Jik's father was clearly their leader. He motioned to his companions to make room for the children, and they sat down. Jik disappeared into the far interior of the cave and returned with a plastic cup of water. Hanna and Ned drank what they needed and handed the cup back to Jik who drained the rest. Fresh drinking water was obviously in short supply this high up the mountain. After a short pause, the men resumed their discussion.

It was frustrating not knowing what they were talking about, but there was no opportunity for Jik to translate. The smoke from the fire made Hanna's eyes sting, and the water she'd drunk had left a nasty metallic taste in her mouth. As the conversation continued, she felt Ned slump against her. He was as exhausted as she was.

Eventually there was a lull in the talk. Jik's father turned to Hanna. He no longer seemed angry, just tense and tired. He spoke to her softly in Bajau. 'My father ask, why do you return to Kaitan Island?' Jik said.

'To look for clues.'

'Clues?'

Hanna struggled to explain the meaning of the word. 'A clue is a thing—*anything*—that will tell us where our mother and father are. Where the pirates have taken them.'

Jik translated. 'My father ask, do these pirates come in big boat or small boat?'

'They came in a small boat with a powerful engine. But they had a bigger boat out at sea, beyond the reef.'

'What colour is small boat?'

Hanna thought back. With the darkness, and the flickering light from the burning hut, everything had looked black, even though she knew it wasn't. 'Green,' she said uncertainly. 'I think it was dark green.'

'Abasa know this dam boat.'

It was like being shot. Trembling with shock, she twisted towards Jik. Had she understood him correctly? Was his father saying that somebody had actually *seen* the pirates?

'Who's Abasa?' she demanded, her heart pounding.

Jik indicated a small, sharp-eyed man sitting opposite.

'What did he see? Ask him, Jik, please!'

Jik went to the man and crouched beside him. They spoke for a long time. Eventually Jik nodded and returned to the children. He looked serious. On the night of the attack, he told them, Abasa had been fishing in his boat on one of the big reefs on the far side of Ular. He'd known nothing about what had happened on Kaitan. Shortly before dawn a strange looking *kumpit* towing a green inflatable boat had approached and drawn up alongside. The crew of the *kumpit* had threatened him, and stolen his last two drums of diesel fuel, plus his entire catch of fish. He'd recognized the men from the way they spoke. They were Tausugs from the island of Tawi-Tawi away to the south, across the Philippine border. Tausug men were very bad criminals—the worst criminals in the whole of the Sulu Sea.

'Was there anybody else on board with them? A white man and a Chinese woman?' Hanna asked frantically.

Jik shook his head. There was nobody else—just the Tausug crew. Abasa was certain of this because they'd forced him to carry the things they'd stolen from him below deck. If anybody had been down there he'd have seen them for certain.

'But they *must* have been there! There was nowhere else they could have gone!' Hanna exclaimed.

Except over the side of the boat, a little voice inside her was saying. Except into the sea where the sharks were waiting . . .

Then the fisherman spoke again. Jik hesitated for a moment before he translated: 'He say there is blood.'

'*Blood?*'

'On *kumpit* deck. Much blood. He say none of the Tausug men is hurt, but there is much blood.'

Hanna felt Ned stiffen. The expression on his face was changing. Horror was rising in his eyes. 'I want to go home,' he said very quietly. 'Hanna, I want to go home!'

Then he was screaming it, tears cascading down his face. '*Hanna! I want to go home!*'

23
Nothing Left to Lose

Ned got to his feet and lurched towards the mouth of the cave. Hanna scrambled after him. There was a steep cliff just beyond the entrance and she was terrified he would tumble over it.

She caught him just in time, wrapping her arms round him, hauling him back. He was sobbing uncontrollably, shaking as if he was freezing cold. She tried to calm him, but it was impossible. 'I want to go home,' he kept repeating, in between sobs. 'I want to go home now!'

'We *can't* go home, Ned,' she told him desperately. 'There's no way we can get back to England. We haven't got any passports. We haven't got any money. We can't even go back to the mainland. We'll be captured and sent to Kuala Lumpur to live with that horrible old man and woman. They'll punish us. We'll be whipped. Locked in a room probably.'

Ned struggled to free himself. 'I don't care!'

'Yes you do. Of course you care!'

'No I don't. Mum and Dad are dead, so it doesn't

matter any more. Nothing matters any more . . . '

Fresh sobs racked his body.

Hanna clung to him despairingly. What could she say—what could she do—to bring him comfort? She could think of nothing except to tell him the truth. To tell him what she knew—what she would *always* know—voices or no voices.

'They're not dead,' she said firmly.

Ned turned to her with accusing eyes. 'You don't know that! You just *hope* they're not dead, and that's not the same thing as knowing! And now there's not even any hope left.'

'They could have been rescued by a passing ship. Anything could have happened to them. Abasa didn't say anything about seeing dead bodies. That's because there *weren't* any.'

'But there was blood. It was Mum's and Dad's blood—I know it was. I want to go home, Hanna. I want to go home right now!'

'Well you can't, because we don't have a home to go to!'

Hanna hadn't meant to shout at him, but she was unable to stop herself. His reaction was immediate. He shrank away from her, pressing himself against the wall of the cave. 'I hate you!' he screamed. 'I hate you I hate you I hate you . . . !'

'My father say to you, please to be quiet!'

It was Jik, hurrying across to the cave entrance.

Several of the men had already gathered there and were staring out into the night. Judging by their expressions something serious was happening. Her ears still ringing with Ned's screams, Hanna peered apprehensively over their shoulders. A string of lights was dancing on the horizon. As she watched, the lights grew brighter and began to merge into each other.

They were flames.

Somebody had set fire to the village on Ular!

The men watched in stunned silence for a moment or two. Then the shouts of fury began. They were literally spitting with rage.

In the gabble of voices Hanna caught a familiar word: *triti.* Jik's father was repeating it over and over again, smacking his hands together as he did so.

What on earth could it mean? Whatever it was, she was convinced that it somehow held the key to everything that was happening.

There was a fresh exclamation from one of the men. She swung her eyes seawards again, following his gaze.

At first it looked like just another reflection of the burning village on the water; but then the ripple of light split into two. They were boats, Hanna realized, and they were heading towards Kaitan!

She could hear the noise of their engines now,

the sound carrying clearly across the calm sea. Suddenly a powerful searchlight flicked on and began to sweep the slopes of the island. Cursing, the men drew quickly back into the darkness of the cave.

There was a momentary flash—like a camera—as the blinding light whipped past; then it was gone. Blinking, everybody returned to the entrance.

The boats were clearly visible now. One of them was a police patrol boat—the searchlight was mounted on its roof. The other was Ahmad's *kumpit*, dangerously overloaded with women and children—the last of the islanders from Ular.

The sight of their families increased the men's fury. As the shouting began once more, Jik's father raised a hand for silence, and began to speak in a hard, determined voice.

'What's he saying?' Hanna asked Jik.

'He say to them to be strong. He say, always the Bajau run, always the Bajau hide. Never fight. Polis take everything. Take our islands. Take our people. But no more. Now we fight.'

'But you can't fight the police,' Hanna said, horrified. 'They've got helicopters. Machine guns. There are hundreds of them—thousands if they bring in reinforcements. They'll call in the army. You can't win!'

Jik shrugged. Made no reply.

'But you'll all be killed!'

'No dam problem. We are dead already.'

He spoke quietly. Too quietly. Hanna stared at him. How long had he felt this kind of anger, this kind of despair? Did all the Bajau feel like him? Was death *really* preferable to life as it was now? Her sadness became almost unbearable.

Outside, the searchlight flicked off, and the two boats began to pick up speed away from the island. She watched until they were lost from view behind Dead Man's Leap, then she turned back to Ned.

He was crouched against the cave wall, his head buried between his knees. She squatted beside him and reached out, trying to draw him to her, trying to give him comfort, but he resisted, stiff and unyielding. He was locked inside himself, grieving for Mum and Dad. Truly grieving.

Eventually, not knowing what to do or say, she gave up in despair. The men were eating now, scooping the soggy tapioca from the big cooking pot with their hands, washing it down with water from the plastic cup. Jik motioned her to join them, but she shook her head. She wasn't hungry, and the way she felt, she didn't think she'd ever be hungry again.

After the meal the discussion resumed, getting rapidly louder and angrier. To escape the smoke and noise, Hanna went and sat at the cave entrance where the air was fresher. The flames on Ular had died down now, with just an occasional dull flicker revealing where the blaze had been. The night was clear and still, the sky shimmering with stars. A silver moon rose slowly above the rim of the ocean away to the east. It seemed impossible that there could ever be a war in such a beautiful place as this.

She was thinking about the men from Tawi-Tawi. They were the real pirates—she was convinced of it now. Everything added up: the time and place; the inflatable boat; the dreadful, horrible blood . . .

In a strange way, the knowledge pleased her. There'd always been a tiny worm of doubt wriggling somewhere deep inside her, but now she *knew* the Sea Gypsies were innocent. It made everything so much simpler, so much easier . . .

Or nearly everything.

It still didn't explain how the Panglima and his sons had come to have her iPod . . .

Or maybe they *never* had it! Maybe the men from Tawi-Tawi had dropped it on the way back to their boat, and the police had found it when they'd come to Kaitan after the raid.

The rest would have been easy. She could imagine the Panglima and his sons being tricked—no, *forced*—into touching it so their fingerprints were all over it. It was the best piece of evidence ever—even better than the 'confessions' that had been beaten out of them, or the statements she and Ned had so shamefully signed. The poor, innocent old man and his stupid sons had stood no chance.

But that still left the biggest question of all unanswered. *Why?*

Why go to so much trouble to condemn three innocent men to their deaths? Why spend a small fortune sending boats and helicopters and armed men to destroy a peaceful fishing village and cart away its inhabitants? There had to be a *very* good reason indeed.

She'd find out sooner or later, she vowed. She owed it to the Panglima and his sons. And when the truth emerged, she'd make sure the Datuk and his pig-faced Superintendent got everything that was coming to them!

She glanced at Ned. He hadn't moved. Her heart went out to him. Without hope he was lost. Without hope there could be no future—and there was nothing she could do about it.

Nothing except coming up with hard evidence to prove that Mum and Dad really were alive and waiting for them somewhere . . .

But where in the world could she find that?

She stared out over the glistening ocean. The

plain truth was, the only people who knew for certain what had happened to Mum and Dad were the pirates themselves, and they were back in Tawi-Tawi.

OK. She'd go and ask them!

It was a stupid idea—perhaps the stupidest idea she'd ever had—but she couldn't think of any other. The Tausugs might be very bad criminals, but they surely had mothers and fathers of their own.

And sons. And daughters.

They'd listen. They *had* to . . .

She'd go alone. It would be too dangerous to take Ned, and Jik was needed here. She'd borrow a boat, get Jik to teach her how to sail, how to read the stars, then head for Tawi-Tawi. If she succeeded, it would be brilliant.

If not . . . so be it. Like Jik, she had nothing left to lose.

24
Nick's Note

Hanna's thoughts were interrupted by a sudden commotion. The discussion round the cooking fire had come to an end and the men were standing up. They fetched spades, pickaxes, and coils of rope from the rear of the cave and began to file quickly outside.

'Where's everybody going?' Hanna asked anxiously as Jik prepared to follow them.

He put a finger to his lips. 'Big dam secret. My father say you must stay here. Not make a noise.'

'But, Jik . . . '

He was gone.

Feeling uncomfortable in the sudden silence, Hanna returned to her brother and sat down beside him. She groped for his hand and held it. Despite the warmth of the night his skin felt cold. 'It'll be all right,' she whispered desperately. 'I know it'll be all right. Please believe me . . . '

He lifted his head, and stared into her eyes. The look of misery he gave her would stay with her for the rest of her life.

The men were gone for a very long time. Eventually, when Hanna had started to think they might never come back, she heard footsteps outside and two of them stumbled into the cave. They were carrying a stout box. It was thick with dirt, and obviously very heavy. They placed it carefully in the middle of the floor and immediately went out again.

More boxes followed. Most were medium-sized, but some were smaller, and one much larger. Hanna counted twenty of them before the men finally returned to the cave.

Jik's eyes were shining with excitement as he came in. 'Dam brilliant!' he exclaimed, wiping at his dirty face with even dirtier hands. 'Dam bloody brilliant!'

'What's in the boxes?' Hanna asked him, consumed with curiosity. Could it be treasure?

Jik's father answered the question for her. He prised open the lid of the nearest one with his *parang*. She peered inside, half-hoping, half-expecting to see the gleam of gold.

It was full of guns.

There were ten of them, each one wrapped individually in a length of oily cloth. The men crowded forward, taking the weapons, unwrapping them and laying them out in a neat line on the floor of the cave. A second box was opened and emptied in the same way. Then a third. Gradually the line of rifles grew.

Hanna peered at the guns. They looked very old-fashioned, nothing like the squat black submachine guns the police used. They were like something out of a museum.

Then she noticed something stamped onto the side of one of them. At first she thought it was Chinese writing, but then she looked closer and realized it wasn't. She turned to Jik. 'Where do these come from?'

Jik consulted his father who was gouging at the lid of one of the smaller boxes. 'My father say Japan. These Japan guns. One time Japan soldiers come to Ular, kill many, many Bajau. Then Melikan soldiers come, take away Japan soldiers in dam ship.'

After a moment's puzzlement, Hanna realized it must be World War Two that Jik was talking about. She remembered Dad telling her how the Japanese had invaded Borneo back then, how they'd tortured and killed thousands of people, and had only surrendered after the Americans had dropped atomic bombs on Hiroshima and Nagasaki. 'So these guns were left behind when the Japanese soldiers went?'

Jik nodded. 'My grandfather bring to Kaitan, hide in secret place. He say, one day the Bajau must fight, one day they must have guns. Now that day come.'

She did a quick calculation. 'But they're more than sixty years old! And you don't have any bullets.'

Jik grinned. 'Got bullets! Many many bullets! Bang bang bang!'

As if to confirm his words, Jik's father finally managed to open the box he was working on. Inside, beneath a sheet of tightly-stretched tinfoil, were hundreds of brass-cased bullets looking as shiny as the day they were made.

It took a long time to unpack all the guns. Eventually Hanna counted more than a hundred of them, occupying almost the entire floor of the cave. The largest box contained a dismantled machine-gun which caused a great deal of puzzlement and comment as the men tried to work out how to put it together.

Hanna felt sad as she watched them. It was so unfair that the Sea Gypsies should be forced into fighting a war with these ancient weapons that probably wouldn't work, or would blow up in their faces. They'd stand no chance at all against trained policemen and soldiers with their lethal modern firepower.

It was getting very late, but the men showed no signs of stopping to sleep. They were cleaning the guns now, trying to wipe away the decades of dirt and grease that encrusted them. They were clearly delighted with the weapons, and were chatting loudly amongst themselves. Suddenly Jik's father issued a curt order and they fell silent.

From outside the cave came a strange groaning noise, ending in a harsh cough. Hanna felt the hairs on the back of her neck rise. 'Goddam monkey,' Jik whispered to her cheerfully.

But it wasn't a monkey. Moments later three wiry men strode into the cave. They had *parangs* slung from their belts and were carrying strings of dried fish over their shoulders. Jik's father and his companions were on their feet in an instant, greeting the new arrivals, embracing them, firing questions. Jik joined in, his face gleaming with excitement. He glanced triumphantly back at Hanna. 'Now we got goddam *army*!'

She was about to point out that three people hardly added up to an army, when more men began to arrive. They came in twos and threes, smiles of greeting on their faces. Several of them were carrying water containers. Others brought sacks of tapioca root and more strings of dried fish. One of them had a large basket of ripe mangoes. Soon the cave was uncomfortably full.

The newcomers were admiring the guns, picking them up, pretending to shoot with them. Apart from an occasional glance in their direction, nobody seemed at all concerned that there was a pair of pale-skinned European kids squatting in a corner. Presumably Jik's father—or more likely the sentry on the mountain path—must have told everybody who they were.

'Where have all these people come from?' Hanna asked Jik, when she finally managed to capture his attention.

He spread his arms expansively. 'Far away.'

'Where's far away?'

'Laparan, Bilingan, Sanga-Sanga. Many island. All come to fight war.'

Hanna's heart gave a sudden lurch. 'Are there any people here from Tawi-Tawi?' she asked urgently.

Jik shook his head. 'No way. Tawi-Tawi people very bad!'

She sucked in a deep breath—now was the moment of truth. 'I'm sure they're not *that* bad, Jik. That's why I want to go there. I want to go and find the men who kidnapped Mum and Dad and ask them where they are.'

Jik's eyes widened in horror. 'Dam big danger! You cannot!'

'Yes I can,' Hanna said determinedly. 'It's the only way I'll ever find out what's happened to them. I don't want you to come with me. Or Ned. I'm going to go alone.'

'You crazy dam girl! They cut your throat!'

'I'll risk it.'

Jik glanced round desperately. 'I tell to my father. He say no!'

'I don't care about your father. He can't stop me . . .'

'*Don't go!*'

Ned's voice was tiny—thin—almost inaudible in the hubbub that filled the cave.

Hanna swung towards her brother. He'd got to his feet and was swaying unsteadily towards her.

'Ned, I've got to go! Don't you see it's my only chance to find out the truth?'

'*Don't leave me here!*'

A harsh sob exploded from his lips. It was as if his entire body was packed so full of misery that it was bursting out of its own accord.

'Oh, Ned!' Hanna pulled him to her. 'I won't leave you. I won't leave you ever!'

She clung to him in anguish.

'*You, sad girl. Very sad girl.*'

It took her some time to realize that somebody was speaking to her. The voice was insistent. '*You, very sad girl. Got kwin.*'

She glanced round, wiping at her tears as she did so. It was one of the newcomers, a small, round-faced man with a balding head and sympathetic eyes. She realized with a start that he was speaking English—of a sort. '*Got kwin,*' the man repeated. '*You like kwin?*'

What on earth was he talking about? Was he trying to tell her he was a *quin*—one of five children all born on the same day?

She turned to Jik, but he seemed as puzzled as she was.

The round-faced man grinned broadly. 'Got kwin! Make happy! You wait here!' He disappeared, and returned moments later with a tattered bag.

He delved inside and produced a small piece of paper. He carefully unfolded it and waved it in front of Hanna's face. 'See!' he said triumphantly. 'Kwin! England kwin! Now you happy!'

It was an English five pound note.

It was tattered, faded, as if it had been put through a washing machine, but there was no doubt that it was genuine. There was the queen's head gazing out at her—the *kwin's* head!

Hanna stared at it in amazement. Where on earth could this man have got a five pound note from?

Then a wild thought occurred.

Could it be Dad's?

Dad always carried a five pound note in his pocket—*always*—even here in Borneo. Mum used to tease him about it, but he said it was for emergencies. If you had a fiver in your pocket you could always get yourself out of trouble without having to beg. It dated from his hippy days, when he'd run out of money once in Katmandu.

She took the note from the man's outstretched hand, peered at it closely.

The front looked like any other fiver.

Then she turned it over. Scrawled across the back were two words:

'Nick's Note!'

It was his! She'd recognize Dad's scruffy handwriting anywhere! He must have written his name on it to stop Mum pinching it when she ran short of change.

'Ned!' she screamed. 'Look at this!'

But Ned was already at her shoulder, grabbing for the note, peering at it closely. When he looked up, his eyes were gleaming. He swung towards the little man. 'Where did you get this?' he demanded.

The man took a step backwards, shocked by the unexpected outburst. He glanced helplessly at Jik. The limits of his English had been reached.

'Jik,' Hanna said desperately, 'this is really important! This is our dad's money. We must find out where this man got it!'

At last Jik seemed to understand. He fired a string of rapid questions at the confused little man, scarcely waiting for his mumbled replies. 'This man name is Tamba,' he explained. 'He is my mother sister husband. When polis come to Ular, he take boat and go to hide on Laparan Island. Now he come back to Kaitan to fight war. He visit his *alul* to catch fish. England money come from there.'

'What's an *alul*?' Hanna demanded.

Jik groped for a translation. 'Like boat . . . but not dam boat.'

Hanna and Ned looked at each other in bewilderment. What on earth was *like* a boat but *not* a boat? Sometimes it was like solving a crossword puzzle understanding what Jik was saying.

Ned supplied the answer. 'Do you mean a *raft*, Jik?'

Jik nodded vigorously. 'Raft! *Alul* mean raft! With little house!'

It was a fishing raft. The children had seen them dotted over the distant reefs. They looked like little floating sheds. Fishermen used them to shelter from the hot sun during the day, and to fish from at night. Somehow, Mum and Dad must have escaped from the pirates and reached one of these *aluls* and left the five pound note there! 'Were there any people on your raft? Did you see a man and a woman?' Hanna demanded.

Tamba glanced at her apprehensively, muttered something. Jik translated. 'He say no people there. Only find money in wall of hut.'

'Is he sure?'

'Dead sure!'

Aching with disappointment, Hanna turned away. For one mad, wonderful moment she'd actually begun to believe in miracles . . .

'We'll find them. Don't worry.'

Now it was Ned's turn to comfort her. He took her hand and squeezed it gently. She glanced down at him. He looked disappointed too, but behind his disappointment she could sense a deep and growing joy. 'They're alive, Hanna,' he whispered.

Then more loudly: *'They're alive!'*

25

The Yellow Cloth

If Mum and Dad weren't on the raft, *where in God's name were they?*

Hanna ran swiftly through the possibilities.

One, they could have swum to a nearby island—but a question to Tamba established that his *alul* was moored on a semi-submerged reef way out in the ocean, far too far from any land for that to be a possibility.

Two, they could have been picked up by a passing ship, and were now on their way to Hong Kong or the Philippines or wherever. But when Jik put this theory to the men, who had gathered round to listen to what was going on, they shook their heads. It was a dangerous reef. The only craft likely to go anywhere near it were Bajau fishing boats, and they'd have heard if anybody had been rescued by one of their own people.

That left only a third—unthinkable—alternative: *that the pirates, realizing they'd escaped, had come back and captured them again.*

Hanna's heart sank. In her mind's eye she could

see Dad and Mum frantically pushing the five pound note into the wall of the *alul* as the pirate's *kumpit* curved back towards them. The pirates would have been angry. Very angry . . .

Yet when the pirates had robbed Abasa, there'd been no prisoners on board their boat, and they hadn't seemed to be searching for any. All they were looking for was food and enough fuel to get themselves back to Tawi-Tawi . . .

It was a mystery.

There *had* to be a logical explanation, and there was only one place to start looking for it: on Tamba's *alul*. The five pound note had been a deliberate clue. If Mum and Dad had left that, they could have left other clues too—things that Tamba probably hadn't noticed. A message scratched on a piece of driftwood perhaps . . .

Hanna swung towards Jik, but Ned had got there first. He was asking—no, *demanding*—that he should take them out to the *alul* in his boat.

Jik went to his father and they spoke for a long time. Tamba, who had reclaimed the five pound note and tucked it back into his bag, joined in the discussion. It was highly frustrating not to be able to understand a word of what they were saying. Eventually Jik turned back to the children. There was a smile on his face. 'My father say to me we can go.'

'Brilliant!' exclaimed Ned.

'Now.'

'Now?' Hanna was astonished. It was the middle of the night.

'Now!' Jik emphasized. 'Then, when the sun comes, we are a long way from Kaitan if anybody see us.'

It made sense. Hanna smiled her thanks at Jik's father. Her smile was returned. The children were given a plastic container of water, and a coconut shell containing several scoops of tapioca from the fresh batch bubbling on the fire. The man who'd brought the mangoes selected three particularly ripe ones and handed them to Hanna with a grin.

Jik hoisted the water container onto his head, balancing it there expertly as though it weighed nothing. Ned took the tapioca, Hanna the mangoes. They were about to leave when Jik's father disappeared into the back of the cave and returned with a small cloth bag. He tied it securely to the belt of Jik's shorts, whispered a few words into his son's ear, then stood back. 'My father say good luck,' Jik explained, as he led the children out of the cave. Hanna asked him what was in the bag, but got no reply.

They took a different path down the mountain. It led through dense undergrowth, and was much steeper than the one on which they'd climbed up. The children groped their way blindly downwards in the darkness, worried that they might fall and break an arm or leg. Twice they met groups of Sea Gypsies on their way up, but Jik didn't stop to speak. He was anxious to be well out to sea before dawn broke.

Eventually the path levelled out and the children found themselves on the fringe of a sandy beach. Keeping to the trees so they left no footprints, they skirted a wide bay, at the far end of which was a dense clump of mangroves. Trying to ignore the insects buzzing round their heads, they clambered over the weird, arched roots that stuck out from the trees' trunks like withered legs. Soon they were wading thigh-deep in water. Then, just as Hanna thought they would have to swim, the mangroves stopped. In front of them, just visible in the fading moonlight, was a small inlet, completely encircled by trees.

It was full of boats—jammed tight with them. Most of them were *dapangs*—outriggers like Jik's, but there were many others, some smaller, some larger. It was like a secret marina, totally invisible from the sea—and probably from the air too.

Jik didn't stop. Still balancing the water container on his head, he began to leap from boat to boat until he reached the far shore. There, stranded on a strip of evil-smelling mud was the familiar water-beetle shape of his own little outrigger.

They swiftly loaded their supplies, and slid it down to the water. It was difficult finding a way out to the open sea with so many boats moored so closely together, but eventually they managed it. Taking a paddle, Jik propelled them rapidly away from the shore, then expertly hoisted the sail. The triangle of striped cloth flapped twice and filled. There was a soft, warm breeze—just enough to send them skimming across the surface of the calm sea.

With alarming suddenness, the moon slipped below the horizon and a deep tropical darkness fell. From her seat near the mast, Hanna could just make out Jik. He was pressed against the steering paddle, occasionally glancing up at the star-speckled sky to check their course.

Ned, who was well on the way to being his old self again, tried to talk to him, asking him questions about the stars and the constellations, but was quickly hushed into silence. On a calm night like this, Jik told him, the sound of voices could carry for miles across the surface of the water. Somebody might easily be listening.

As if to confirm this, the children saw a point of light flare, then fade, from the direction of Ular. Somebody had obviously been left behind to guard the smoking ruins of the village and had just lit a cigarette.

It was a strange feeling sailing in an invisible boat over an invisible sea—dreamlike, halfway between sleeping and waking. Slowly Hanna's eyes began to close . . .

She awoke in the grey light of dawn. Ned was sprawled in the bottom of the boat, mouth open, sound asleep. Jik, who had apparently not moved all night, was still pressed against the steering paddle.

He caught her eye and smiled. 'Good sleep?' It was obviously OK to talk now.

Hanna nodded. 'Where are we?'

The boy pointed behind him. There, faint in the early-morning haze, was the distant outline of Ular. They had come a long way in the night, further than she could have believed possible. 'Salim bring good *habagat*,' Jik explained cheerfully.

'Who's Salim?' Hanna asked, puzzled.

'Salim is *saitan* of sea. Very big dam spirit . . . '

There was a sudden scraping noise and the boat jerked to a halt. Ned sat up, rubbing his eyes. 'What's going on?' he demanded.

'No dam problem!' Jik exclaimed, and promptly jumped overboard.

Hanna stared at him, amazed. They were in the middle of the ocean, and yet the water was only knee-deep! Jik gave the boat a sharp shove and it slid free from whatever had been gripping it. Then he flung himself back on board, re-set the sail, and they were once more on their way.

Hanna peered over the side, and suddenly everything became clear: they were sailing on top of the largest reef she'd ever seen!

It stretched for miles in every direction—in some places just below the surface, in others plunging down into deep crevasses.

As the sun rose, the whole reef came to life. It was like a vast underwater garden. Shoals of brilliant blue and yellow fish twisted and swirled between the outstretched coral branches. Striped clown fish patrolled fields of waving sea-anemones, challenging any creature brave enough to venture close. Giant purple-lipped clams lay gaping in the shallows, siphoning plankton from the rich, warm water. The reef at Kaitan had been wonderful—but this was in a different league. Hanna found herself wishing she had her snorkel and mask—or that Jik's boat had a glass bottom!

'Look!' Ned's sudden exclamation made her glance up. On the horizon was what looked like a small, thatched garden shed sticking up out of the water.

It was an *alul*!

'Is that one Tamba's?' Ned asked, his eyes flashing with excitement.

Jik shook his head. 'That one is my uncle.'

'*My uncle's*,' Hanna corrected, trying to hide her disappointment.

Jik rolled his eyes and made no reply.

The *alul* was the first of a dozen fishing rafts they passed in the next couple of hours. Some of them were neatly maintained, others little more than semi-submerged heaps of driftwood. None of them was Tamba's. The rafts had obviously been positioned with care, because large shoals of fish were invariably gathered beneath them, rootling in the soft white sand of the reef bed.

They'd just passed the final one when Jik suddenly stopped steering and hauled down the sail. 'What are you doing?' Hanna asked crossly, not wanting any delay.

He grinned. 'Wait, see!'

He reached down inside the boat and slid out a slender bamboo pole. It had a viciously-barbed metal tip. He went to the bows and stood motionless, staring intently into the water.

For long minutes the boat drifted gently across the surface of the reef. Then, with a sudden explosive movement, he hurled the spear downwards.

He hauled it up with a whoop of glee. Writhing

on the end of it was a large scarlet fish speckled with vivid splashes of electric blue. *'Ista pula!'* Jik said triumphantly. 'Red fish!' It was the most beautiful fish Hanna had ever seen.

He fetched a heavy piece of wood and put the creature out of its agony with a swift blow to its head. Then he took a sharp knife and expertly filleted it into thin, almost transparent strips. 'Good,' he said, smacking his lips. 'Eat!'

'But it's not cooked!' Ned exclaimed, examining the slice he'd been handed with distaste.

'It's like sushi,' Hanna told him. 'Japanese people eat it all the time.' They'd had sushi once when they'd been on a trip to London, and she remembered Ned complaining about the fish being raw even then.

Reluctantly he put the slice into his mouth and chewed. Hanna followed suit. The fish was tough, salty, but fresh tasting. It was a funny feeling knowing the mouthful she was swallowing had been swimming about under the boat only moments before.

In the end even Ned ate quite a lot of the fish, and they followed it up with some tapioca and a mango each. The mangoes were delicious—juicy and perfectly ripe. All things considered, it was not a bad breakfast.

Still licking the mango juice from his lips, Jik

cleaned his spear and replaced it in the boat. Then he hoisted the sail and they were off again. Knowing it would soon start to smell in the heat, Hanna dropped the remains of the fish overboard. There was a sudden violent splash as some unseen creature rose from the depths and swallowed it in a single gulp.

A short while later, Jik took his hand from the steering paddle and pointed away to the right. '*Tamba alul*,' he announced.

The children peered intently in the direction he had indicated. For a moment or two they could see nothing; but then, slowly emerging from a thickening haze that obscured the line between sea and sky, they spotted the outline of a raft.

It was one of the scruffiest *aluls* they'd seen. Part of its roof was missing, and it seemed to be floating very low in the water. It looked as if it could sink at any minute.

But that didn't matter. It had saved Mum and Dad, and that made it the most beautiful raft in the world!

The wind, which had been fading for a while, dropped even further. 'Can't you make this thing go any faster?' Ned urged, jerking frustratedly at the sides of the boat.

Jik tightened the sail, but the outrigger still crept with agonizing slowness across the glassy surface of the sea. Eventually the boys abandoned wind-power altogether and grabbed the paddles, pounding at the water while Hanna attempted to steer.

It seemed to take for ever, but eventually they drew close to the sagging platform. Ned was the first on board, abandoning his paddle and diving overboard to swim the final few metres. Jik threw him the mooring line which he tied to a post. Then Hanna and Jik scrambled across to join him.

Hanna stared round her in excitement.

And her excitement died.

The *alul* was completely empty.

It was just a creaking, swaying bamboo platform, black with age and rot, with the tattered remains of a hut perched on top.

She and Ned began a frantic search, concentrating on the walls of the hut. Any clue—any *message*—that Mum and Dad might have left would surely have been placed up here amongst the crudely woven palm fronds, out of reach of the waves. This was where Tamba had said he'd found the five pound note . . .

But apart from a rusting fish hook with a section of frayed line attached, they found nothing.

They were turning away in despair, when Jik, who'd been making his own search of the fishing platform outside, suddenly announced that he'd found something.

The raft tilted alarmingly as the children scrambled across to him. 'What is it?' Ned demanded.

Jik held up what appeared to be a dead, crumpled leaf. He knelt and dunked it in the sea. What looked like brown paint flowed off it. 'Blood,' he said decisively. 'That goddam blood!'

Dad's blood—it had to be! Or maybe Mum's . . .

It was a small section of coarsely woven cotton cloth. As Jik rubbed at it, its true colour began to show through.

It was a dull yellow.

He lifted the cloth out, spread it carefully on the bamboo floor. Then he looked up at the children. There was wonder in his eyes. '*Manai Liha come here*,' he said softly.

26
Salim Bring

'But I thought you said Manai Liha was dead?' Hanna exclaimed.

'I think so too,' replied Jik in an awed voice. 'But she is live! This Manai Liha cloth. Only dam big *umboh* like Manai Liha wear special yellow cloth.'

'You're certain it's hers?'

'Dead dam certain! She come here.'

'That's crazy!' Ned put in. 'Her boat was sinking. I saw it. It was falling to pieces! It didn't even have a sail or engine. How on earth could she have come all this way?'

Jik stared reverently at the piece of cloth. '*Salim bring*,' he said simply.

Salim! Hanna's head was reeling. Was Jik really saying that Manai Liha had been brought all this way by a *sea spirit*? It was ridiculous—preposterous! Yet how else could she have got here? What kind of ocean current would carry her all the way from her rickety mooring to this distant reef?

It defied logic—but then, out here on this strange

sea, with this strange boy, nothing seemed totally logical any more.

She thought back to that unforgettable night in the old woman's evil-smelling boat: the chanting and jostling; the two wooden figures with their strange staring eyes. And those voices, those amazing, scary, familiar voices . . .

Jik had promised that Manai Liha would find Mum and Dad.

Now it looked as if she had!

Hanna imagined their astonishment as the ancient craft bumped alongside the *alul*; imagined them gratefully accepting Manai Liha's offer of a piece of her precious yellow cloth to soak up the blood from their wounds; imagined them tucking Dad's five pound note into the wall of the hut at the very last minute before climbing into the old woman's battered, leaking boat . . .

Then what?

Presumably the same current that had brought Manai Liha to them had carried them away.

But where to?

She desperately tried to visualize Dad's tattered map of the Sulu Sea. As far as she could remember there were no more islands for hundreds of miles. Had Mum and Dad managed to escape the pirates, only to drift out into the deep ocean and drown as the floundering boat slowly sank beneath them?

No! That was not possible! She would not *allow* it to be possible! Not after all this time. Not after everything they'd been through . . .

Then Jik did something very strange. He dropped to his knees and pressed his forehead against the blackened floor of the raft, muttering something rapidly beneath his breath. After a short while he straightened up, reached for his belt and untied the bag his father had given him. Inside it were three small rice cakes, a tiny jade carving of a fish, and five old Chinese coins with holes in the middle—like the ones Mum kept in the little box on her dressing table back home.

He carefully arranged the objects on Manai Liha's yellow cloth. Then, after muttering another prayer, he scooped up everything, and with a quick movement, threw it into the sea.

The fish and coins sank instantly, curving down to the sea bed below; but the rice cakes and the cloth floated, dancing slowly away from the *alul* as the wavelets caught them.

He turned to the children. 'Now we go,' he announced.

'Go where?' Ned asked, mystified.

'Find your mum and dad! Find Manai Liha!' Jik was already unhitching the mooring line of his boat, gesturing for them to climb on board.

When they'd done so, he leapt in beside them, and sat down. *'Brilliant!'* he exclaimed. *'Goddam brilliant!'*

Except it wasn't.

Absolutely nothing happened.

The boat bobbed up and down next to the *alul*, occasionally bumping against it; going nowhere. The sun beat down on their heads, making Hanna long for her battered old straw hat which had disappeared somewhere during her travels. After a short while Ned became impatient. 'Jik, hoist the sail for God's sake!'

Jik stared at him as if he was mad. 'For what?'

'So we can go and find Mum and Dad like you said.'

'Not need dam sail! Salim bring!'

Hanna and Ned peered at him in disbelief. Was he *seriously* proposing that they should just drift about over the surface of the ocean until they *happened* to end up wherever Dad and Mum might be? Did he have *that* much faith in this sea spirit of his?

Apparently he did. He reached down inside the boat and took out a rolled-up grass mat. Using a couple of paddles as support, he quickly rigged up a crude awning. Then he dived underneath it, lay down on his back and closed his eyes. A few seconds later he was fast asleep, snoring loudly.

Hanna and Ned stared at one another helplessly. There was no point in waking him, they realized. Even if they forced him to hoist the sail, where would they sail to? There were three hundred and sixty degrees worth of direction to choose from and not a single clue to guide them. Prayers or no prayers, Jik was right to let them drift, because that was all Manai Liha's crippled boat would have been able to do. Only by abandoning themselves totally to the sea, would they have any chance of finding out where Mum and Dad had gone.

But would Jik's plan succeed? For them to follow exactly the same path over the open ocean, wind and tide would have to be exactly identical. Was that even remotely likely after so many days?

It wasn't. But what other alternative did they have? Not being able to do *anything* was the worst feeling in the world!

It was too hot to stay where they were, so they joined Jik underneath the awning and lay down. Maybe a little shut-eye *was* the answer . . .

Hanna's eyes flicked open in alarm. A loud rumbling noise had woken her. Was it thunder? Dreading a storm like the one that had smashed into the ridge above the Istana, she lifted a corner of the awning and stuck out her head. While they'd slept, they'd drifted a long way from Tamba's *alul* she saw. There was no way they'd be able to reach shelter if a major gale struck.

Then, sickeningly, she realized where the noise was coming from.

Flying fast and low towards them, its sinister black shadow expanding and contracting as it slid over the wave-tops, was the helicopter!

She ducked swiftly back inside and nudged the boys awake. Jik let out a curse and pulled away the paddles that were supporting the mat. It collapsed suffocatingly on top of them. 'Stay still!' he hissed. 'Maybe they think boat is empty!'

He was right, Hanna realized, pressing herself as flat as she could. With no sail up, and with nobody apparently on board, they might easily be mistaken for a boat that had drifted away from its mooring somewhere.

But as the huge machine reached them, the mat began to leap and flap. '*Grab it!*' Jik yelled above the roar of the engines.

The children tried to do what he asked, but it was hopeless. The wind from the machine's rotors whipped the awning from their hands and sent it spiralling away into the sea. Peering upwards, Hanna could see the pilot and co-pilot clearly.

The co-pilot made a sharp gesture with his right hand, and as he did so, her blood ran cold. Despite the helmet and intercom concealing most of his face, his hard, reptilian gaze was unmistakable.

It was the Datuk!

The rear door of the machine slid open and a winchman—the same blank-faced man who had snatched them from the collapsing walkway that desperate night on Ular—twisted down towards them.

Hanna grabbed a paddle and thrust it into the water. The little outrigger picked up speed, but the helicoper turned with them, dropping ever lower, its black belly only inches from their mast-tip.

Escape was impossible.

The winchman swung in low and fast towards them. It was Hanna he was aiming for, and he caught her squarely, sending her paddle flying, wrapping a sinewy arm round her waist. This time there was going to be no harness, she realized. He was going to rely on brute strength to hold her as she was hoisted upwards into the machine.

She fought with him, but it was hopeless. His flat brown face, inches from hers, was hard, mask-like. His breath smelt sour, like an animal's.

Then, without warning, his expression suddenly changed. His eyes widened, and he let out a harsh scream.

He released his grip on her, and she fell heavily back into the boat. Glancing round, she saw the reason for his cries of pain. Ned, his eyes blazing, had grabbed Jik's fishing spear and was thrusting up at him with all his strength.

Again and again he jabbed.

Again and again the winchman screamed, as the needle-sharp point ripped through the thin material of his uniform.

He signalled frantically to the helicopter, and was whisked away out of range—but not before Ned had managed a couple of final hard thrusts into his bloodstained backside.

'Got him!' Jik yelled triumphantly. 'Got him where it goddam hurt him most!'

Bleeding heavily, the winchman was pulled inside the cabin, and the door slammed shut. The helicopter hovered for a few seconds more, then tipped and headed rapidly back towards the mainland. Looking upwards in those last moments, the children had seen the cold fury in the Datuk's eyes. He'd be back, they knew; and next time he wouldn't be so easily defeated.

Ned was celebrating now, leaping up and down, giving Jik high fives, making the little boat rock wildly.

For a mad moment Hanna joined in, but then she pulled away. 'We've got to get going!' she said urgently. Out on the open ocean they were sitting ducks.

But Jik continued to leap and dance. 'Salim bring!' he shouted cheerfully. 'No dam problem!'

She glanced at Ned. He'd stopped dancing and looked as astonished as she was. Despite everything that had happened, despite the danger they were in, Jik was still proposing to let them drift!

'Jik, please . . . ' she began.

Then stopped. She was staring in disbelief at the sea.

Something very strange was happening . . .

27

Gripped

It was as if the boat had been gripped by an unseen hand. It was whirled around once—twice—then dragged swiftly away to the north. The water was seething and boiling all around them, forming strange humps and vortexes. As Hanna watched, a floating palm frond was up-ended and sucked instantly from sight.

They were in some kind of violent tidal race. If anything happened now—if they hit a submerged rock or a reef, and capsized—they would be instantly dragged down to their deaths. There was no way even the strongest swimmer could survive in a sea like this.

Hanging on for dear life as the boat bucked and pitched beneath her, she glanced back at Jik. Had he known this was going to happen? Had he been expecting it? Was this what he'd been *praying* for?

His expression told her it was. He'd grabbed the steering paddle to keep them straight and was staring ahead expectantly. There was a look almost of awe on his face. Ned seemed to have caught the mood too. *'Wicked!'* he was repeating quietly to himself over and over again. *'This is wicked!'*

Hanna, too, stared up ahead, but she could see nothing. The haze, which had been closing in all afternoon, had now turned into a fog, thickening by the minute, blotting out the sun. At least the helicopter would be unlikely to return in conditions like this, she thought.

She shivered. A cool breeze had sprung up from somewhere, churning the fog into wave-like billows that exactly matched the movement of the sea. Mum and Dad must have been swept away by this same violent current too, she realized, but how could they have possibly survived it in Manai Liha's rickety old boat? There were large pieces of driftwood in the water now, leaping and twirling in a mad circular dance. Would the next thing thrown to the surface be a dead body?

Terrified by the thought, she turned away. She was helpless. There was nothing more that she—or any of them—could do.

How long they were whirled along through the fog she had no means of knowing. It was as if time itself stood still. Occasionally she heard Jik muttering—praying she supposed—above the noise of the waves. And once she felt a heavy thump as something large and hard collided with the underside of the boat.

Then, as suddenly as it had seized them, the current let them go. The fog was as dense as ever, but the sea had become flat, motionless. Hanna had the unsettling feeling that they had somehow become separated from the rest of the world—that they were *inside* something. Her anxious eyes sought Ned's, but she could read nothing from his expression.

That was when they heard the clapping.

The sound was soft at first—indistinct—like somebody applauding in a distant room. But then it swelled rapidly, and seemed to circle them, before dying away to a gentle murmur.

Again the clapping came. And again.

Hanna was conscious of her heart beating painfully. Was she going crazy? Had they some-how—magically—been transported into the middle of a large football match?

Of course not! The thought was too stupid to even contemplate. But if not, what? Who were all these clapping people? What were they applauding? And where were they?

A glance at Jik told her that he knew the answer. '*Lotau*,' he said in a scared voice. 'This *Lotau*.'

'What's *Lotau*?' Ned sounded as frightened as Jik.

The boy looked profoundly uncomfortable. His face was beaded with moisture. '*Lotau* mean . . . '

he groped for the right word. '*Lotau* mean . . . ghost. We come to *Ghost Island*.'

Ned gulped, squinted into the mist. 'There's no such thing as ghosts,' he said uncertainly. 'They're just make-believe.'

Jik shook his head wildly. 'No! No! They are real dam thing! Many ghost in this place. Many *saitan*! Now we go!' He sprang forward and began to unfurl the sail.

'But we've only just got here!' Hanna said frantically. 'Surely we should check out—'

'We go!'

The breeze, which had died away to nothing, suddenly picked up, making the sail flap and crack. Instantly the applause began again—building to a thunderous crescendo.

Could those *really* be ghosts that were clapping?

Like Ned, Hanna didn't believe in the supernatural. But what other explanation could there be for the noise? If ghosts could groan and rattle chains, they could no doubt clap as well.

She shivered. Maybe Jik was right. Maybe they should get out of this weird place!

Jik was wrestling with the sail, trying to make it fill properly. 'Which way are we heading?' Ned shouted above the roar of the applause.

Jik looked confused, scared. 'I don't know which dam way! Too many ghost! Too many *saitan*!'

261

At that moment, buffeted by the rising wind, the fog began to lift.

The children stared around them wide-eyed. Emerging slowly from the gloom was one of the strangest islands they'd ever seen. It consisted of a circular ridge of jagged black rock surrounding a small lagoon, in the middle of which their boat was floating. On the far side of the lagoon was a narrow gap leading to the open sea. They were inside the crater of an extinct volcano, one that had long ago been flooded by the waves.

But it wasn't its shape that made the island so strange. Attached to the scrubby trees that clung to its flanks were hundreds—no, *thousands*—of small green and white flags. Some were tattered and faded, as though they had been there for a long time. Others looked fresh and new.

As the wind blew, they fluttered and flapped, making a noise exactly like people clapping.

'What are they?' Ned asked in an awed whisper.

Jik's reply was almost inaudible. '*Pangi*. They are call *pangi*. Make ghost happy.'

Hanna tried to visualize what happy ghosts would look like, but failed. 'Who puts them there?'

'People.'

'What people?'

'People who get sick. People who go to die. Now we go. Big dam danger!' He swung the boat round, aiming its bow towards the gap that led to the open sea.

'Look!'

Ned had spotted something on the shore. It was high up on a strip of black sand close to the tree-line. At first sight it seemed to be just a heap of driftwood, a jumble of old planks and branches. But then Hanna made out the curve of a boat's hull. There was something familiar about its shape.

Her excited eyes met Ned's. Could it be . . . ?

He was in no doubt. 'That's Manai Liha's boat,' he yelled. 'I know it is!'

Hanna felt a tightness in her chest. It was suddenly difficult to breathe. If this really *was* the old woman's boat . . .

She turned to Jik but he refused to meet her eyes. He was gripping the steering paddle, urging his little boat onwards. 'Too big danger,' he hissed. 'We go!'

Hanna and Ned couldn't believe what they were hearing. They'd come so far, been through so much, and now he was proposing to just sail away! 'Mum and Dad are on this island, I know they are!' Hanna exploded. 'Steer towards that boat!'

'Too many ghost!'

'I said steer towards it! Now!'

He ignored her. He tugged at the sail, trying to

get more speed as they skimmed towards the open sea.

That was when Ned hit him.

He launched himself across Hanna's out-stretched legs and crashed into Jik's chest. The two boys collapsed into a struggling, yelling heap in the bottom of the boat.

Swiftly Hanna grabbed the steering paddle and swung the boat round. It tipped violently, then righted itself. The sail jerked across, filled, and within seconds they were racing towards Manai Liha's boat.

The struggle was over almost as soon as it had begun. Suddenly all the fight seemed to go out of the Sea Gypsy boy. His eyes were wet with tears. He was truly terrified, Hanna realized, and not just for himself. For all of them.

'Let him go,' she said to Ned, who had him pinned against the mast.

He obeyed reluctantly.

She told Ned to steer, and clambered across to Jik. She put an arm round him and pulled him close, conscious that he needed her strength, her certainty, every bit as much as Ned did. She spoke softly to him: 'Those people you were telling me about, the ones who put all those flags up, how come *they* aren't scared to come to this island?'

Jik sniffed. 'Always they come with *umboh,*

come with Manai Liha, never come alone. She talk to ghost, talk to saitan, tell them they must not harm these people. Tell them they must depart from the bodies of the sick people so they can get well again.'

'And they listen to her?'

'Always they listen to her. Manai Liha is very big dam *umboh.*'

An inspired thought suddenly occurred to Hanna. 'If that's the case, don't you think Manai Liha will have already *told* the *saitan* about us? If that's her boat, if she came here with Mum and Dad, she's bound to have explained everything. They're probably *expecting* us. After all, Salim brought us here, and he's a *saitan*. He knew *exactly* where to bring us. I bet Manai Liha arranged everything with him too.'

Jik looked up into her eyes. 'You really think that?'

'I do.'

She felt him relax a little. He risked a glance at the approaching beach, at the wrecked, stranded boat. 'Salim bring,' he said, with growing confidence. 'Salim bring!'

28
Ghosts

It *was* Manai Liha's boat. Any doubts there might have been disappeared the moment their little outrigger crunched onto the coarse black sand next to where it was beached. Hanna and Ned were out in an instant, sprinting towards it. Maybe Mum and Dad were still on board. Maybe they were using it for a shelter or something . . .

They weren't.

The boat was completely empty. But worse than that, *it had no bottom.*

All that remained were a few jagged planks resting on the bare sand. A large land crab, which had made its home inside the rotting hulk, eyed them evilly before scuttling away.

Hanna and Ned began to panic. It had been dangerous enough getting here in Jik's sturdy little boat. God only knows what it must have been like in this sagging wreck. They could imagine its floor opening up suddenly, like a trapdoor, shooting Mum and Dad and the old woman down into the swirling depths. They could imagine . . .

'*Find foot!*'

Jik's voice. Hanna glanced wildly at Ned.

He'd found a foot? *Just a foot?*

Dreading what they might be about to see, the two children scrambled out to join him.

Jik was pointing downwards at the sand.

It wasn't a foot he'd found, but a footprint!

A large, adult footprint.

Casting round excitedly, they found others— quite a lot of them. They were blurred, indistinct, obviously made some time ago. Could the larger prints be Dad's? And the smaller ones Mum's?

Ned had no doubt whose they were. He peered through the fog at the fluttering, flapping hillside, inflated his chest and let out a massive shout. '*Mum!*' he roared, his face purple with the effort. '*Dad! It's ussss . . .* '

His shout ended in a strangled gasp as Jik clapped a hand over his mouth. 'No dam noise! *Saitan* get angry!'

Ned wrenched himself free, furious. 'I don't care about your stupid *saitans*! They're just make-believe! I'm going to make as much noise as I like because I want my mum and dad back, and shouting's the only way they'll ever know we're here. *Mum! Da—*'

It was Hanna's hand now, across his mouth. 'Ned, please, do what Jik says. It's important. We can't take chances, not now we're so close.'

'You believe in those stupid ghosts too, do you?'

'It doesn't matter what I believe.' She glanced around desperately, trying to find something—anything—to stop this pointless argument. There was a gap in the undergrowth beyond the wrecked boat. Could it be the start of a path? The footprints seemed to be heading in that direction. She ran towards it.

It *was* a path, narrow and ill-defined, zigzagging upwards from the beach. And at its entrance was the distinct outline of a human foot. 'Over here!' she said excitedly. 'They went this way, I'm sure of it!'

Ned raced to join her, glanced quickly at the footprint, then thrust past, determined to be first up the hillside.

'Come on, Jik!' Hanna called, anxious to follow.

He didn't move. He was still fearful, despite their conversation in the boat. She hurried back to him; smiled reassuringly. 'It'll be safe, Jik. I know it will!'

He resisted for a moment longer. Then reluctantly, slowly, he allowed himself to be led to the path.

It was a steep climb, and got steeper by the minute. The mist had swirled in again, threading itself between the dripping branches, blotting out what little sunlight had managed to break through earlier. Hanna shivered; gripped Jik's hand more tightly. It was easy to believe this place really was haunted.

A sudden gasp of fright from Ned. Hanna and Jik scrambled up to join him. He was staring at the gnarled trunk of an ancient tree. Attached to its base—seemingly growing out of it—were two carved wooden figures. They had staring, cowrie-shell eyes. Tufts of black hair stuck out of the tops of their heads.

They were exactly like the two figures Manai Liha had produced on that terrifying night on her boat—the ones she said had turned into Mum and Dad.

Except these were bigger. Much bigger.

'*Ta'au-ta'au*,' Jik said in a scared whisper. 'Very dam powerful *saitan*.'

Hanna wanted to run, to get as far away from these evil-looking things as quickly as possible, but it was as if all the strength had been sucked from her body. Ned obviously felt the same.

'Must make respect!' Jik dropped to his knees, pressed his forehead to the ground. He began to mutter loud prayers.

Not knowing what to do, Ned and Hanna followed suit. '*Our Father*,' Hanna heard herself saying, '*which art in Heaven* . . . '

She didn't get the chance to finish. Jik was on his

269

feet again, backing slowly away from the statues, never once taking his eyes off them. Then he turned and ran. Hanna and Ned scrambled after him.

The path continued to twist upwards, the fog thickening all the time. There were more *ta'au-ta'au* carvings, some standing alone, others ranged in groups around the trunks of trees. Each time, the children paused to pay respect, before hurrying onwards. Though Hanna knew they were only made from seashells, their eyes seemed to move, to follow them as they went. She half expected their wooden mouths to jerk open and mad, evil laughter to ring out.

Could Mum and Dad *really* have climbed this horrible path? Surely it would have been much easier for them to stay down at the beach, near the boat. And what about Manai Liha? She was old. She wouldn't have had the strength to make it this far . . .

She was about to call out to the boys, to suggest they turn back, when she saw the ghost.

The fog suddenly parted and it was there, standing on the path maybe fifty metres ahead. It looked nothing like the black, menacing *ta'au-ta'aus*. It was slender, human-shaped, a delicate silvery-white. It seemed to be made from the mist, and to float upon it. In the instant before the fog closed in again, Hanna caught a powerful feeling of sadness flowing from it; a bleak, desperate sadness that brought tears to her eyes.

'*Lotau!*' Jik whispered, terrified, beside her. '*Ghost!* We go!'

'No, wait!' There'd been something familiar about the apparition's shape, Hanna realized. Something about the way it held its head, the way it moved . . .

She turned to Ned. 'Do you think . . . ' she began.

But he wasn't listening to her. He was staring fixedly into the fog. 'I'm going to take a closer look,' he announced.

'No, you mustn't.' She grabbed at his arm in alarm. 'It might be . . . *anything.*'

'I don't care. I'm going to find out.'

He wrenched himself free, and thrust past her. '*Ned, for God's sake!*'

But he was gone, swallowed up by the fog.

'Stupid dam boy,' Jik muttered unhappily.

'He can look after himself,' Hanna replied, with a confidence she didn't feel.

Had what they'd seen been an optical illusion? A trick of the light? If so, Ned might spend hours stumbling around the mist-shrouded hillside, getting more and more lost. He could end up pitching over a ravine . . .

Then she heard his voice.

It was faint, fearful, almost drowned out by the flapping of the prayer-flags. It was impossible to make out what he was saying. Urging Jik ahead of her, she scrambled up towards him.

He was standing on the path, staring into a deep, rock-strewn gully that fell away to one side. He looked profoundly distressed. 'She went down there,' he said unsteadily.

'*She?*'

'Mum.'

Hanna's heart lurched. She felt suddenly sick. The creature in the mist had certainly *looked* like Mum—only now did she dare admit it to herself. 'Are you sure it was her?'

'Dead sure. She's dressed in a weird sheet thing. I spoke to her, but she didn't say anything. She just hurried off down there.'

Hanna shivered. For so long she'd dreamed of finding Mum. She'd imagined her running towards them along a wide, flat beach, her arms outstretched, her eyes sparkling with happiness.

But not this. She'd never dreamed of anything like this. Ned must have got it wrong. He *must* have! 'Did you see her clearly?' she demanded.

Ned nodded numbly. 'She looked so weird, Hanna. So pale and sad. What if she's dead? What if she really *is* a ghost? What if this is all that's left of her?'

Hanna fought back her alarm. 'Don't be stupid! You don't *believe* in ghosts! You're always telling me that.'

'But you didn't see her close up. Not like I did.' All his bravery was gone. Tears streaked his cheeks. 'Why didn't she speak to me, Hanna? Mum's not shy. She'll speak to anybody.'

'There must be a good reason. A really good reason.'

'But what? What sort of reason could she have?'

Hanna had no answer. She peered desperately into the gully. It was impossible to see where it led to. To go down into it would be like stepping off the edge of the world. But Mum was down there— somewhere. And she was no ghost. She took a deep breath: 'I think we should go and find out, don't you?'

Followed by the two boys, she began to pick her way gingerly downwards. There was no path, just loose, slippery pebbles that shifted constantly underfoot. Here and there strange outcrops of black volcanic rock loomed out of the fog, looking like twisted, agonized faces. Large green lizards sat on fallen logs, eyeing them evilly as they passed.

After a while the ground levelled out and the loose rocks disappeared. The going became easier, the surface smooth and hard, as though many feet had passed that way. Suddenly Jik, who had been

273

walking increasingly slowly, stopped dead. *'Nunuk,'* he whispered to Hanna. 'Big dam danger.'

'What's a *nunuk*?'

'Ghost tree.'

'A *ghost tree*? You mean it's not real?'

'Real dam tree. But many ghost. Many many *saitan!*'

'I don't want to be here,' Ned announced unhappily.

'Nor me! We go!'

Jik twisted, preparing to run. This time Hanna didn't try to stop him. 'OK, you go!' she hissed. 'But I'm staying here, ghosts or no ghosts!'

The boys hesitated, not knowing whether to go or stay.

There was a strange, sweet smell, like an old woman's perfume. The feeling of loss and desolation had returned. Hanna edged forward a few more metres and the fog thinned . . .

It was a tree—but nothing like any tree she'd ever seen. Its massive trunk had been split in two by a lightning strike sometime in the distant past. Every branch—every *twig*, it seemed—was hung with dangling aerial roots that cascaded down to bury themselves in the soil at its base. It looked like a huge evil spider, crouching ready to pounce. Its lower limbs were festooned with fluttering green and white flags, and stacked amongst its knotted roots were hundreds of *ta'au-ta'au* statues, many of them life-sized, as gnarled and ancient as the tree itself.

Jik began to mutter prayers, backing away as he did so. Hanna ignored him. She was staring hard at the tree. Was it an illusion? Had there been a flash of white as something—*someone*—had moved, deep inside its dense curtain of hanging roots?

'Did you see what I saw?' she whispered to Ned, who was standing beside her, rigid as one of the statues.

He nodded numbly. 'It's hiding in there.'

'It?'

'The ghost. Whatever it is.'

An unexpected fury gripped her. *'It's not a ghost! It's not! It's Mum! You know it is!'*

No longer caring what kind of danger she might be in, she raced towards the tree, dodging the *ta'au-ta'au* statues, ignoring the yelps of terror from Jik. She heaved frantically at the knotted roots. It was like trying to wrench her way through a tangled fishing net. Eventually—suddenly—they parted, and she stumbled forwards into a dimly-lit open space, strewn with twigs and dead leaves.

Mum was there.

She was standing close to the twisted trunk of the tree, her face half-hidden in the gloom.

'Hanna?' she said hesitantly, in a strange, cracked voice. 'Is that really you, Hanna?'

'Of course it's me, Mum! Who did you think it was?'

'I thought you were dead . . . I thought you were dead, Hanna.'

She was going to say more, but she had no chance. Hanna was screaming, yelling, hurling herself into her arms. 'Ned!' she was screaming. 'It's Mum! She's here! She's real! We've found her! We've finally found her!'

29

Survivors

Ned exploded through the curtain of roots like a small rocket. He was whooping with delight. His impetus, as he flung himself at Mum, sent all three of them staggering back against the tree. They would never let her go again, Hanna told herself, as they clung together, their faces shiny with tears. Never, ever . . .

But where was Dad?

As Hanna put the question, the joy in Mum's eyes died. 'He's . . . not well,' she said hesitantly. 'He was hurt when the pirates attacked. Quite badly.'

'We know that. There was blood.'

'They slashed him with a *parang*. His arm . . . ' She broke off.

'Mum where *is* he?' Hanna beseeched.

She drew a deep breath. She looked so thin, so old, draped in the stained white sheet she must have found from somewhere. 'You'd better come,' she said quietly.

She led them behind the tree to a shallow cave.

Dad was lying on a crude bed made from ferns and leaves. The upper part of his left arm was wrapped in a bloodstained bandage, obviously torn from the same dirty white material that Mum was wearing. His eyes were closed, and he was breathing heavily. The strange, sweet, old lady smell the children had noticed earlier was stronger now. It was the smell of decay, Hanna realized. Decay and death.

She shivered violently. Ned, she saw, was biting his lip, not knowing whether to go any closer or not.

Mum dropped to her knees near the bed. 'Nick!' she whispered urgently into his ear. 'Nick! It's the children. They're here! Can you hear me, Nick? *It's the children!*'

Dad's eyes slowly opened. 'Don't be stupid,' he said in a slurred voice. He sounded drunk even though he wasn't.

'I'm not being stupid, Nick. I'm not! They're alive. They've found us. Somehow they've found us. See? They're here!'

Dad shifted his body, groaning as he did so. His eyes, usually so bright and sparkling, were dull with pain. 'I'm dreaming this,' he said. 'Tell me I'm dreaming this.'

'You're not, Dad,' Hanna told him, her voice tight with anxiety. 'This isn't a dream. We're really here. And now we're going to rescue you.'

Not daring to hug him, she leaned forward and kissed his cheek. His skin was burning hot. She loved him so much it was like a physical pain. 'We'll get you to hospital,' she whispered. 'We'll get you better!'

'Sounds like a good plan to me.' For an instant— a magical instant—a smile flickered at the corners of his mouth, lighting up his whole face. Then his eyes closed, and the harsh breathing began again.

'I stitched up his wound, but it got infected,' Mum said helplessly. 'He needs treatment— antibiotics—otherwise . . . ' She stopped, unable to continue.

Hanna reached out to her, trying to bring her comfort. 'We'll save him! Somehow we'll do it!'

'We've got a boat, Mum!' Ned told her, his words tumbling out in his anxiety. 'It's got a blue and white sail. It goes really fast. We can take him to hospital in that! Jik's a brilliant sailor. We'll get him there in no time!'

'Jik?'

'He's our friend. He's a Sea Gypsy. Remember that boy in the boat we gave a Liquorice Allsort to? It's him. He brought us here. He's amazing. He's brilliant. He can do anything! I'll go and fetch him, he's just outside!' Ned charged out through the curtain of roots and disappeared.

Mum stepped back to get a better look at

Hanna's face. Her eyes were misted with love and tears. 'I still can't believe you're alive! We thought you were dead. The old woman told us . . . '

'Old woman?'

'Manai Liha. She rescued us. She said you'd been in her boat, but there was a big storm and you went up into the sky. We thought she was telling us you'd died and gone to heaven.'

Hanna laughed. 'We did go up into the sky, but we weren't dead! It was a helicopter! It captured us. It took us back to Tamu, but we managed to escape. Is that why you didn't speak to Ned when you saw him out there in the fog? Did you think he was a ghost?'

Mum nodded. 'I thought I was going crazy.'

'*He* thought *you* were a ghost too! How weird is that?' Hanna glanced round. 'Where is she?'

'Manai Liha?' Mum's expression changed. 'She's dead. She was old. The strain of the journey was too much . . . She insisted on bringing us to this tree. She told us that the *saitan*—the spirits of this place—would look after us, that we'd be safe here. Then she sat down and just stopped breathing. I think she'd deliberately come here to die. I made a grave for her on the other side of the path. It was difficult. I didn't have a spade, and your dad was too weak to help.'

'It must have been horrible.'

Mum shrugged. 'There have been so many horrible things, Hanna. It was just one more to add to the list.'

There was a sudden chorus of shouts and grunts. It was Ned returning, frog-marching Jik through the tangled roots. The Sea Gypsy boy was wide-eyed with terror. 'It's OK,' Ned was saying in a firm but reassuring voice. 'This is my mum. She's real. She's not a ghost. Honest she's not! There's nothing to be worried about!'

Mum dropped to her knees in front of the petrified boy, and spoke softly to him in Malay. She spoke for a long time, and he listened in silence, nodding his head every so often. Slowly he seemed to calm down. Eventually he muttered something and turned away. His eyes were wet. 'I've explained that it's safe here, and I think he believes me,' Mum said, getting to her feet. 'He's sad about Manai Liha. She was his granny.'

'He never told us that,' Ned said.

'I don't tell you dam everything!' Jik retorted through his tears.

Mum led them outside to the old woman's grave. It was a simple mound of black stones, on which she'd placed some white flowers from a nearby tree. The three of them waited on the path while Jik approached it and stood motionless, his head bowed.

Eventually he turned back to them. His eyes were shining. 'Manai Liha speak to me,' he said in a quiet voice. 'She tell me everything you say is dam true. *Saitan* keep us safe. Now we are OK!'

'So you're not scared any more?' Ned asked.

'No dam way!'

'Cool! Isn't that cool, Mum?'

'Pretty dam cool,' Mum agreed, and smiled a wonderful, sunshiny Mum-smile. A smile that for so long Hanna and Ned had feared they'd never see again.

There was a hoarse exclamation from Dad. He needed water. Mum thrust a cracked earthenware pot into Hanna's hands and she ran to fill it from a spring that was trickling between the roots of some large ferns nearby. The water was cool and clear. She helped raise Dad's head while Mum pressed the bowl to his lips. He took a sip, coughed, grimaced with pain. *'Don't you dare die,'* Hanna told him silently as she brushed away a lock of hair that had fallen across his face. *'Don't even think about it. I won't allow it!'*

She glanced up sharply at Jik. 'How long to get to the mainland in your boat?'

The boy shrugged. 'Three, four days if wind is good. Maybe one week if not.'

'Is the wind good?' Mum asked.

The boy shook his head sadly. 'No dam good. In

this month always the wind is from south. We need wind from north.'

'But we've got to try!' Ned said desperately.

'Dad's too weak to spend days in an open boat,' Mum put in quietly. 'He'll never survive.'

'Well, he won't survive here either will he? Nobody's going to come and rescue us.'

'Manai Liha told us that Sea Gypsy people come to this island often to pray.'

'They won't come any more,' Hanna said bitterly. 'There are no Sea Gypsies left.'

Mum looked puzzled. 'None left? How can there be none left?'

'They've been taken away by the police. We don't know where to. Jik's mum and brothers and sisters were taken with them. There's nobody living on Ular now. The police have burnt the village.'

'But why?' Mum asked, aghast.

'They said the Bajau were pirates. They said it was them who attacked us.'

Jik exploded: 'That is big dam lie!'

'The pirates were Filipinos,' Mum said firmly. 'I'm quite certain of that. From Tawi-Tawi Island.'

'We know that too,' Ned told her. 'The Sea Gypsies are completely innocent.'

'Goddam polis better believe it!' Jik shouted furiously. 'If not there is big dam war!'

283

Dad stirred, groaned. Mum put a finger to her lips. 'Please, we're making too much noise. It's vital Dad gets as much sleep as he can.' She stared down at her husband for a short while, then turned back to the children. She had obviously reached a decision. 'If what you're telling me is right, there's no point in staying here. We must try to get him to the mainland in Jik's boat. Dad's tough—that's why he's still alive now. Maybe he'll be tough enough to make the journey.'

'Jik'll sing a wind song,' Ned said enthusiastically. 'That always works to make the wind blow. We'll go like a rocket. Isn't that right, Jik?'

Jik nodded. 'Sure dam thing! Like goddam rocket.'

'Let's hope so.' Mum peered out anxiously through the curtain of roots. The fog was finally beginning to lift—the sky to the west streaked with pink. 'We'll need to rig up some sort of stretcher to get him down to the beach. I only hope the four of us can lift him without dropping him—I'm not as strong as I used to be.'

Jik volunteered to make the stretcher, and he and Ned raced off downhill to cut bamboo for the poles. When they had gone, Mum turned to Hanna. 'We ought to eat something,' she said helplessly, 'but there's no food. We had a little rice from Manai Liha, but I gave that all to Dad.'

Hanna put on a reassuring smile. 'Don't worry, Mum. We ate earlier—Jik speared a big fish on one of the reefs. I'm still full from that.'

It was a lie. She *wasn't* full—far from it—but she could live with it. She looked her mother up and down. 'You told me about Dad, but what have *you* been eating, Mum?'

'This and that.'

'Like what?'

'This and that. I just said.'

'You've not been eating *anything*!' Hanna exclaimed, horrified. 'You're starving!'

'Please, Hanna, there are more important things to talk about!'

Mum gave a sob. She was close to collapse, Hanna saw. She took her in her arms. It was like hugging a skeleton. 'We'll get home again,' she said to her softly. 'All of us. We're survivors. You must believe that.'

It was a funny feeling comforting Mum. It was the wrong way round, somehow. It was like it must be when your parents got very old, and relied on you utterly.

30

Revelations

The boys came back soon afterwards. They were carrying lengths of stout bamboo, and had strips of creeper slung across their shoulders. Ned wore a triumphant expression. 'Look what we've got!' he exclaimed, pointing.

Dangling from the poles, their claws tightly bound with creeper, were two enormous blue crabs. 'Jik caught them. He just dived into the lagoon and came up with them!'

'They try to bite me but I am too dam quick!' the Sea Gypsy boy said proudly as they put down their load and straightened up. 'I bring this too. I keep in my boat.' He produced a cheap cigarette lighter.

'That means we can have a *cooked* supper!' Hanna exclaimed. 'How about that, Mum? Isn't Jik brilliant?'

Mum nodded in amazement.

The children hurried off to gather leaves and dry branches, and within minutes a fire was blazing. The crabs, which Mum expertly divided into

286

manageable chunks, were roasted on skewers of green bamboo, then bashed with rocks to break their shells. Inside, the succulent white meat tasted of wood-smoke and the sea. It was utterly delicious. Mum saved some of the tastiest pieces for Dad, and Hanna persuaded him to swallow a couple of mouthfuls. It was almost like old times.

Almost . . .

Darkness fell, a swollen red sun dropping swiftly beneath the sea to the west. Jik piled more wood onto the fire to give them enough light, and began to rapidly construct the stretcher. It was like making a fish trap, he explained, only easier, showing Ned how to weave lengths of flexible creeper between the rigid bamboo poles.

Despite the heat, the light from the fire was comforting. Even the faces of the *ta'au-ta'au* figures ranged around the tree didn't seem quite so scary as usual. 'What happened after the pirates took you away, Mum?' Hanna asked, as they crouched, watching the boys work.

Mum's haunted look returned. 'I don't think . . . ' she began. And stopped.

Ned glanced up from the knot he was tying. 'Please tell us, Mum!' he beseeched. 'We need to know!'

Mum was silent for a while, obviously debating the wisdom of agreeing to their request. Then she took a deep breath. 'OK. Where do you want me to start?'

'From the beginning. From when you went to help Dad.'

She spoke softly—so softly that the children had to strain to hear: 'Dad was having a big argument with the pirates about money when I got to him. He'd offered them all the cash we had, but they said it wasn't enough. I tried to calm things down, but they took no notice. Then one of the men grabbed me and tried to steal my rings. I remember noticing he had six fingers on one of his hands, which was weird. He was very rough. Dad ordered him to stop, but he wouldn't, so Dad punched him in the face. There was a big fight. The two of them were rolling about in the sea. Then one of the pirates took a *parang* and slashed Dad on the arm . . .'

Hanna shuddered. 'Was that when you screamed?'

Mum nodded. 'You heard it?'

'Ned wanted to go to you but I wouldn't let him.'

'Thank God you stopped him! All the time I was praying you'd stay hidden and not show yourselves.'

'So what happened next?' Ned asked.

'I thought the man was going to kill Dad, so I

tried to pull him away, but he threw me down and kicked me. I must have blacked out, because the next thing I knew I was lying in the bottom of the pirates' boat with Dad slumped on top of me. He was unconscious. Blood was gushing out of his arm. There was so much blood. The whole boat seemed to be full of blood . . . '

Mum paused, wiped at her eyes. 'He would have been dead in a few minutes—nobody can lose that amount of blood and survive—but luckily I managed to find a piece of cloth and tie it round his arm. The bleeding stopped. Soon after that the men came back. They'd stolen all our stuff and set fire to the hut. They had a big boat anchored further out in deep water and took us to that. They threw us onto its deck and told us they'd kill us if we moved. Then they started the engine and we went away.'

'Where to?'

'Out to sea somewhere, I don't know where. After a while we came to another boat. It was obviously waiting for us. Remember the boat that took us out to Kaitan when we first arrived?'

Hanna was astonished. 'You mean *Ahmad's* boat?'

Mum nodded. 'Ahmad was in it, and when he saw Dad and me he got very angry. He had a big row with the pirates. They were speaking Malay so

I could understand what they were saying. Ahmad wanted to know why they hadn't killed us like they'd been paid to do.'

'They'd been *paid* to kill you?'

'They'd already been given half the money. The pirates told him they wanted to hold us for ransom, but he said they wouldn't get the rest of the money unless we were dead. His boss needed evidence, he told them.'

'Did he say who his boss was?' Hanna asked urgently.

'Somebody called Kamal.'

'The Datuk!' the children chorused. Now, for the first time, there was proof of what they'd suspected for so long. His evil, scheming brain was behind everything!

'You know this man?' Mum asked, surprised.

'Oh yes, we know him!' Ned exclaimed. 'He told us you were dead, and tried to put all the blame on the Sea Gypsies!'

Mum looked puzzled. 'But why? I don't understand.'

'Nor do we, but we'll find out, won't we, Hanna?'

Hanna nodded. 'Somehow! Tell us how you and Dad escaped from the pirates, Mum.'

'Dad was conscious by this time, and when I told him what was happening, we decided our only chance was to try to swim to safety. So we climbed

over the side of the boat. The pirates were still arguing and didn't notice what we were doing.'

'But you were in the middle of the ocean!'

'What choice did we have? If we'd stayed where
we were we'd have certainly been killed. Dad
thought there might be some reefs nearby and we
could reach one of them.'

'How did he manage to swim with only one
arm?' Ned asked, horrified.

'He couldn't. All he could do was float. I supported him, kept his head above water. I learnt
how to do it on my life-saving course, remember?
There was a strong current running and we drifted
quite a long way from the boats. After a while the
pirates realized we were gone and started shining
lights on the water, trying to spot us. Every time a
light came near us we held our breaths and
ducked under. Eventually they gave up and went
away. They obviously thought we had drowned.'

'So what did you do then?'

'We just floated. The sea was quite warm, but
Dad was getting weaker all the time, and kept slipping under. He told me to leave him and try to save
myself, but I refused. There was no way I was going
to let him go . . . '

Mum's voice had become hoarse. Hanna
fetched some water and she took a sip. After a few
moments she was able to continue. 'Eventually it

began to get light. I was pleased about that until I saw the sharks. I hadn't thought anything about them up till then. There were lots of them circling round us. They must have been attracted by the blood from Dad's arm. They got closer and closer. Then one of them headed straight towards us. I didn't know what to do, so I kicked at it with my bare feet. I must have surprised it because it swerved away . . . '

'Did it attack again?' Ned asked, wide-eyed.

Mum shook her head. 'No, thank God. The water had got too shallow. We were on a reef. We must have floated onto it in the darkness without realizing. There were big flat pieces of coral just beneath the surface. Then Dad spotted the hut . . . '

'It wasn't a hut, it was a raft,' Ned said excitedly. 'It's called an *alul*. We've been there.'

'You've *been* there?' Mum looked astonished.

'It's a long story,' Hanna put in. 'So how did you get to the *alul*?'

'We walked, floated. It took a long time, because Dad was so weak. But eventually we reached it and managed to climb on board. At last we were out of the water.'

'You were safe!' Ned said triumphantly.

Mum shook her head. 'I thought so, but we weren't. I thought there'd be fishing boats out on the reef and we could attract their attention, but we didn't see a single one. I managed to get Dad inside the hut, into the shade, but he became unconscious again. He'd lost too much blood, and his arm was still bleeding. I knew I had to do something quickly or he'd be dead. I found a fishing line in the hut. It had a hook attached. I used the hook as a needle and stitched him up with the line. He didn't wake up while I was doing it, thank God . . .'

'You're amazing, Mum,' Hanna whispered. 'Truly amazing.'

'You can do anything when you're desperate.'

'Then what happened?' Ned asked.

'Dad needed fluid to replace all the blood he'd lost, but we had no water at all. It got hotter and hotter as the day went on. It was like being baked inside an oven. I tried to keep him cool by splashing sea water on him, but it didn't do any good. By the time night came he was hallucinating.'

'What's hallucinating?'

'It's when you see things that aren't there. He thought you and Hanna were on the raft with us. He kept talking to you. He kept saying: "Hi, kids".'

'*We heard him!*' Ned said excitedly. 'Or at least we thought we did! That was the night we were on Manai Liha's boat. Were *you* calling out to us as well, Mum?'

'I don't know. Maybe I was. Maybe I was

hallucinating too. I was so exhausted. So thirsty. I knew that if we didn't get water soon we'd both be dead. I remember getting Dad's five pound note out of his pocket and hanging it up inside the hut so if we didn't survive at least people would know we were from England . . . '

'Then Manai Liha arrived?' Hanna asked gently.

Mum nodded. 'I must have passed out, because the next thing I knew she was standing beside me. How she found us I don't know. She had a plastic bottle with water in it. I gave some to Dad, which he managed to swallow. All the time the old woman was muttering in a strange language I couldn't understand. Then she produced two small statues. One of them had Dad's sweatband wrapped round its head. The other was wearing my lucky pendant. At first I thought she must be in league with the pirates, because how else could she have got hold of our things? Then she told me about you.'

'I thought you couldn't understand what she was saying?' Hanna said.

'She spoke some Malay. Just enough. She told me you'd been to visit her on her boat and there was a big storm. She said you'd gone up into the sky. I honestly believed she was telling me you were dead. It was the worst moment of my life. Up till then I'd thought you were safe. Up till then I'd thought somebody would come and rescue you. Now there was no hope left. No reason to go on living . . . '

Mum paused, wiped at her eyes. 'I don't remember much after that. Somehow we must have got your father onto the old woman's boat and reached this island. Somehow we must have climbed up to this tree. Before she died Manai Liha told me it was called a ghost tree. I became one of its ghosts.'

'You certainly looked like one when we first saw you,' Ned said quietly. 'You really scared us.'

'But you're *not* a ghost!' countered Hanna fiercely. 'And none of us is *ever* going to become one . . . '

'*Boat come!*'

Startled, they swung towards Jik. He had finished making the stretcher, and was staring intently out across the lagoon.

At first, all they could hear was the clapping of prayer flags and the buzzing of cicadas.

But then came another sound—faint, but getting rapidly louder.

It was the roar of a powerful engine.

31

Trapped

There was enough light to see—just. A three-quarter moon had broken through the clouds and was projecting a silver pathway across the ink-black waters of the lagoon. As they watched, a sharp-nosed speedboat surged through a gap from the open sea and curved to a halt close to where Jik's outrigger was drawn up.

Their hearts leapt. Had somebody—some-where—finally realized what was going on and raised the alarm? Was this a rescue mission?

Then a light flicked on inside the cockpit and the terrifying truth was plain. The boat's driver was a short, stocky man wearing a police uniform. His companion was thinner, with a beak-like mouth. It was the Superintendent—and he had the Datuk with him!

Hanna's mind was racing. How had these two evil men known where to find them?

As she turned back to the others, the answer became sickeningly clear. It was their fire! It was blazing fiercely, and must be visible for miles across the open sea. If they'd rigged up a giant flashing sign reading 'WE'RE HERE!' the message couldn't have been plainer.

'*Put it out!*' she yelled, pointing at it.

The boys rushed to obey her, but it was too late. The men in the speedboat were peering intently in their direction. The Datuk made a sharp gesture, then climbed out of the boat and waded to the shore. The Superintendent followed. Both of them were carrying vicious-looking sub-machine guns.

Hanna began to panic. 'They'll be here in a minute! They mustn't find you, Mum! They'll kill you!'

But Mum didn't understand what was happening. She was staring down at the boat. 'It's the police!' she said, with mounting excitement. 'I recognize that man's uniform. They can get your father to hospital . . . '

'NO!' Hanna wrapped her arms around her, terrified that she'd give herself away. 'You mustn't go down there! They'll kill you if they see you. They'll kill both of you!'

'But they're *police*. I know they are!'

'There's no time to explain. One of those men is the Datuk, the man Ahmad works for. He's the one who paid the pirates to have you killed. Go back inside the tree with Dad. We'll try to lead them away from you!'

At last Mum seemed to understand. 'I can't allow you to do that,' she gasped. 'I can't allow you to take that risk!'

'*Mum, do what we ask!*' It was Ned. He'd planted himself squarely in front of her, blocking her exit. 'Those men are looking for *us,* not you. They think you and Dad are already dead. They don't want to kill us. They just want to catch us and send us back to Kuala Lumpur. We'll be fine.'

'You're sure?' Mum said doubtfully.

'Dead sure! Now go back inside with Dad and don't let him make any noise. Come on, you two!'

Without glancing back, Ned hurdled Manai Liha's grave and disappeared into the undergrowth. Jik followed, and then Hanna, after she'd made certain that Mum was safely back inside the tree. The grunts and heavy footsteps of the men could be clearly heard now as they climbed the steep path from the beach.

It was dark in the jungle—cold—the leaves still wet from the day's fog. Hanna found it hard to catch up with the boys who had raced ahead, taking a route roughly parallel to the beach. She was about to call out to them when she heard Ned's voice ring up into the night sky: '*Nah nah! Nah nah! You can't catch us! We're over here!*'

It was his school playground chant, high-pitched and piercing—one she'd heard a hundred times before—challenging other kids to give chase. Only this time it was grown men his words were aimed at—grown men with guns!

Hanna raced towards the boys, joining in with the chorus as she did so: *'You can't catch us! We're too fast! You're too slow! Nah nah! Nah nah! Slow and stupid!'*

Powerful torches flicked on, their beams slicing through the undergrowth. There were shouts, crashes, curses as their pursuers turned off the main path and began to stumble in their direction. Hanna exchanged a triumphant glance with Ned as she caught up with him. Their plan was working! The Datuk and Superintendent were being led further and further away from Mum and Dad. Every second was adding to their safety.

She felt a surge of exhilaration. She could run all night—and all next day if she had to—before she needed to stop for breath.

But then what?

The terrible truth hit her. Even if they led the men as far away from Mum and Dad as it was possible to go, it still wouldn't be far enough. It was a small island. In a few hours it would be light. There was no way Mum and Dad could stay hidden for ever, and Dad was in so much pain he was bound to groan or shout out some time. Sound carried a long way . . .

There *had* to be a solution. But what? It was so hard to think clearly when you were running and shouting at the top of your voice.

Suddenly there were no more trees, just slabs of bare, black, volcanic rock split into deep canyon-like gullies. What looked like a path twisted up through one of them. The boys took it, still running at high speed, their gleeful voices bouncing off the sheer walls: *'Nah nah! Nah nah! You can't catch us—'*

And then their shouts stopped.

As Hanna caught up with them she saw why. The path ahead of them was blocked by a huge rock-fall. There was no way out except the way they'd come in.

They were trapped!

Ned's wild eyes met his sister's. 'What do we do now?'

Hanna felt as if her brain had frozen solid. 'I don't know . . . ' she began helplessly. And then she heard herself say: 'Nothing. We do nothing.'

'Nothing?'

'It's us they're looking for, not Mum and Dad. We must let ourselves be captured. Once they've got us they'll take us straight back to their boat and not bother to go anywhere else. We can get help once we get to the mainland.'

'But Dad needs . . . '

Ned's protest died on his lips. The Datuk and

the Superintendent had rounded the final bend and were charging towards them. The beams from their torches blinded the children. They felt like rabbits caught in a car's headlights.

'Stay where you are! Don't move!' The Datuk's voice was harsh with fury. 'Your game's over.'

'It's not a game—' Hanna began.

'Shut up!'

She gasped with fear as he thrust his face close to hers. She could feel the wetness as he spat his rage at her. 'You think you're smart? You think you can make a fool out of me? Well, you're wrong! Nobody makes a fool out of me. *Nobody!* It's over. Finished!'

She fought to stay calm. 'We've been looking for our mum and dad,' she just managed to say. 'We thought they were still alive. You can't blame us for that . . . '

'Your excuses don't interest me. You had your chance, but you refused to take it. Now get moving!'

'You're taking us back to Tamu?' It was Ned's voice—uncertain.

The Datuk twisted towards him. 'You think we're stupid? We're going for a boat ride. A nice little boat ride . . . '

'But I don't understand . . . '

Hanna did. Suddenly she understood perfectly well. They were going to be taken out to sea, killed, and dumped overboard for the sharks. That way there'd be no evidence. If anybody asked awkward questions they'd no doubt produce Jik's boat, say they'd found it floating upside down, say there must have been a tragic accident. She could see the Datuk and his evil wife facing the TV cameras with crocodile tears in their eyes, explaining how they'd done everything they could. How kids would be kids . . .

'You heard what the Datuk said! Get moving!'

The Superintendent jabbed his gun into Hanna's back. She yelped with pain and jerked forwards. Jik, who'd been silent up to now, protested loudly in Malay. He was sent sprawling by a vicious blow. 'Gypsy scum!' the Datuk snarled, lashing his foot into the boy's ribs before jerking him to his feet and sending him staggering after Hanna.

Ned still didn't understand. 'Where are we going? I want to know where we're going!' he demanded, as he too was thrust forwards with the others.

The gully narrowed near its entrance, the path splitting into two just beyond it. Uncertain which way to go, Hanna hesitated. The two boys, who were following close behind, pitched into her. 'Keep moving!' the Datuk roared, and lashed out again.

There was a scream.

At first Hanna thought it was Ned who was screaming, but then immediately she knew it wasn't. It was a different voice—harsh, demoniacal—coming from somewhere high above them . . .

Glancing up she saw a gleam of white amongst the jumbled rocks on the edge of the gully.

Ned had seen it too. 'That's my mum,' he announced loudly. 'That's my mum you can hear!'

Hanna stared at him in horror. Had he gone completely mad? Was he trying to get everybody killed?

She was about to protest when the Datuk grabbed Ned, jerked him up close. 'You stupid child!' he snarled. 'Your mother is dead!'

'Of course she's dead,' Ned replied matter-of-factly. 'You paid those men to kill her, so you should know. Well, now she's come back from the grave. It's her ghost that's screaming. It'll haunt you for the rest of your life—every single minute, every single hour, every single day. Then, when you die, it'll still go on screaming at you while you burn in hell!'

'You're crazy! You're a mad boy!' The Datuk thrust Ned away. He sounded shaken, unsure of himself.

Hanna shot her brother an admiring glance. Sometimes he could be utterly brilliant! Knowing Mum would be able to hear them from her perch up on the rocks, she said loudly: 'Ned's telling the truth. We've seen the ghost lots of times since we got here. It speaks to us. It's promised us that if any harm comes to us, the person responsible will die a slow, agonizing death. His whole body will start to rot. First his face . . . '

'Then the rest of him,' added Ned with relish. 'There it is!'

He pointed upwards. For an instant Mum had stepped out from the cover of the rocks. Her skin gleamed silver in the moonlight. *'Murderers!'* she screamed down at the two men. *'Murderers! Harm those children and you die!'*

Then she was gone.

She was just in time. The Superintendent, his face distorted with fear, swung his gun up. Bullets whined off the rocks and into the surrounding trees.

A burst of maniacal laughter from Mum told the children she was unhurt.

'You can't kill her! She's already dead!' yelled Ned gleefully. 'You're in big troub—'

He stopped.

A new noise had filled the night. It was coming from behind them this time, from the opposite side of the gully—not a scream, but a deep, menacing roar of rage. It was as if some maddened beast was about to launch an attack.

Hanna spun on her heels. Jik was staring upwards in terror. *'Saitan come!'* he gasped. *'Saitan come!'*

High above them, its carved face grimacing evilly, its cowrie shell eyes flashing in the moonlight, was the biggest *ta'au-ta'au* statue Hanna had ever seen.

It was moving!

Jerking from side to side, it waddled slowly towards the lip of the gully.

The Superintendent had lost all self-control now. Wrenching his gun round, he fired wildly. Splinters flew, but still the massive statue continued to move . . .

There was a sudden loud click. His gun was empty. He groped frantically for fresh ammunition, but he was too late. With a final, furious bellow the *ta'au-ta'au* launched itself into space. Hemmed in by the rocks, the policeman had nowhere to go. The huge statue slammed down onto him, crushing him to the ground.

Hanna stared in amazement—but she had no time to work out what had happened, or why. The Datuk was twisting towards her.

As if in a dream she saw him raise his gun, saw him aim it at her chest, saw his finger tighten on the trigger . . .

Then the boys hit him.

Ned and Jik slammed into him low and hard, like a pair of miniature torpedoes. Bullets howled skywards as the gun flew out of his hands and spun away into the rocks. Punching and kicking, they wrestled him to the ground, rolling over and over in the dust.

But they were no match for a grown man. There were yells of pain as the Datuk fought back. Jik was sent tumbling away, clutching his face. Then the Datuk's hands were round Ned's neck, squeezing, squeezing . . .

Hanna had never held a real gun before, never fired one, but as she raced to pick up the Datuk's fallen rifle, she didn't care. It felt surprisingly light, almost like a toy. She turned with it, gripped the trigger. 'Get off him!' she screamed.

The Datuk didn't seem to hear her. Ned was choking, coughing—close to unconsciousness.

'I said get off him!'

Now he heard. He released his grip, stood up slowly. He stared first at Hanna, then at the gun. There was a smile on his face—a malevolent, sharp-toothed, crocodile smile. 'Give me that,' he said softly, extending both hands. 'You're not going to fire it, so give it to me.'

He took a step towards her. Then another. She was just a young girl, he was obviously calculating. She wouldn't dare to kill anybody.

He calculated wrong.

The surge of hatred that Hanna felt at that moment was like nothing she'd ever experienced before. It was cold, hard, shocking in its intensity. *'Stop right there!'* she yelled.

She raised the gun to her shoulder; peered along its barrel. She was aiming at his heart—or where his heart would be if he had one.

32

The Terrible Truth

'*No, Hanna, I'll deal with this!*'

Mum was suddenly next to her, taking the gun from her hands, putting it to her own shoulder. With her hollow cheeks and sunken eyes she looked like a walking corpse.

The Datuk glanced wildly round, obviously seeking to escape, but a sharp command stopped him. 'Try anything and I'll kill you,' Mum hissed. 'And believe me, you won't die slowly!'

He shrank back. For a brief moment all the fight seemed to have left him. 'You're dead,' he said numbly. 'I know you're dead. I don't understand . . .'

A grim smile played on Mum's lips. 'There's nothing to understand. Just accept that sometimes ghosts come back to life. And when they do they get very very angry!'

Hanna felt a rush of relief. Would she have pulled the trigger? Could she have? Now she'd never need to find out. Mum was once more taking charge, and that was the way it should be. She hurried to help the boys. Jik's left eye was badly swollen, and Ned's neck was streaked with angry red marks where the Datuk's hands had gripped it, but otherwise they seemed OK. Jik was staring awestruck at the *ta'au-ta'au*, which was still wedged across the motionless figure of the Superintendent. '*Saitan do this!*' he whispered. '*Saitan do this!*'

'I just hope it *was saitan*,' Mum said grimly.

Hanna stared at her in alarm. What on earth was she implying? Then the terrible truth dawned.

Surely it wasn't possible!

She pushed past the boys and scrambled frantically up the tumbled rocks to the top of the gully, to the place where she had first seen the giant *ta'au-ta'au*. She spotted a dark shape close to the edge.

It was Dad.

He was lying face-down, motionless.

Sobbing with terror, she raced up to him. Blood was seeping from beneath his body. The Superintendent had fired so many shots he must have been hit. 'Dad!' she screamed. 'Dad!'

He groaned.

He was alive! Thank God he was alive! Gingerly, Hanna turned him over. It was the wrong thing to do, she knew, but she had to find out.

To her huge relief she could see no bullet holes. The blood was coming from the wound on his arm, which was now gaping open. Mum's stitches, she saw, had been ripped violently from the flesh.

There was only one way it could have happened.

Somehow Dad had dragged the massive statue to the edge of the rocks and sent it hurtling down onto the Superintendent below!

His eyes flicked open. For a brief second he was her do-anything, stop-at-nothing Dad once again. '*Got him!*' he murmured, and smiled. '*Smacked him flat!*'

Then his eyes closed and his head fell sideways.

Not knowing what to do, Hanna fumbled for his wrist, searching desperately for a pulse. To her relief she found one. It was weak, but it meant his heart was beating. There was still hope. 'Mum!' she was screaming. 'Ned! Jik! It's Dad! He's up here!'

The boys scrambled up to her. Mum followed moments later, thrusting the Datuk in front of her with the barrel of his gun.

She glanced down at her husband. 'I knew it,' she said bitterly, her anxiety coming out as anger. 'I just knew he'd do something like this!'

'But he saved us, Mum!' Ned protested.

'The *saitan* gave him strength,' Jik chimed in. 'No dam way will he die now!'

'Not now we've got the boat,' Ned added triumphantly.

The boat!

Hanna glanced down at the lagoon. It was clearly visible, bobbing gently at anchor, its polished hull gleaming in the moonlight. It looked very fast. With any luck Dad could be in hospital within hours, getting the antibiotics he so desperately needed. She turned urgently to Mum. 'Do you know how to drive a speedboat?'

'I'll find a way.' Mum spoke tersely, not taking her eyes off the Datuk. Her finger was tight on the trigger of the gun. She was taking no chances.

The boys sped off to get the stretcher, and helped by Hanna, eased Dad carefully onto it. Mum thrust her gun into the Datuk's stomach. 'Pick it up!' she ordered.

'But Mum!' Hanna protested.

'If he's got his hands full, he can't make any trouble. Drop my husband and you're dead!' she hissed at him.

'You're the one who's going to be dead,' the Datuk snarled, his venom returning. 'And next time I'm going to kill you myself.'

'I said pick it up!'

Reluctantly, the Datuk bent and took the front handles. The two boys hurried to take the ones at the back. At Mum's sharp command they began to shuffle forwards.

It was dark beneath the trees, impossible to see clearly. Terrified they might trip and fall, Hanna raced back to the gully to fetch one of the torches the men had dropped. She found one, still gleaming brightly amongst the rocks.

She led the way, her torch trained on the Datuk. Mum followed with the gun. The path was steep, twisting sharply, laced with exposed roots. Twice the Datuk stumbled, but the boys, clinging desperately to their handles at the rear, managed to steady him. They should have tied Dad on to the stretcher, Hanna realized, as he pitched dangerously from side to side.

The sky was lightening in the east by the time they'd passed the last of the *ta'au-ta'au* statues and reached the beach. Dawn was not far off. At Mum's command, the Datuk and the boys waded out to the boat and hoisted Dad on board. Hanna scrambled in next to him and made him as comfortable as she could on the passenger seat. He was still bleeding, but less heavily now. *'You can do it!'* she whispered to him. *'You can do it, Dad!'*

There was no response.

The exhausted boys climbed in next, followed by Mum, who handed the gun to Hanna as she did so. 'Shoot him if he moves,' she said, indicating the Datuk, who had been ordered away from the boat, and was standing knee-deep in the lagoon. He was drenched with sweat, his once-immaculate white shirt caked with mud and filth.

His face was purple with fury. 'You're dead!' he was screaming at them. 'You're all dead! Every single one of you . . . '

Mum ignored him, and pressed the starter. The engine roared into life. Jik scrambled to raise the anchor and they moved forwards, slowly at first, then picking up speed as Mum grew accustomed to the controls.

As they headed out towards the open sea Hanna glanced back. The Datuk was still standing in the water, but he was no longer looking in their direction. He was fumbling in one of his pockets. To her horror, she saw him take out a small hand-held radio, extend its aerial, and begin to speak urgently into it.

33

Life or Death

'Which way?' Mum yelled, as they surged out beyond the shelter of the island into the vicious, swirling current.

Nobody knew. During the mad white-water ride that had brought them here, the children had lost all sense of direction, and the speedboat had no navigation system to help them. East was where the dawn was breaking, that much was obvious, but where exactly they were on the vast expanse of the Sulu Sea was another matter. Ned checked the fuel tank. It was just over half full—enough to get them to Tamu if they headed straight towards it, but not enough to cover any error. It would be the ultimate disaster if they ended up out of fuel, drifting helplessly miles from land, miles from the hospital that Dad so urgently needed.

'What about the stars?' Hanna asked Jik.

He shook his head. A thin layer of silvery cloud had extinguished their already fading light. They were truly lost.

They decided to head south. Borneo was so big they'd be bound to spot it eventually.

As Mum eased the throttle forward, Hanna glanced back at Ghost Island. It was already fading from view, melting into its shroud of mist as though it had never been.

It was impossible to go fast. The boat, designed for just two people, was overloaded with five of them on board, and each time they picked up speed, water surged into the cockpit. Dad was semi-conscious now, groaning loudly as the spray hit him. Hanna spotted a bottle of water wedged next to the driver's seat, and managed to get some of it between his parched lips. After that they all took a sip, not daring to drink deeply, concerned about what the future might bring.

Hanna told the others about the Datuk, and his radio.

'We should have searched him!' Ned exploded. 'We should have forced him to empty his pockets!'

'Well, we didn't,' said Mum tersely. She'd allowed herself to relax momentarily, but tension was once more gripping her face.

'So what do we do now?' Hanna asked.

'The only thing we *can* do. We get Dad to Tamu as quickly as possible. It's the only place on this coast with a hospital.'

'But the police will be waiting for us. We'll be arrested.'

'What for?' Ned demanded. 'We haven't done anything.'

'We've stolen this boat for a start. And threatened people with guns.'

'They won't dare to deny Dad medical help,' Mum put in. 'And even if we're arrested we can somehow get word out. Once the world learns the truth about what's happening here . . . '

'What if it never does,' Hanna said quietly.

Mum half turned, not taking her eyes off the sea ahead. 'I don't understand.'

'What if they don't *allow* us to get to Tamu?'

'I don't see how they can stop us.'

Hanna told her about the sinister police patrol boats with their big machine guns. There was no way they could outrun or outfight those. 'They'll blow us to bits,' she said quietly.

'*No dam way!*' Jik, who'd been listening intently to the conversation, reacted with fury. He'd been given the Datuk's gun to hold when they'd come on board and was waving it about dangerously. 'Goddam polis! I shoot them! I kill them! Every goddam one!'

Mum glanced at him sharply. 'Throw that thing overboard!' she ordered.

Jik looked horrified. 'You crazy?'

'*I said throw it overboard!*'

'But, Mum!' Ned protested.

'It's served its purpose. The surest way to get us all killed is to have any kind of gun on this boat. Now throw it overboard!'

Jik gritted his teeth, gripped the gun more tightly.

'You'd better do what she says,' Ned told him. 'She won't take no for an answer. She never does.'

There were tears in Jik's eyes—tears of rage and frustration. This was his best chance ever to hit back at his mortal enemy, and now it was being denied to him!

'Please, Jik,' Hanna said softly, and reached for the gun.

He resisted for a moment or two, then slowly released the weapon. 'Goddam crazy woman!' he muttered, as Hanna dropped it over the side.

'Better crazy than dead,' Mum said, unmoved.

Hanna was thinking about the Datuk and his radio. She'd seen him talk *into* it, she was sure of that. But had he received any reply? The radio had looked very small, and Ghost Island was a long way from anywhere. She could imagine his fury if he failed to get any response to his frantic calls for help.

She felt a sudden surge of optimism. They were going to make it now. Nothing could stop them!

As if in response to her mood, the sun suddenly

burst above the rim of the sea. A new day was beginning. A new, fresh day.

'Look!' Ned was pointing away to the east.

Hanna narrowed her eyes against the dazzling light. On the horizon was a familiar triangular shape, like the fin of a shark sticking above the water.

It was Kaitan!

And in front of it, just visible, was the snake-like curl of Ular!

Now it really was just a matter of time.

A choppy sea had sprung up. Mum throttled back, but there was no way she could avoid Dad being thrown around as the boat pitched into the waves. Hanna was trying to steady him when he let out a sudden cry of pain. His face had become sheet-white, his lips a dangerous shade of purple. He slumped sideways, gasping for breath. Her terrified eyes sought Mum's. 'There's something wrong!' she yelled.

Mum glanced down fearfully. 'Oh my God! I think he's having a heart attack! Hanna, you take over!'

Mum flicked the controls into neutral and thrust past the boys. With the boat rocking wildly, Hanna scrambled for the empty driver's seat.

Mum was astride Dad in an instant, feeling for his pulse, then easing his head back, pinching his nostrils, clamping her lips to his mouth. His chest rose and fell. Again she blew into his mouth. And again.

'Get going!' Mum yelled in between breaths.

'But I don't know how to drive . . . ' Hanna began.

She stopped herself. There was no way she was going to let Dad down now! She gripped the steering wheel with one hand. With the other she reached for the throttle lever.

The engine roared, and they surged forwards. 'Faster!' Ned shouted, his face shiny with tears. 'We've got to go faster! He's going to die!'

Hanna took a deep breath. It was now or never. 'Hold on tight!' she yelled. It was like being shot from a catapult. Water lashed at her face, blinding her, filling her mouth, stopping her breath. She'd seen clips on TV about speedboats flipping over; seen them soar up into the air before slamming upside down onto the waves and smashing themselves to pieces. Any moment it would happen to them, she was convinced. Hunched over the wheel, her hair whipping at her face, she fought to keep the boat level. An *alul* whizzed past. Then another. They must be close to the reef. If they hit the coral going at this speed it would be like hitting a brick wall . . .

Ular sped towards them, its charred palm trees pointing skywards like so many blackened fingers. Beyond it was Kaitan, massive and brooding.

And beyond that was the mainland!

Dad was getting worse. Mum was thrusting desperately at his chest now, using both hands. He was slipping away from them—Hanna could sense it. *'Don't die!'* she screamed at him. *'Don't you dare die!'* If only they had a bigger engine, her tortured brain was telling her. If only they could fly . . .

Then something caught her eye—something from her worst nightmare.

Speeding out towards them from the shelter of Ular was a sinister black craft. It had a single word painted on its side: 'POLIS'.

34

The Miracle

Hanna tried to race it, but there was no way they could escape. With its massive engines, the huge vessel easily outpaced them. As it closed in, she throttled back in despair and the little speedboat came to a halt.

Jik was weeping with rage and frustration. 'Goddam polis!' he was yelling. 'I kill them but I got no dam gun!'

'Stop it!' Mum told him sharply, in between thrusts at Dad's chest. 'Just put your hands up! Everybody put your hands up so they can be seen!'

The children obeyed reluctantly.

The patrol boat was closing in fast, the machine gun on its foredeck aimed directly at them.

'*Berhenti! Jangan tembak!*' Mum shouted desperately in Malay, trying to make herself heard above the roar of the engines. '*Stop! Don't shoot!*'

There was no response.

Hanna closed her eyes in those last few seconds. She didn't want to see what was coming. To her surprise she felt no fear. Just anger—a deep,

321

profound anger. To have come so far, to have got Mum and Dad back against all the odds, and for it to end like this was so unfair—so desperately, sickeningly, crushingly unfair. If there was a God in Heaven he should hang his head in shame . . .

And then the miracle happened.

Instead of gunshots there was a voice.

'God dammit is that you, Jik?' the voice called out.

Hanna opened her eyes in amazement. The patrol boat had slowed, and was edging alongside them, its engines rumbling.

The voice came again. 'It *is* you! And who's that with you? Well, I'll be damned—it's the Bailey family! I just don't believe this!'

Hanna stared upwards. A blonde-haired woman was peering down at them from the patrol boat's deck. Her face seemed familiar.

But who . . . ?

Jik supplied the answer. *'It's goddam Annie Weir!'* he shouted, leaping up and down with excitement. *'She's come to save us!'*

Now Hanna remembered. It was the face from the photograph—the American woman who'd spent a year with the Sea Gypsies; who'd taught Jik to speak English.

But what was she doing in a police patrol boat? And how did she know their names? 'Be careful, Jik!' she began.

But it was too late. A ladder was lowered, and Jik was already scrambling up it. *'Annie! Annie! Annie!'* he was shouting at the top of his voice, as he flung himself into the woman's arms.

He pulled away instantly. 'Man hurt!' he told her breathlessly. 'Man hurt real bad!' He began to bang his hands on his chest, imitating Mum's heart massage.

Annie Weir glanced down at Mum, who was still working desperately on Dad, then turned and issued a series of sharp orders in Malay. Seconds later two uniformed medics were abseiling down the ladder onto the speedboat. After a brief examination, they strapped Dad onto a stretcher and hoisted him up onto the deck. Mum, Ned, and Hanna followed at a run as he was taken to the wheelhouse, where electrodes were swiftly attached to his bare chest. 'What are they doing?' Ned asked, panic-stricken, as the medics adjusted a small machine.

'It's a defibrillator,' Annie Weir told him. 'It'll give him an electric shock. Restart his heart.'

Mum's voice rose in an anguished shout: 'He's stopped breathing! For God's sake hurry!'

Dad's whole face was turning blue. It was lack of oxygen, Hanna knew. How long before his brain was damaged? How long before . . .

There was a loud beep. Dad's body jerked as the electric current slammed into it. One of the medics

323

checked his breathing, shook his head. A second jolt hit him. Then, moments later, a third.

Suddenly, incredibly, Dad gave a loud sigh, his chest heaved, and he began to breathe again!

'Dad!' Hanna was screaming at him, half-laughing, half-crying. 'Dad, are you OK?'

He tried to say something to her, but no sound came out of his mouth. An oxygen mask was strapped to his face and he was eased onto his side, into recovery position.

Mum was crying now, big tears dripping onto the polished wooden deck at her feet. She crouched next to him, took his hand. 'Tell me he's going to be all right,' she said to nobody in particular. 'Please tell me he's going to be all right!'

'It's too soon to say,' one of the medics told her gently. 'It depends on how tough he is.'

'Oh, he's tough,' Hanna said, through her own tears. 'He's as tough as old boots.' As she spoke the engines roared, and she felt the boat begin to turn. 'Where are we going?' she asked, her apprehension—forgotten during the fight for Dad's life—flooding back.

'The mainland,' Annie told her. 'As fast as ever we goddam can.' She looped an arm round Hanna's shoulders. 'Come, we've got things to talk about. Your father's in good hands here. Give these guys space to work on him properly.'

Hanna was led reluctantly to a table and sat down. Ned and Jik followed. Eventually Annie persuaded Mum to join them. Dad was hooked up to a heart monitor, and after an unsteady start the *beep-beep* of his pulse became reassuringly regular.

It was all too good to be true. 'Why are you helping us if you're working for the Datuk?' Hanna asked Annie suspiciously.

The American let out a snort of derision. 'Me? Work for that dam murderer? I'd rather work for the Devil himself!' She indicated the crew, clustered round the controls as the boat gathered speed. 'These guys are Federal Police, not the Datuk's men. They've taken over at Tamu. They've got an armed patrol out hunting for the Datuk right now.'

They were joined by a small, intense-looking man with swept-back hair. 'This is Encik Hassan,' Annie said. 'He's from MACA—the Malaysian Anti-Corruption Agency.'

'What's corruption?' Ned asked.

'It's when powerful people cheat and lie to get money,' Hassan explained. 'We've had our eye on Datuk Kamal for quite a while. We knew he was up to no good, but he's very clever and we've never been able to pin anything on him.'

'Well, perhaps you can now,' Mum said softly. 'I think we can give you all the evidence you need.'

A crewman arrived with a tray heaped with sandwiches. There was ice-cold Coke too, which tasted like nectar when Hanna sipped at it. While they ate and drank, Mum and the children told their story. Annie's and Hassan's astonishment turned to fury as the full details of the Datuk's murderous plot emerged. 'But why pick on us?' Mum asked. 'We're just an ordinary family. I don't see what possible motive he could have for wanting us dead.'

'It was greed,' Annie said bluntly. 'Pure dam greed. He had plans to turn Ular and Kaitan into a luxury holiday resort.'

Hanna was horrified. *'A holiday resort!'*

'He stood to make millions out of it. But first he had to get rid of the Sea Gypsies.'

'But I still don't understand what it had to do with us,' Mum said.

'Because of goddam triti!' Jik told her in an exasperated voice.

The *triti* again! Maybe now the mystery could be solved once and for all. 'What *is* this *triti*?' Hanna asked urgently. 'Is it some kind of statue?'

Annie looked astonished. 'A *statue*? Whatever made you think that? No, *triti* is the Malay word for a *treaty*—a signed agreement. A hundred years ago the Sea Gypsies—who *were* notorious pirates back then—signed a treaty with the government of the day which gave them legal ownership of Ular and Kaitan Islands for ever, on condition that they gave up piracy for good. I came across the treaty by chance during my researches and discovered that it was still valid. The Datuk was furious, but he couldn't get it over-ruled. There was no way he could get his greedy hands on those islands to build his dam resort.'

'Unless he could get the Sea Gypsies convicted of piracy?' Mum asked.

'Exactly. And I guess you were just the opportunity he was looking for. When he heard there was a British family staying on Kaitan he contacted a gang of Filipino pirates and paid them to carry out an attack. They were told to kill you and your husband, destroy everything, and disappear back across the border. After that he would mount a police raid on Jik's village on Ular and come up with "evidence" that the Sea Gypsies were responsible.'

'It nearly worked,' Mum said quietly.

'Except you and Dad weren't dead,' Hanna said. 'And we refused to believe you were.'

'And we knew the Sea Gypsies were innocent,' Ned added. 'Right, Jik?'

Jik nodded, his mouth full of sandwich.

'But how did you get to hear about all this?' Hanna asked Annie. 'Don't you live in America?'

'I do. But I've been working with Hassan for some time, gathering evidence against the Datuk, and a few days back he sent me this.' She pulled an e-mail from her shirt pocket. It was a copy of the newspaper report Hanna had seen that day at the market, with her tear-streaked picture plastered across the front page. 'When I read about the pirate raid on Kaitan, and how the Datuk and his brave men had rescued you guys from the evil Sea Gypsies, I smelt a big rat. I know the old Panglima well—there's no way he'd get involved with anything that would put his precious *triti* at risk. So I got on the first plane and came over, and was horrified at what I found.'

'They took everybody away from Ular!' Jik said bitterly. 'Everybody!'

'And put them in goddam filthy, unsanitary camps on the edge of town. I managed to track down Jik's mum in one of them and she told me what had happened. She told me there was going to be big dam trouble out at the islands. I could see the Sea Gypsies losing everything, so I contacted Hassan and we decided to act before it was too late.'

Hassan nodded. 'We put out an arrest warrant for the Datuk and his Superintendent of Police, but somehow they got wind of what was happening and escaped by boat. My guess is they decided to track you children down and eliminate you, so you couldn't give evidence against them.'

'*Eliminate.*' It was such a cold, clinical word. Hanna shivered. They'd been so close to disaster. Only now did the full horror of what had happened begin to penetrate her exhausted brain. Jik and Ned had saved her life with an act of extraordinary bravery. How many people of any age—let alone kids—would dare to tackle a man with a loaded gun? And as for Mum with her ghost imitations, and Dad with his giant *ta'au-ta'au* . . .

She looked at them with awe.

The shrill of an alarm. A sudden flurry of activity from the medics. Dad's heartbeat had become irregular again. 'We've got problems,' one of them said in a worried voice. 'He needs hospital quick. How long to Tamu?'

Hassan glanced through the window. The coast was clearly visible now, getting closer by the second. 'Twenty minutes maybe.'

'Tamu hospital's no good,' Annie cut in. 'It's just a goddam tin-roofed shack, OK for minor injuries, nothing more. The money that should have been spent on it has gone into the Datuk's pockets.'

'We should have killed him!' exploded Ned. 'Shot him dead!'

'That's enough!' Mum was back at Dad's side. 'What do we do now?' she asked, anguished.

Hassan was hurrying towards the radio. 'We'll casevac him out.'

'What's casevac?' Hanna asked, her heart pounding.

'An emergency airlift. We'll fly him to the nearest big hospital—that's in Kota Kinabalu.'

Things happened quickly after that. It seemed like seconds—not minutes—before they were roaring across the bar into Tamu harbour, scattering fishing boats in their wake. At the jetty—the same jetty where they'd smuggled themselves on board Ahmad's boat—an ambulance was waiting, its doors open.

Dad was slid swiftly inside. Hanna, Mum, and Ned leapt in after him. 'You're not coming with us?' Ned called out to Annie and Jik in the moments before the doors were slammed shut.

Annie shook her head. 'No room! Good luck!'

'Dam good luck!' yelled Jik.

As the ambulance accelerated out of the compound Hanna became aware of a crowd gathered at its gates, of lights and television cameras, but they roared past without stopping.

Despite the oxygen, Dad was having big problems breathing—his chest jerking painfully up and down. The dressing the medics had put on his wound was already saturated with blood and pus and needed changing. How long would it take to get to Kota Kinabalu, Hanna wondered. An hour? Two? Now they'd really find out just how tough he was.

Suddenly Ned pointed outside. 'Look!'

She followed his gaze. They were speeding towards a pair of large white gates. As they approached, they swung open.

It was the Istana!

Dodging the police cars that cluttered the drive, they squealed round to the front of the house. A helicopter was waiting on the helipad, its rotors already turning. It was the Datuk's helicopter—the same machine that had been hunting them for so long!

But now it had a new crew—fast, efficient, helpful. Dad was swiftly transferred on board and strapped in securely. Hanna, Ned, and Mum scrambled for their seats.

As they lifted off, Hanna glanced down at the house. A beautiful woman, dressed in immaculate white, was being led out towards a waiting police car.

For an instant—a brief instant—their eyes met.

35

So Dam Happy!

It was the best pool ever—even better than the one at the Istana—because you could sit on stools and have drinks at a bar while you were still in the water! Hanna and Ned were alternately sucking on pineapple smoothies, then racing each other to the far end and back again, waving at Mum and Dad as they did so. It was bliss!

It had been a long three weeks—the longest Ned and Hanna could remember.

The television people who'd interviewed them had called them heroes, but they hadn't felt like heroes—they hadn't felt like *anything*—not while Dad was still in intensive care. There'd been operations—two of them so far—followed by anxious days and nights while they and Mum had taken turns to sit by his bedside. But slowly, stubbornly, Dad had fought the infection, and *miraculously*— that was the word one of the doctors had used— he'd pulled through. And now today, for the very first time, he'd been allowed out of hospital! It called for the biggest celebration ever.

Now they could really enjoy the posh Kota Kinabalu hotel they were staying in!

They were racing up the pool for the third time—Hanna attempting her butterfly stroke—when she was suddenly dive-bombed from above. Coughing and spluttering, she peered around crossly to see who had done it.

It was a boy—a brown-skinned boy in bright red shorts—swimming swiftly under water. His head broke the surface. He was wearing an enormous grin.

It was Jik!

Ned, who'd been trailing Hanna up the pool, let out a great shout of glee, and instantly the two boys were rolling and tumbling in the sparkling water like a pair of boisterous seals.

It was so brilliant to see him again!

A peal of laughter from the terrace. Hanna glanced up. It was coming from Annie, who was crouched next to Dad's wheelchair, her eyes sparkling. Dad had obviously cracked one of his jokes—they were always really bad, but somehow even funnier because of that.

'They've come for lunch,' Mum told Hanna, laughing too, the dark circles gone from her eyes. 'We'll have it up here when you three are ready.'

While they ate, Annie and Jik told them how they'd returned to Kaitan with Hassan once the ambulance had left, and had met up with Jik's father and his men. It had taken a lot of talk, a lot of persuasion, but eventually the Sea Gypsies had agreed to surrender their weapons and have them destroyed. In return the village on Ular would be rebuilt.

'So everything will soon be back to normal!' Hanna said, overjoyed.

Annie sucked in a deep breath. 'No . . . not *quite*. The old Panglima has decided to give up his post— he and his sons still haven't fully recovered from their treatment in jail. Jik's dad has been elected in his place and he's keen for changes to be made.'

'What changes?' Hanna asked, suspiciously.

'They want to build their own holiday resort on Kaitan.'

'But they can't! They mustn't!' Hanna cried out in anguish. 'It'll ruin everything!'

'It'll be on a very small scale, and I'll work closely with them to make sure it has a minimum effect on the environment. But it will be *their* resort, not some greedy developer's. With the money they make they'll be able to build a school and a clinic on Ular. They'll be able to replace their old fishing boats with efficient new ones . . . '

'Get dam fast speedboat!' Jik exclaimed joyfully.

'That is *not* what I goddam meant,' Annie said severely.

Jik caught Ned's eye, and giggled. 'Later you come and stay in our dam resort,' he said.

'And we jump off Dead Man's Leap!'

'And we go fish for *ista pula* . . . '

A sudden thought struck Hanna. 'What's happened to the Datuk and the Superintendent? Did you catch them?'

Annie shook her head. 'When Hassan's men reached Ghost Island it was deserted. Jik's boat was missing. They found it later, floating upside down in the tide race outside the lagoon. One of its outriggers had snapped off. The two men must have tried to escape in it and capsized. No bodies were found, but they're almost certainly dead.'

'*Salim* make happen!' Jik exclaimed joyfully. 'I am so dam happy!'

'And me!' said Ned, giving his friend yet another high five.

Hanna finished the ice cream she was eating, put down her spoon and looked at the familiar, smiling faces round the table. She was happy too—but her happiness had nothing to do with the Datuk. He was history.

She was thinking about the future. A future that—against all the odds—was now theirs to share together.

About the author:

David Miller was born in Norfolk. He has worked in advertising as a copywriter, and later as a creative director.

He has travelled widely all over the world, and has lived and worked in Malaysia and Singapore. *Shark Island* was inspired by his experiences while visiting a small island off the east coast of Malaysia.

David now writes full-time and lives in Hampshire with his wife, Su'en and his daughter, Hanna. *Shark Island* is his first novel for children.

Coming soon from
DAVID MILLER
SEA WOLF

A thrilling new adventure awaits . . .

Hanna, Ned and Jik are back on
Shark Island and in search of lost
treasure when a tropical storm
catapults them into trouble.

Soon they're racing through
underground island tunnels,
fighting a deadly shark attack,
and encountering a dangerous man
known as the **SEA WOLF** . . .

TURN THE PAGE FOR A TASTER
AND PREPARE TO BE SWEPT AWAY

1

Missing

The storm didn't just break, it exploded.

Everything disappeared in an instant. It was as if a massive dam had burst and was sweeping away everything before it. Hanna clung desperately to the mast as an avalanche of water thundered down on top of her.

The tiny boat began to surf madly down into the vast wave-troughs gouged out by the gale; before climbing again, higher and higher, to meet each wind lashed crest.

Dear God, let this not be a typhoon, she prayed, as she fought to keep her grip. Let this just be an ordinary storm that'll be gone as quickly as it came . . .

But it was no ordinary storm.

As the wind rose to an unholy shriek, her hands were ripped from the mast and she was sent tumbling along the length of the boat. Sharp things—paddles, fishing rods, a rusty anchor—scraped at her flesh. She was going overboard.

An arm locked onto hers.

It was Jik. He was wedged against the steering paddle, fighting to keep the boat level. She pushed herself up beside him, clutching at the paddle, adding her own weight, her own strength to his.

But where was Ned?

She squinted desperately through the lashing rain. It was impossible to see anything clearly. She prayed that her brother was still safe, that he'd managed to cling on with a tighter grip than she had. Was that dark shape hunched under the outrigger poles him, or was it a bundle of ropes that had burst out of one of the lockers? 'Ned!' she screamed. 'Is that you, Ned!'

But her words were swallowed by the wind. There was no way he would ever hear her.

Then the big wave came.

It wasn't so much a wave as a solid black wall of water. It was taller than a house—taller than the tallest building in the world, it seemed to her—as it raced towards them with the speed of an express train. Not even a large ship could survive a wave like this—let alone a tiny, flimsy sailing boat.

Hanna just had time to suck in a lungful of air before the dapang shook itself like a dog, swerved sideways, and somersaulted high into the air.

For a second she was flying, but then the wave grabbed her and crushed her into itself, and she was whirling round and round in a mad tangle of spars, ropes, sails and another flailing, gasping human body.

Down she went, further and further down into the blackness . . .